SUNRISE OVER PEBBLE BAY

DELLA GALTON

Boldwood

First published in Great Britain in 2021 by Boldwood Books Ltd.

Copyright © Della Galton, 2021

Cover Design by Debbie Clement Design

Cover Photography: Shutterstock

A CIP catalogue record for this book is available from the British Library.

Paperback ISBN 978-1-83889-110-7

Large Print ISBN 978-1-80280-874-2

Hardback ISBN 978-1-80280-875-9

Ebook ISBN 978-1-83889-111-4

Kindle ISBN 978-1-83889-112-1

Audio CD ISBN 978-1-83889-229-6

MP3 CD ISBN 978-1-80280-928-2

Digital audio download ISBN 978-1-83889-109-1

Boldwood Books Ltd
23 Bowerdean Street
London SW6 3TN
www.boldwoodbooks.com

For my very dear friend and fellow 4 a.m. writer of emails, Molly Carney, with my love.

1

Olivia Lambert closed her eyes and took a deep breath. The smell of cake filled her senses. The glorious sweetness of vanilla, almonds and sugar with an underlay of richly spiced fruit. Gorgeous. She never got tired of that smell. It helped that she adored fruit cake, every single delicious bit of it, from the exotically dark sticky fruit to the sweetness of the thick fondant icing, she'd loved it all since she was small and had learned to mix the ingredients in Aunt Dawn's kitchen. Her mother was a fine cook, but baking cakes had never come into her top ten list of things to do on your day off. Baking cakes, and indeed icing them, was one of Aunt Dawn's many passions. Aunt Dawn had been the Queen of Cake Makers in their family until she had handed Olivia her crown.

Olivia opened her eyes. This cake, which was a gloriously unashamed celebration of pink – no gender-neutral theme here – was three tiers high. The bottom and middle tiers were pale pink with a string of gold beads encircling them at their base – these were disguising the gap where the tiers were temporarily joined – and there was a big, slightly brighter, pink bow wrapped around the centre tier. The bow was made of sugar paste, beautifully crafted so it was impossible to tell it wasn't real. The top tier, the smallest of the three, was ivory. A trail of pink roses cascaded over one side; the roses painstakingly fashioned, petal by petal, in delicate curves and dotted with diamanté sparkles. Proper bling, Olivia's mother would have said, but classy with it.

On top of the cake, in pride of place, looking for all the world as though they'd been carelessly discarded there, nestled a pair of pink sugar paste baby shoes with white sugar paste flowers fashioned to look like daisies on each buckle. The shoes were a little smaller than life size, but they were adorable and just looking at them brought a lump to Olivia's throat. One day she would hold her own little girl in her arms and pop her foot into a tiny pink shoe made of some satiny material.

Olivia blinked away the images swiftly. Creating christening cakes, especially for girls – not that she'd have minded a boy – always made her broody. She was now thirty-nine and very aware that her biological clock was ticking.

She continued with her inspection, checking for imperfections, making sure everything was just as it should be. Sitting inside one of the baby shoes was a tiny caramel-coloured teddy bear with chocolate drop eyes and a heart-shaped pink nose. He'd been fiddly, especially his jacket, but, wow, he looked the part.

The words, Arabella's Christening Day were piped around the outside of the cake, above a date, 6 March, which was this coming Saturday. Today was Thursday.

Olivia smiled. The cake was gorgeous – even if she did say so herself. Arabella's parents were going to be very pleased.

She hooked out her iPhone, took a series of pictures for the gallery on her website and then carefully separated the tiers, ready to put them into the three cardboard carrying boxes that lay waiting on her worktop. The work wasn't quite over. The most nerve-wracking part of her job, by far, was the delivery. Whenever she could, she asked her clients to come to her, but Arabella's parents, the Greys, had asked her to deliver this one. She was slightly regretting agreeing to that.

The Greys lived in a very upmarket house (the type with griffins on stone pillars either side of the drive) in the pretty Dorset village of Puddletown. Olivia lived and worked close to Weymouth Quay in a mid-terrace house that overlooked a car park. According to the app on her phone, it was a twenty-three-minute drive, door to door. This was her next job, to deliver the cake safely, assemble and finish it on site, to gracefully accept the thanks of another happy customer – she hoped – along with the balance owing on their purchase and to wish them well for Arabella's christening day.

She leaned forward and gently lifted the top tier into the box, taking equal care with the other two. Then she lidded them all up carefully and pushed them back on the worktop, just to be safe. With infinite care, she carried the first box through her open front door, nudging it back with her hip as she passed, and into the March sunshine. She crossed the footway that ran alongside the public car park that abutted the row of terraced cottages, of which number five, where she lived, was the middle one. It was a lovely afternoon for March. Not as warm as yesterday, but apparently it was getting warmer at the weekend, which would be good for spring holidaymakers and perfect for Arabella's christening, which was being held in a marquee in the Greys' back garden.

Olivia's white van, which sported the sign 'Amazing Cakes – you imagine it, I'll create it,' was in its usual space. There were advantages of living beside a car park, especially in the narrow streets around here that she and her aunt Dawn, who lived a few minutes away, dubbed the back streets of Weymouth.

In the height of summer when the kids were off school, this car park got packed. At weekends, Olivia occasionally had to use her aunt's spare space, which was behind Vintage Views – her aunt's vintage clothes shop which fronted the quay. Vintage clothes, like cakes, were another of Aunt Dawn's passions. Parking at her aunt's wasn't too much of an inconvenience. The trip back to number five on foot took less than three minutes, even including hurtling over Town Bridge, which was the lifting bridge across the harbour.

Weymouth was jam-packed with pubs, cool cafes, interesting shops and a plethora of places to eat freshly caught fish and diver-caught scallops, not to mention fish and chip takeaways patrolled by hungry seagulls. There was even a handy Indian takeaway on the other side of the car park, which came in useful when she didn't want to cook. She could also hire a dive boat or a jet ski, should she ever feel the urge. Olivia felt extremely lucky to live in such a fabulous spot.

As she ran back to collect the next cake box, she caught a whiff of cardamom and garlic wafting on the breeze and her mouth watered. Maybe she'd get a takeaway later. She tried to restrict them to one a week, but it was tricky when she lived so close and was working flat out.

Fortunately, one of her favourite ways of unwinding was to head off on regular 10K runs, which helped to offset a diet of king prawn madras, fish and chip suppers and cake.

Olivia was on the third and final journey from kitchen to van when disaster struck. She tripped as she went out of her front door. She wasn't even sure how it happened. She wasn't hurrying. Knowing her tendency to be clumsy, especially when stressed, she never rushed a cake transportation, but somehow her foot caught on the raffia Welcome mat and the next thing she knew she was stumbling over her threshold. For a split second she thought she might save herself – or, more importantly in that moment, the top tier of Arabella's christening cake. She stumbled, righted, then didn't quite manage it and stumbled again clumsily and unstoppably, feeling as though she were falling in slow motion towards the tarmac walkway.

There was nothing slow motion about the thump as she hit it. She yelped as pain shot through her wrist which she'd put down to save herself. The cake box landed a few feet away. The box, which was clearly a lot less sturdy than it looked, burst apart, and the cake bounced out and was now in more than one piece. Several ivory-edged fruit chunks on the dirty pavement.

For a few seconds, Olivia stayed where she was, half lying, half sitting. The shock of the fall, the hurt in her wrist and the distress of wrecking so many painstaking hours of work competed for top place. The wrecked cake won hands down. She had a strong urge to burst into tears. She swallowed it down. Tears were not going to help. In her bumbag, which was strapped around her waist, a permanent fixture when she was working, she both heard and felt the buzz of her mobile.

More immediately vying for her attention was an elderly female passer-by. Olivia had an impression of a greying head and a purple jacket arriving beside her. The woman was wheeling a tartan shopper and her kindly face was anxious.

'Are you all right? Oh dear. Your lovely cake.' As she spoke, she bent down as if to pick up the pieces. 'It's probably not as bad as it looks...' Now crouched at the same level as Olivia, she broke off and bit her lip uncertainly. Even to the most optimistic of observers, it was clear she was wrong about this. The cake was a complete write-off. She turned her attention to Olivia. 'Are you hurt?'

'No. I'm fine. Thank you.' Olivia rubbed her wrist and realised, thankfully, that this was true. Apart from the initial shock and the ignominy of falling over, she didn't seem to have done any lasting damage – small blessings – but she was aware that other people in the car park and on the walkway were now looking in their direction. The last thing she needed was a bigger audience.

With a small sigh, she got carefully to her feet.

The woman, who'd been so verbose at first, was now clearly unsure what to do. She was still shaking her head.

'It's nice of you to stop,' Olivia told her. 'But I'm fine, honestly.'

'If you're really sure.' The woman sounded relieved.

'I am.' Olivia retrieved the split box and began to gather up the broken chunks of cake, even the quite small bits. A few feet away, an opportunist seagull was waiting hopefully. It hopped a couple of steps closer as the woman grabbed the handle of her trolley, gave Olivia one last sympathetic nod and went on her way.

One of the baby shoes was damaged. The other was still in one piece. The teddy bear had lost an arm and now seemed to be eyeing her with a look of mild reproof.

'I'm sorry,' Olivia told it. Oh my God, now she was talking to a sugar paste teddy bear. She was definitely losing the plot. Aunt Dawn must be right after all. She'd been working too hard. She'd been burning the candle at both ends. It was a bad habit of hers. This week had been frenetic – every single second of her time had been accounted for, up to and including all day tomorrow – especially tomorrow.

Oh my God – tomorrow.

Again, she fought the urge to cry as she took the remnants of the cake back inside, then retrieved the other two tiers from her van and carried them carefully into the kitchen. She could hardly rock up at the Greys' with two thirds of a christening cake.

Back in her sunny kitchen, the enormity of the disaster hit her.

Delivering Arabella's cake would have finished her working week – at least as far as Amazing Cakes was concerned.

Olivia's other profession, the one that didn't pay as well as baking, but was where her heart truly lay, was acting. She'd been to drama school after passing her A levels and she'd had a fair bit of success. She'd earned her equity card, and had several small parts on television, as well as playing on stage when the opportunity arose. Last year, she'd played Gertrude in *Hamlet* with a small but brilliant company she'd acted with before – they'd done the summer at Brownsea Island. But all of this paled into insignificance compared to tomorrow.

Tomorrow morning, she had a return ticket on the 6.55 a.m. Weymouth to London Waterloo to audition for a part in *Casualty*, the BBC's award-winning hospital drama. She'd sailed through the first audition. This was a callback. Her agent's voice echoed in her head, 'They absolutely love you, darling. You're perfect for the part.' Now, she was down to the last two. She and another actress had been shortlisted. It was the door to her future and it had opened a tantalisingly big crack.

She could not blow it. It was what she'd dreamed of since she was thirteen and had told her startled parents that she wanted to be a prostitute when she left school – having just watched *Pretty Woman*. They'd been mightily relieved when they'd found out she meant an actress.

Olivia looked back at the wrecked cake. She had never, in the five and a half years since she'd launched Amazing Cakes, let anyone down and she didn't intend to start now. But she could not be in two places at once. *Casualty* or Amazing Cakes? She was going to have to choose.

2

In her kitchen, Olivia ran through the conversation in her head with Arabella's mother, Juliet Grey.

Olivia: 'I'm so sorry, but due to unforeseen circumstances, I'm afraid I can't now deliver your christening cake.'

Juliet: 'Oh that's fine, dear. I'll pop into Waitrose and pick up another one.'

Except, of course, she was not going to say that. Even in Olivia's wildest dreams – which she had to admit, could get pretty wild – and no matter how much it cost her, she knew she had to somehow honour the promise she had made. The promise that was written on the side of her van – 'You imagine it, I'll create it.' And, in the Greys' case, 'I'll deliver it.'

Her mobile buzzed again and she hooked it out of her bumbag. Two missed calls. One from Aunt Dawn and one from Juliet Grey, who she'd spoken to so often during the design and creation of this cake that she'd put her number in her contacts list. There was also a text from her boyfriend, Phil Grimshaw.

Hey you. I've wangled tonight off. Shall I come over and make you some tea while we do a last-minute run through of the script?

What a darling. Phil was in the 'profession' like her. They'd met last year on the set of *Hamlet*. He'd played the best Claudius she'd ever seen. He was the perfect villain – dark and brooding, with a natural presence both on and off stage. He'd been brilliantly malevolent as the evil Claudius and the audience had fallen silent every time he was in the spotlight. And Olivia had simply fallen for him.

His other job – every actor Olivia knew had more than one job – was maître d' at The Bluebell Cliff – a posh boutique hotel in Swanage. He must have pulled some strings to get tonight off to help her. That was lovely of him. He knew, better than anyone, how stressed out she'd been about tomorrow's audition and usually the idea of seeing him would have made her heart leap. Half an hour ago, she'd have texted back, 'YES!' immediately. But this was not now going to happen.

It was 4.20 p.m. She needed to make another cake, which would take about three hours to mix and bake and another three or four hours to cool and then she would be up all night decorating it. She'd be lucky if she was even done by the morning, not to mention delivering and setting up. No way would she be finished in time to catch the 6.55 to London, all fresh-faced and bright-eyed for the most important audition of her life.

Her phone informed her that she had two voicemails, so one of them must be from Juliet Grey. A wild surge of hope swelled up. Maybe the christening had been cancelled. Maybe the vicar had double-booked. Or the catering company had failed to live up to Juliet's incredibly exacting standards. Maybe there had been some freak weather in Puddletown and a small tornado had ripped through the Greys' acres of posh garden and demolished the hired marquee and it would be too late to get a replacement. Or the harpist who was playing background music while the christening guests mingled and ate canapés had suddenly found that she was indisposed.

Olivia knew so many details about the christening she felt as though she was practically family. Her palms sweated as she dialled her voicemail and heard Juliet's plummy voice say, 'Good afternoon, Olivia...'

All her hopes for a stay of execution were dashed with her client's next words.

'I'm just phoning to let you know that when you come into the private road, it forks to the left and right. You need to take the left-hand fork, and as I said, we're the house with the griffins on the stone pillars. I wasn't sure if I told you this and I didn't want you to get lost. Thanks, love.'

Juliet Grey was nice, as well as being plummy and pernickety. That somehow made it all feel so much worse.

The phone rang again in her hand. Olivia dropped it in alarm on the worktop and then leaned forward nervously to look at the display.

It wasn't Juliet. It was Aunt Dawn.

She snatched it up, shaking with relief.

'Darling, I'm not interrupting you, am I, only I'm in a bit of a quandary...'

'What quandary?' There was something in her aunt's voice that made Olivia's heart clench. *Oh no, please not more problems.* 'Are you OK?'

'I'm fine, but Emmeline isn't, unfortunately. I've just got in my car to take her to the vets, but it won't start and I wondered maybe... but only if you're free...'

Olivia's heart sank. She glanced at the digital clock on her oven and swallowed.

'Um... yes, I'm free.' She wasn't in the habit of lying. But Aunt Dawn knew how hectic her life was and she never asked her to do anything unless it was really, really important.

Emmeline may only be a chicken, but her aunt doted on her little flock of ex-battery hens, all of which were named after famous women she admired, from Emmeline Pankhurst to Claudia Winkleman. They were right up there at the top of her list of passions, ahead of fabulous cakes and even vintage clothes.

'She's in a box,' Aunt Dawn continued a little breathlessly. 'I'm right here with her. I'll start walking. Save time.'

Blimey, it must be urgent.

Olivia bit her lip. 'OK. I'll meet you in the car park in five minutes.'

Her aunt disconnected and Olivia stared at the wrecked pink cake box on the side. Phoning Juliet would have to wait. Making another cake would have to wait too. She would need a miracle to resolve this one. Preferably in the next five minutes.

But right now, she needed to focus on Aunt Dawn. She grabbed her keys and dashed out of the door.

Deciding her aunt must be really worried to be in such a rush, she didn't wait in the car park but started jogging towards Weymouth Quay to meet her. Hens may be almost as light as air, but it would still be awkward manhandling a cardboard box up across Town Bridge and down the stone steps.

Today the water in the harbour looked green. It sparkled in the afternoon sun. Not that much different than the green-painted underside of the bridge itself. Aunt Dawn wasn't difficult to spot. She was halfway across and was wearing a long red and white polka dot skirt and her favourite vintage denim jacket, which had gorgeous pink and red beaded flowers all over it, although her top half was mostly obscured by the cardboard box.

She was puffing slightly when Olivia reached her and didn't see her until the last minute.

'Oh hello, darling. I'm so sorry. I don't want to hold you up.'

'You're not.' When had she become such an accomplished liar? 'Shall I take her?' Olivia opened her arms for the box, which was punched with air holes in both sides, and her aunt reluctantly relinquished her precious cargo.

Dawn's face was flushed. That must be worry, Olivia surmised, because she was one of the fittest sixty-two-year-olds she knew. Tendrils of dark curly hair escaping from a workmanlike plait framed her pretty face. 'Thank you.' Worried brown eyes that Olivia knew were a mirror image of her own met hers. 'I'm so grateful you could step in.'

'We'll soon get her sorted out.' Olivia hoped she was right. Chickens were fragile creatures. And she needed to make that cake. Her stomach crunched with anxiety as they fell in to step on the bridge.

They were the same height, five feet nine and a half, and they were the spitting image of each other. Instead of inheriting her mother's fair hair and English rose colouring like her sister Ruby had, Olivia looked like her aunt. They had the same dark brown, unruly hair, except Olivia's was longer, slightly olive skin and delicate bone structure. They were often mistaken for mother and daughter. Although Aunt Dawn declared that Olivia was the spit of *Coronation Street*'s Alison King (she was a big fan of Corrie) and she proclaimed herself to be Alison King plus a lifetime of laughter lines. A pretty accurate description.

Olivia dragged her thoughts away from soap dramas – despite the fact today seemed to be turning into one – and concentrated on negotiating the stone steps off the bridge. She definitely couldn't afford to drop another box of precious cargo. A few moments later they were back at her van. She put the boxed-up Emmeline gently on her aunt's knees as requested. At least something good had come out of the cake catastrophe. If this afternoon had gone according to plan, she wouldn't have been able to do this for at least another hour and a half and that might have been too late.

'What do you think's wrong with Emmeline?' she asked as they sped along the back streets. 'You are still using the same vet, aren't you?'

'Yes, Mike Turner. The white building on the corner of Park Street.'

'I know the one.'

'I'm not sure what's wrong with her. She may be egg-bound. She's been in the coop on her nest, poor little thing. I thought she was struggling at lunchtime. I'm hoping I haven't left it too long.'

'I thought you'd be working in the shop.'

'I was, but luckily I went out the back about half an hour ago. To check on Emmeline.'

Olivia nodded. Her aunt lived in the flat above her shop, which was like a Tardis and had a lot more space inside than there looked to be from outside. At one end of the building was a fire exit that led out onto a six-foot square terrace, which in turn led down into what Olivia had called the secret garden when she was small. It was an idyllic space full of pots and hanging baskets and it dropped down in a series of levels that were connected by steps and narrow pathways until you got to the lowest level, which had a wall around it and a gate that led to the back of the shop.

A fluttering and a scratching from the boxed-up Emmeline reminded Olivia of their rescue mission as she drew into the vet's large car park and found a space.

Mike Turner, who reminded Olivia a bit of her old science teacher but who had a lot more charisma, turned out to be brisk and efficient. He confirmed the egg-bound diagnosis, administered a calcium shot to the docile hen and gave them a list of instructions.

'She should be fine. She's very healthy,' he reassured. 'Keep an eye on her for the next couple of hours.'

Her aunt looked hugely relieved as she stroked Emmeline's silky black feathers.

Olivia had been so focused on the rescue mission that she hadn't thought about her own problems, but now they flicked back into her mind with a vengeance.

The vet trip had taken less than an hour. It was nearly 5.30. Just before they left the vet's, she checked her phone. There were no more calls from Juliet Grey, thank God. But there would be soon, she was sure. She needed to phone her and explain why she hadn't arrived at the scheduled time and she needed a plan of action. She still couldn't bear to think about tomorrow.

'You're very quiet,' Aunt Dawn murmured on the journey back. 'What's going on? Is it that new man of yours?'

'No, Phil's fine. He's lovely.' She remembered she hadn't answered his text either. Neither was he very new – they'd been seeing each other nearly ten months, but in Aunt Dawn's world, anything less than a year was 'just the other day'.

'So what is it?'

There was no point in beating about the bush, her aunt knew her too well. She told her what had happened.

'Mmm,' Aunt Dawn said when she'd finished. 'Awkward. I don't suppose you've got another cake in stock you could use?'

'Not fruit no. Not so many people want it, these days.'

'Why were you taking the cake today anyway if the christening's not until Saturday?'

'It's a long story, but one of the reasons is that they have a photographer coming tomorrow to take snaps for the family album of a relative who can't make Saturday because they're out of the country. They're doing a mock-up of the christening. It's that kind of family. They've got a marquee in the garden, a harpist, caterers coming in...' She broke off. 'It's kind of irrelevant anyway, isn't it? I'd agreed to drop the cake off today. And now I can't.'

'But first thing tomorrow would be OK?'

'I think it would.' They could still do the photo shoot. 'We said today to allow for unforeseen circumstances. Juliet Grey is a risk-averse kind of lady.' She shook her head as they pulled up at a traffic light. 'It's just as well she is.' She took a deep breath. 'I'm going to have to tell her. Then I'm going to have to make another top tier and re-ice it.'

'I can help you.'

'What about Emmeline? The vet said you needed to keep an eye on her.'

'We can do that at yours. We'll go back to number five.'

Olivia opened her mouth to protest that having Emmeline in her kitchen broke every hygiene and health and safety law in the book and then shut it again, Aunt Dawn knew that.

'What about the shop? Is Lydia there?' Lydia Brooks was her aunt's right-hand woman; a small, bustling, smiley woman in her fifties, who was a specialist in lace and brocade – what she didn't know about vintage fashion wasn't worth knowing.

'No, she's off today. I closed up early. It's fine. The shop would be shut in another half-hour anyway and I'm not expecting any deliveries or pick-ups. Passing trade will come back if they want something.'

Olivia stopped arguing as they arrived back at number five. Fortunately, her space was still free.

As they went into the kitchen, complete with Emmeline, who was clearly feeling better because she shifted in her box and clucked with indignation as they moved her again, Olivia spotted some crumbs of pink icing scattered like confetti around her back step. A reminder of her clumsiness.

'I'll put Emmeline in the lounge, shall I, love?'

It was a rhetorical question. Her aunt had already disappeared. A few moments later, having left the recuperating hen with water and making sure she was comfy, Dawn was back again. They both washed their hands at the small sink that Olivia had installed in addition to the main one to comply with the endless regulations there were when you baked commercially from your kitchen.

'What else are you supposed to be doing this evening?' Dawn enquired. 'And tomorrow morning?' She clapped her hands over her mouth. 'Oh lord, your *Casualty* audition. That's tomorrow. How did I forget that?'

'You've had other things on your mind.' Olivia shook her head. 'I need to cancel it. I'm not going to make it. Even if I could do another cake in time, I still need to deliver it first thing. I can't be in two places at once.' She sighed. 'I haven't even told the client what's happened yet. It was literally just before you rang that I dropped the cake.'

'Oh, my darling, and you didn't say a word. Bless you. That is so typical of you. Did you hurt yourself?'

'I don't think I did my wrist much good. But no lasting damage.'

'Let me look.'

Olivia held up her hand. 'Not even bruised – see? It's fine.'

'Good. Right then.' Aunt Dawn straightened her shoulders apparently satisfied. 'Don't worry.' Her dark eyes were soft as she touched her niece's arm. 'We've got this.'

'We have?'

'Absolutely.' She gestured towards the laminated sign over the cooker. *The impossible we can do at once. Miracles might take a little longer.*

Olivia's mobile rang. It was Juliet Grey again. Panicking, she dropped it like a hot baking tray onto the worktop. 'That's the client. What shall I say?'

'Well, usually I'd say full disclosure is best. But I'm guessing you don't want to panic her.'

'I don't. I can't.'

'Shall I speak to her.'

Olivia mouthed an uncertain yes and Dawn picked up the mobile before she could change her mind.

'Good afternoon, Amazing Cakes, how may I help?'

Olivia held her breath as her aunt listened to what was clearly quite a long babble of words from an anxious Juliet.

'May I stop you there for a second,' she said. 'I was just about to phone you. There's been a family emergency which Olivia is dealing with now. Your cake is done, but we will have to defer delivery until first thing tomorrow morning. I understand you need your cake tomorrow, so would 9 a.m. sharp suit?' Her voice was a mixture of calm and authoritative. Then she listened to the response carefully. 'Thank you for being so understanding. Yes, these things happen. Quite. Thank you. That's very sweet of you. I'll pass on your regards. We'll see you at nine.'

She disconnected.

'Not a problem,' she said and glanced at the clock. It was approaching 6 p.m. 'Have you got all the ingredients, love?'

'I think so. I'd better cancel the audition and I really need to tell Phil not to come round tonight – unless he wants to help us make sugar paste roses.'

'Don't cancel anything.' Aunt Dawn had fire in her voice. 'I can deliver your cake in the morning. And I can do the finishing for you on site. Your Mrs Grey was very understanding.'

'Are you sure?' Olivia felt a fizz of hope thread through her despair.

'Damn right, I'm sure. Let's get cracking.'

3

An hour later, the ingredients were weighed out and mixed and the six-inch cake was in the oven. The timer was set for 10 p.m. which was the earliest it would be ready. The kitchen was beginning to fill up with the rich sweet scents of slowly baking fruit cake.

While Aunt Dawn had made the cake, Olivia had been cutting shapes out of pink sugar paste icing at the kitchen table. She had a pattern for the baby shoes and had completed a new pair in record speed. There were just the sugar daisies on the buckles to make. Then she would start on the teddy bear. Briefly she'd contemplated repairing the original, but it was too risky. If even the tiniest bit of grit had got into the sugar paste, it would be a disaster.

A huge amount of time went into making her kitchen a sterile place to work. It wasn't just about the Environmental Health inspections, which could happen at any time, it was about her reputation. She had a dread of a hair ending up in a cake – or something else that wasn't supposed to be there.

The cake itself would take between three and four hours to

cool enough to be rough iced. Rough icing a cake is the equivalent to putting primer on a wall you're painting. It's unseen but essential in order to make the final version perfect.

She couldn't rough ice until the early hours, but fortunately a lot of the decorative work could be done in advance.

She was trying not to think about the roses. Even with both of them working, they'd be struggling to finish them before midnight. Olivia hadn't realised she was frowning until her aunt came across to the table. She smoothed down the apron she'd borrowed, which was white, with the words Head Cook emblazoned on it, and said, 'Don't look so worried. Apart from the fact that we're working against the clock, I really enjoyed that.'

'Thanks again. I really appreciate this. I'll make some more coffee. Phil should be here soon. He said he's always wanted to make sugar paste roses.'

'I can do the coffee.' Aunt Dawn went to the sink. 'The more I know about your Phil, the more I like him.'

Olivia softened. 'Phil's great. He also said he'll bring supplies for the chefs, something we can eat while we work, being as time is of the essence.'

'So then...?' Aunt Dawn's voice had gone ultra-casual. 'While we're on the subject of your Phil, how is it going? Is it getting serious? Or is this just a casual fling? Not that I want to pry, darling – tell me to mind my own if you like?'

'When have I ever told you to do that? No, it's fine. It's going great actually. He's amazing. He's thoughtful, kind, smart, not to mention amazingly hot. Sorry, too much information...'

'I'm not completely blind. I can see the boy's hot.' She rolled her eyes. 'And it must be good going out with a fellow thespian – is it?'

'Yes, it is. He totally gets it. The hope. The heartbreak. He's had the whole acting bug thing as long as I have. He's just as obsessed as I am. We both have the same dream – one day we'll get that breakthrough role. Even though we haven't yet...' She sighed. 'It's different for men – there's always lots of good parts for guys. Age isn't so much of a thing.'

As they'd been talking, Olivia had been fashioning the sugar paste daisies for the baby shoes and now she stuck them gently onto the buckles.

She was aware that her aunt was back at the kitchen table and they both looked at the finished shoes.

'Age isn't so much of a thing for guys when it comes to starting a family either,' Olivia said softly. 'It doesn't matter that Phil's forty-one. He can probably father children right up until he's in his seventies and beyond, but it matters that I've just turned thirty-nine. I feel as though every month that goes past lessens my chances of being a mum...'

Suddenly she couldn't speak. There was too much of an ache in her throat. She hadn't realised until she'd said the words how much she cared. And something darker was in her heart too – fear. She was so afraid it would never happen. That she'd never get the chance to hold her own baby in her arms. That her dreams of having her own family would break apart and fall into the dirt like the smashed christening cake.

She felt a tear roll down her cheek and she closed her eyes. Bloody hell where had this come from? She heard the scrape of chair legs at the table and Aunt Dawn sat beside her and put an arm around her shoulders.

'Oh my darling, I didn't know you were feeling like this.'

'Neither did I until we started talking about it.' Olivia laid her head against her aunt's bony shoulder. 'I'm sorry. I'm just tired – and stressed out. And I feel as though the clock's ticking...' She glanced at the oven and bit her lip. 'In more ways than one.'

'Hey. You've got plenty of time. Lots of women start their families in their forties, these days.' She pulled a pristine white hanky out of her pocket. She always had hankies. White monogrammed vintage ones.

Olivia sniffed and took it and wiped her face.

'I know they do, but I've never even been pregnant. Some of my friends have had scares, but I haven't. And after what happened with Tom...' She broke off. Tom Boyd was her ex and one of the reasons she hadn't yet started a family. But the subject of her ticking biological clock and Tom's laissez-faire attitude towards it were the last thing she wanted to be talking about when Phil arrived. 'I'm sorry. Can we change the subject?'

'Of course we can. I'll get started on the roses?'

'That would be brilliant. Are you really sure about taking the cake tomorrow? We're not going to get much sleep.'

'I've always thought sleep's overrated,' Aunt Dawn said briskly.

'Thank you,' Olivia whispered, 'So much. Not just for the cake.' Her aunt's eyes softened in acknowledgement as Olivia slid out of her chair and escaped to the bathroom. She wasn't a good crier. Her skin always went blotchy. She splashed water onto her cheekbones and then retied her dark hair back up on top of her head.

Now Tom was in her mind, it was hard to get him out again. They'd met in 2010 when she was twenty-eight and he was thirty-three at a wedding exhibition at Olympia. At the time, she'd been baking cakes for a wedding planning company, prior to setting up her own cake making company, and he'd been selling diamonds.

Tom was a brilliant salesman. He had one of those faces that people trusted and he could literally sell anything, although she'd discovered later that he tended to focus on high-end commodities. In his career to date, he'd sold Sunseeker boats, shepherd's huts to rich landowners and holiday homes in Iceland.

He'd asked her for a coffee when they had a break at the exhibition and they realised they actually lived within five miles of each other, in Weymouth, and had a mutual friend who was a member of the same gym they were. Not that either of them went. They laughed about this. They laughed about a lot in that half an hour, and when he'd asked rather shyly whether he could take her to dinner the following weekend, Olivia had agreed happily.

She was only slightly fazed when he took her to the most expensive restaurant in town. They both laughed when he told her he was just trying to impress her and after that it would be McDonald's all the way.

It wasn't though. Tom Boyd was very wealthy – that quickly became apparent – but he wasn't ever flashy and neither did he take it for granted. 'I work really hard and I've also been lucky,' he told her. 'I like nice things. But I may not always have money. I'm only as good as my last commission. Let me spoil you while the going's good.'

Olivia had always been fiercely independent, but she had to admit it was lovely being spoiled.

Their relationship had slowly become more serious. They wanted the same things. Stability, socialising with friends. They both loved their work. He liked the fact she was an actress and had actually been in things he'd heard of. He liked showing her off. They both wanted kids – one day in the future when the time was right. There was no rush.

Seeing as they both worked and operated in the wedding biz scene, neither was keen on marriage. They'd both seen it as an unnecessary label. It had been Olivia who'd changed her mind first, just after she'd turned thirty-three.

She'd mentioned it to him in passing, in a 'wouldn't it be nice' kind of way, and he'd seemed hesitant. Then, to her surprise, three weeks later when they were on a weekend away in Florence, he'd proposed.

It had been the most incredibly romantic proposal. Tom was the king of big romantic gestures. They'd just been for lunch in a gorgeous open-air trattoria, and they'd been walking back towards their hotel across Ponte Vecchio, the famous bridge lined with goldsmiths and jewellers, when Tom had grabbed her hand and pulled her towards a shop window.

'What is it?' she'd asked, slightly alarmed when he'd dropped to one knee on the pavement and grinned up at her.

'Marry me, Olivia? Live with me forever and be my wife?'

Several passers-by stopped to watch. The Italians did have a reputation for being the most romantic of all Europeans after all. Hadn't they invented the language of love? And it was obvious to everyone exactly what was going on.

'Of course I'll marry you,' Olivia had said, tugging him to his feet and kissing him, to the delight of the crowd of cheering, applauding onlookers.

She realised that they had stopped outside the most expensive, most exclusive jewellers and they went straight in to buy Olivia a ring.

'Why didn't you buy it in advance?' She had teased as they'd browsed the trays of diamonds. 'Did you think I'd say no?'

'I wanted you to choose,' he'd murmured, touching her cheek. 'I didn't want to make a mistake.'

The romance of that weekend had shone brightly over the next year and had only tarnished slightly when another two years had passed without them actually setting a date for the wedding.

'There is no rush to set a date for the wedding,' Tom had said and she had agreed. Even though she was beginning to think this was the longest engagement in history.

Five years after the engagement, when even Aunt Dawn had begun asking whether they still planned to get married, Olivia had raised it with Tom and that, she'd finally realised with hindsight, had been the beginning of the end.

'I'd like us to start a family, Tom,' she had said one evening when they were eating at Harbour Views; their favourite fish restaurant, which was contemporary and served gorgeous food but had cold tiled floors and modern, slightly uncomfortable furniture. 'I know it's old-fashioned, but I'd really like us to be married when we do.'

They'd just finished their main course – seafood linguine, which was to die for and all sourced locally.

Tom reached across the glass table and took both her hands in his and there was something in his face that had stilled her. 'I've been thinking about families, Olivia.' He frowned and chewed absently at the corner of his lip and then he'd dropped a bombshell. 'The thing is, I'm not sure whether I actually want one.'

She looked at him in shock. 'But you've always wanted kids. You've always said that when the time's right...' She broke off.

He was nodding but his blue eyes were shadowed. 'I know what I said. And, believe me, I meant it. But it's been on my mind a lot lately and I don't think I do. I love my life – our life – as it is. I don't need kids to complete it. In fact, I don't think they would complete it. I think ... Well, I think it might be the opposite.'

He'd rubbed at the five o'clock shadow on his chin while Olivia stared at him in disbelief. She couldn't believe what she was hearing. This was such a complete turnaround.

Or was it? Suddenly, his reluctance to set a date for the wedding made a lot more sense.

'How long have you been feeling like this?' she'd asked.

'I don't know. Six months. Maybe a year.' He shrugged. 'Does it matter?'

'Yes, I think it does.' She knew suddenly that it had been much longer than a year. He must have had doubts for ages. She pulled her hands from his.

'It doesn't affect us,' he said, looking anguished. 'I still want to marry...'

'Of course it affects us,' she cut across him. 'I do want a family, Tom. It's what I've always wanted, as you know. But I can't have one by myself, can I?' She was shocked at the bitterness in her own voice and he'd clearly heard it too.

He looked stricken. 'I know, but...' He blew out through his teeth. 'Look at what happened to Alfie and Lin.'

For a second, she'd paused and her heart gave a wild swing of hope. Maybe that's what this was all about. Alfie and Lin were two of his closest friends – he'd been best man at their wedding – they'd married when they were both in their thirties but had trouble conceiving. After five rounds of IVF, they'd finally got their much-wanted twins, who'd been born premature, but the trauma of the whole thing had been so great that they'd ended up splitting up and were now in the throes of an acrimonious divorce.

'You've been talking to Alfie?' she asked.

'Yeah. A lot. Having a family hasn't brought him any joy. *Au contraire*. He's totally messed up.'

'That doesn't mean it's going to happen to us, Tom. I might fall pregnant straight away. We've never even tried. I've never even missed a pill.' That wasn't quite true, but it hadn't happened often and she'd always made sure they'd used some other form of contraception if it had.

Her mother had a lot to answer for in this respect, as both herself and Ruby had been conceived the first time she'd tried to get pregnant, which had left both of them with the impression it would be incredibly risky to do as much as breathe while a boy was present.

She had held Tom's gaze and he'd nodded slowly and for the longest moment Olivia had thought he was considering what she'd just said. She went on quickly. 'When my parents wanted a baby, they got pregnant the first time they tried. And here I am – the living proof. Same with Ruby. They didn't split up. They've always been blissfully happy.'

Tom lowered his eyes. 'I don't want a family. I'm really sorry – I truly thought I did, but I've made up my mind. Please don't walk away from me. Just say that you'll think about it for a while. Think through the pros and cons.'

Olivia didn't walk away. Not at first. They'd talked and they'd cried, but neither of them had budged an inch. She was desperate for a family. Tom was completely against having one. In the end, the only possible solution had been to end the relationship. They'd been together for just over ten years. She had been shocked to the core. His complete turnaround had devastated her. She didn't think she'd have felt any worse if he'd gone off with someone else.

The sound of her doorbell flicked Olivia back into the present and a few moments later she heard voices in her kitchen.

Phil must have arrived.

Hurriedly, she rubbed away some smudged mascara and reapplied foundation. She and Phil were still at the stage where she wanted to keep the illusion of having perfect skin and being beautiful. She'd never decided whether this was insecurity or vanity. After all, he already knew what she looked like with no make-up on. They quite often woke up in the same bed at weekends.

When she got back to the kitchen, Phil was chatting to her

aunt. She felt a twang of lust. He was gorgeous. Even with his black hair a bit windswept – in fact, especially with his hair a bit windswept – and still in his work jacket that fitted snugly over his broad shoulders. Her sister Ruby reckoned he looked like Aidan Turner in *Poldark* and it was true.

He broke off when he saw her. 'I see that Operation Save The Day is in full swing. How's it going?' He dangled a carrier bag from the fingers of one hand. 'I nipped into M&S and got "not just nibbles". I'll put them on plates and we can help ourselves – yes?'

'Brilliant. Thanks.' She went across and kissed him, aware that her aunt had busied herself making coffees.

'I'll just stick my jacket in your lounge,' Phil said, shrugging it off as he spoke. 'Save cluttering up the kitchen.'

He disappeared but was back very quickly, wearing a slightly bemused expression.

'Did you know there's a chicken sitting on your sofa?' he asked Olivia. He opened his fingers to reveal something in his palm. 'And she seems to have laid you an egg.'

4

A disgruntled and loudly protesting Emmeline was recaptured and returned to her box and Aunt Dawn moved her into the darkened bathroom and came back into the kitchen with an apologetic look at Olivia. 'Sorry about that. She'll roost now it's nighttime anyway. I'm just so relieved she's OK. I should have known she'd escape from that box. When I first got her, she was forever trying to escape from the coop, and once, she got herself stuck in the netting on the gate. I called her Emmeline in the first place because she's such a feisty little thing.'

Phil looked mystified at this announcement until Olivia explained. 'Emmeline Pankhurst – the suffragette who's famous for chaining herself to the railings in protests.'

'Of course. How did I not clock that?' He banged his forehead. 'Doh.'

They all laughed and then turned their attention to the nibbles he'd bought.

Included were miniature pizzas the size of tablespoons, a selection of olives with Manchego, cherry tomatoes stuffed with mozzarella, gherkins which Phil and Olivia both loved and cocktail sticks to eat everything with so they didn't have to use their fingers.

'I figured they'd be quick to eat and not create any more mess,' Phil said.

'How thoughtful,' Dawn glanced at Olivia. 'I'd say he's a keeper, this one.'

Olivia didn't answer. Not because she didn't agree but because she didn't want to come across as clingy or heavy.

She'd been on the rebound when she'd met Phil. She'd split up with Tom less than a month earlier and another relationship had been the last thing on her mind. She was totally focused on *Hamlet*, which had come along at exactly the right time.

Relationships were not even on her radar, she'd told Phil when they were having a coffee one Saturday. Even that had been accidental – a few of the actors had got together for a social evening after rehearsal and they'd been the last to leave.

'I'm not looking for a relationship either,' he'd told her. 'In fact, technically I'm seeing someone.'

'Technically?' she had asked, intrigued despite herself.

'We met via a dating show,' he'd explained. 'It's an unusual situation as in we've never actually been on a date, but we will be going on one. It's going to be filmed and then hopefully aired on Netflix.'

'I hope it works out for you both,' she'd told him sincerely.

But as time had gone on, they'd found themselves drawn more and more to each other and Phil had finally explained that neither he nor his prospective date thought their relationship had a future. And that, actually, the lady in question had her eye on someone else too.

So, Olivia had agreed that a date might be fun. As long as they took things ultra slowly.

'I don't want anything heavy,' she'd said.

'Let's just have some fun,' he'd replied. 'See how things go.'

'Yes, we can take it a day at a time. We're both really busy.'

'Sounds good to me. No strings.'

All of those little phrases that gave both of them a get-out clause, Olivia had thought at the time. But it was true they were busy. They both had two jobs for a start – and they didn't live on each other's doorsteps. Phil was in Brancombe, which was on the outskirts of Swanage. It was twenty-six miles, door to door – a fifty-minute drive if there was no traffic. Not exactly a long-distance relationship, but also not quite in the 'pop by for a coffee' range either. At least not without a prior arrangement.

Rehearsals for Hamlet had started in April and they'd started dating in May, but only casually. By Christmas, they'd decided they'd be exclusive, as in neither of them wanted to see anyone else. But they hadn't yet ventured into discussions about commitment. Neither of them had ever said, 'I love you.' It had been on the tip of her tongue sometimes, Olivia thought, when they'd been snuggling up after a film night or he'd cooked her breakfast at his. But she'd never voiced it. Nor had she discussed her hopes for a family. Even though she was acutely aware that the clock was always ticking.

It seemed to get harder – not easier – to mention the c word. She was happy and she knew he was happy too and a part of her was scared of rocking the boat. Why risk the loveliness that they had?

* * *

By 10 p.m. the cake was cooked and cooling on her worktop. You can't rush the cooling of a cake. Not if you planned to ice it so soon after making it.

By 11 p.m. she and Aunt Dawn were three quarters of the way through the sugar paste roses.

Phil was yawning, but stoic and supportive, keeping them supplied with caffeine and encouragement. At eleven thirty, Aunt Dawn said, 'You should go to bed, Olivia. You need to be at your best tomorrow. I'll finish the icing. I can work from the photos you took of the original. To be honest, love, it feels great to keep my hand in.'

'Your aunt's right,' Phil agreed. 'I'll drop her home with Emmeline when it's done.'

'I'll take the cake to the Greys in the morning,' Dawn said. 'Don't forget to give me the address.'

'What about your car?' Olivia asked, suddenly remembering. 'What if it doesn't start in the morning?'

'I've got that covered. Lydia's in tomorrow and she's happy for me to take her car. I texted her earlier.'

'Are you sure?'

'A hundred and one per cent. Now shoo.'

'Get to bed,' Phil said.

They both looked at her with expressions that dared her to argue. Phil's was mock stern and her aunt's was uncompromising.

Olivia felt like a child. 'I can't thank you enough. You've both been so brilliant.'

'It's not a big deal,' Phil said.

'Now be off with you.' Dawn waved a palette knife at her. 'Night, night, darling.'

Phil came across and gave her a lingering goodnight kiss. 'I'll be thinking of you tomorrow. Break a leg.'

She was feeling all emotional again but for different reasons. It was another of those occasions, she realised as she drew away from Phil, in which she'd have liked to say, 'I love you.'

Olivia thought she'd have trouble sleeping, knowing that the pair of them would still be in her kitchen, but she must have gone out like a light because she didn't even hear them go.

When her alarm woke her at 5.15 a.m. and she went, bleary-eyed, to get coffee, there was barely a sign they'd ever been there. They'd cleared up after themselves too, the darlings. Her kitchen was spotless.

There was a note on the side in Aunt Dawn's loopy handwriting. 'Let me know how it goes. I'll text you when the cake's safely delivered.'

She was half hoping Phil might have added a line, but there was nothing. She chided herself for being disappointed. Phil was more of a 'sending texts' kind of guy than the 'writing notes' kind.

* * *

Her train was due to arrive at Waterloo at 9.53 and the tube journey would take about forty minutes. Her appointment wasn't until midday, but she never left anything to chance. Knowing her tendency to get clumsier than usual when she was nervous, she'd even put an extra top into her backpack, in case there should be an incident with a takeaway coffee – this had happened once before – along with the script and directions. She was wearing her lucky necklace, a multicoloured stone on a long silver chain which went with nearly everything she owned, which might well be the reason she always had it on when anything good happened. After Phil and Aunt Dawn's heroic efforts to ensure she'd make today's audition, she was extra determined to make it a success.

As the train sped through patches of countryside interspersed with the long back gardens of houses, glimpses into other people's lives, Olivia fantasised about getting the part. She would be playing Alison Brown, a consultant with issues, a formidable strong, stroppy woman with a secret daughter she hid from the world and a dysfunctional family. A consultant with secrets that would emerge one by one as the character developed.

It was the usual high-octane kind of stuff that went on in hospital dramas and Olivia was really excited about it. Much of her acting career had involved non-speaking or very small speaking parts on television. In the early days, she'd done shed-loads of work as an extra. But since she'd got her agent, Clarice Munroe, who was herself a formidable strong, stroppy woman, her profile had gone up considerably. She'd had several minor speaking parts in soaps and a couple of call backs for bigger roles, but she still hadn't had her big break.

Clarice had run her own agency for forty years and had a reputation for being tough and uncompromising. There was a standing joke in the business,

Question: What's the difference between a rottweiler and Clarice Munroe?

Answer: A rottweiler knows when it's beaten and lets go.

Olivia had been a little nervous the first time they'd met, but she'd found Clarice to be fair as well as brusque.

'My job is to find you the opportunities. Your job is to turn up on time and impress them. It couldn't be simpler.'

Now she was finally on the train, Olivia allowed herself to think about Clarice's reaction if she had cancelled today. She'd probably have been dropped like a hot cake tin.

Thank God for Aunt Dawn and Phil.

She was on her second tightly lidded coffee when a WhatsApp message came through from Aunt Dawn.

Cake safely delivered and finished. The Greys are thrilled. They gave me a nice tip for you.

There was a picture of the cake in situ. Olivia blew it up to have a good look. It was perfect. Just like the original. Her heart swelled with relief and gratitude.

She texted back.

The tip's yours. You've definitely earned it. Thank you so much for last night. You saved my life. Were you very late?

She got a smiley face emoji back and no answer to her question. If she'd had a better signal, she'd have phoned, but they were clearly in a bad area. Her mobile hovered between one bar and none.

The next time she had a signal, she texted Phil too and thanked him profusely. His reply came back almost immediately.

Break a leg, my lovely. Call me when you're done.

The signal disappeared completely. She would thank them both properly later. She owed them big time.

Now she knew her customer was happy, she began to relax.

To her relief, the train was on time too and the venue was easy to find. Everyone knew where the London audition studio was. When she arrived, fifteen minutes early, she discovered there were several other people waiting. They must be casting more than one role today, which was maybe why they were auditioning in London, not Cardiff, where *Casualty* was filmed.

Some of the auditionees looked calm, some were chatting to each other. Olivia didn't know anyone, although she could guess who her competitor was. There was only one other woman who was anywhere near old enough for the role of Alison Brown and that was debatable – she was at least ten years younger than Olivia. She was wearing a suit and carrying a Mulberry bag, which could have been a fake. Olivia watched her surreptitiously, which wasn't that difficult as she was sitting opposite and didn't look at anyone, just tapped incessantly into her phone.

She allowed herself a brief fantasy in which she was so famous that she no longer had to go through the ordeal of attending auditions. Not that she really minded the auditions, it was the nerves and anxiety before and the waiting to hear afterwards that she hated.

In her fantasy, her agent just sent through texts that said things like: Channel Four have asked if you'll consider doing…

She didn't know anyone who got texts like that, although she had once known an actor who was famous for getting the lead in police dramas. The first time he hadn't been called to go to an audition he'd been worried, but then his agent had phoned and said, 'They didn't ask you to audition, darling, they assumed you'd know you'd got it.'

OK, so she didn't know whether this was actually true. It could have been an industry myth. But she was so immersed in her fantasy that her name was called twice before she heard it.

'Olivia Lambert, please.'

'Sorry.' She got up and fell over her feet. Good start! Then, with her heart beating on triple time and her face hot with embarrassment, she followed the woman with the clipboard into an adjoining studio.

5

As Olivia walked up to the microphone, Clarice Munroe's voice echoed in her mind. *Focus totally. Be the best you can be.*

She gave it her all. The adrenaline of the last twenty-four hours was coursing through her and it was a relief to have an outlet. Days of preparation and a few moments in the spotlight. At least that's what it always felt like and today was no different. It was over so quickly that she couldn't remember much about it.

It was impossible to know how her portrayal had gone down. There were three people in the room and their faces were pretty much impassive, although one of the women did smile and give her the thumbs up at the end.

'Thank you so much for coming, Olivia. We'll be in touch.'

As always, time had disappeared during the audition and she was amazed to find that almost an hour had passed, by the time she emerged back onto the busy London street. She was hit by a cacophony of noise, blaring horns, diesel engines, voices and a crush of people plugged into smartphones and indifferent to everyone else.

Sidestepping Boris bikes, she crossed the road. She found

London vaguely threatening – the lights, the city smells, the huge volume of traffic, the crowds of people rushing about, most of them in a huge hurry, unsmiling and all totally focused on where they were going.

Yet she felt strangely calm now it was all over. This could be the role that properly launched her career. Or she could fade back into obscurity until the next opportunity. All or nothing. It was the thing she both loved and hated about the business.

She got the tube back towards Waterloo and for the first time she wished she wasn't alone. Phil had offered to come with her, but she'd stopped him. Train tickets that got you to London early cost a fortune and it would have meant him taking a day off work. There was no sense in two of them running up a big bill.

'If I get it, you can take a day off then and we can properly celebrate,' she'd suggested and he'd agreed, but right now she really wished he was here.

When she got off the tube, she bought an extortionately priced sandwich from a trendy open-air café and sat on a bench by the Thames to eat it. She wasn't that familiar with London. She wouldn't have wanted to live there full time. Fortunately, with *Casualty* filmed in Cardiff, she wouldn't need to. She allowed herself a brief fantasy about getting the role and what would happen next, which she and Phil had already discussed, although not in too much detail because they were both too superstitious about jinxing it. She wouldn't need to move to Cardiff, but she wouldn't be able to make so many cakes. 'I could still do part-time cake baking. I'd just need to be careful what I took on. Downsize the business. One of the perks of being self-employed.' She still couldn't quite believe she'd got this far; that she was on the brink of making that decision.

Her phone pinged with a text and she jumped out of her skin. That could be Clarice now. She hardly dared look.

It was not Clarice. It was Juliet Grey, thanking her for the wonderful cake and hoping that the family emergency had been resolved and promising to recommend her to everyone she knew.

There were also messages from Ruby and her parents wishing her luck for today.

Olivia texted a thank you to everyone, finished her sandwich and got back to her fantasy. What would be the outcome of today? She really had no clue. She swung between elation and despair.

Her dreams of making a real name for herself as a serious actress, like her dreams of becoming a mother, seemed to get a little more elusive as each year passed. She would be forty in November and while she knew that you didn't have to be young to do either of those things these days, it sure as hell helped.

Knowing that the rest of her family – this included her younger sister Ruby and their parents, James and Marie – were all happily and successfully established doing what they'd spent their entire lives wanting to do didn't ease the pressure.

Ruby, at thirty-four, was an art dealer – a hugely successful one who'd made it big two years ago after being engaged by a handful of London celebrities for whose art collections she now had total responsibility. She had started in London but now worked from her beautiful home on the outskirts of Weymouth, with regular trips back to the capital. Ruby earned more in a month than Olivia earned in a year. She was organised, single-minded and sensible. Olivia loved her to bits, but they didn't have much in common and didn't see that much of each other despite being so close geographically.

Their parents were archaeologists. They had met on a dig when they were in their early twenties and had been inseparable ever since. United by their love of the past, fossils and a passion for dinosaurs, they had both been brought up near Bridport, which was close to Dorset's famous Chesil Beach and not a million miles from Lyme Bay, one of the best places in the country for fossil hunters, and it had been clear from the beginning that they were the perfect match. When they'd met, James had owned a cat called Tyrannosaurus – Rex for short – which had bemused everyone except Marie, who got him and the name, totally. It was a story that got trotted out on every anniversary.

'It was dinosaurs that brought us together,' Marie was fond of saying. 'Dinosaurs and a cat.'

Marie and James were currently on a dig in the Outer Hebrides. They had rented out their house for six months and were having a great time.

'Not that we don't miss you girls,' her mother told her every time they spoke. 'But you're busy too, aren't you?'

Olivia always agreed this was true and she was pleased that her parents were doing what they loved best and weren't needy and clingy or nagging her about giving them a grandchild, which was the case with one or two of her friends. That hadn't happened so much lately. She only had one other long-term friend, Hannah, who didn't have children and that was because she said she preferred puppies to babies. Hannah didn't even live close by any more. Her mum had moved to Cornwall a couple of years ago and Hannah had moved closer to her soon after. She must remember to message Hannah with an update or maybe call her for a proper catch up when she wasn't working.

Olivia called Phil as she'd promised and the sound of his gorgeous deep voice grounded her instantly.

'How did it go? How do you think it went?' he asked.

'Good, I think. It's so hard to tell, isn't it? I guess it depends what they're looking for.'

'I bet you smashed it. Fingers crossed. Are you coming

straight back or are you going off to do something cultural while you're up there?'

'I might have a bit of a wander around. I've got to get on a train before 4.30. Thanks again for last night. Were you very late?'

'It was about two-ish, I think. I didn't know there was so much involved in icing a cake. Your aunt is amazingly skilled.'

'I know. It was Aunt Dawn who taught me to ice. She's brilliant. But, oh my goodness she must be tired. And she must have got up early too. I got a text from her saying the cake got there fine.'

'Dawn's great. I really like her. She's like an older version of you.'

'Everyone says that. But she's much more sensible than me. And not as clumsy. I still can't believe I dropped that cake!'

'Stop beating yourself up. You've got two jobs and neither of them are exactly coasting-along kind of jobs, are they? They're both full on, high-octane gigs. You wouldn't be human if you didn't make the occasional mistake.'

'You always say exactly the right things.'

'I try.' She could hear him breathing. He must be out walking. 'Are you near the Thames?' he asked.

'I am.'

'So tell me what you can see.'

This was a game they sometimes played when they were in different places and wanted to connect.

Olivia looked around. 'Well,' she began, 'I'm sitting on a bench. Wooden with ornate metal armrests. Not far from the river.'

'What colour's the river?'

'Pink.'

He laughed. 'I'm being serious. I thought it was always dirty brown.'

'It is quite brown actually.' She stood up to get a closer look. 'Greeny brown. You wouldn't see much if you were swimming in it.'

'Is anyone swimming in it? Do people go wild swimming in the Thames. I've always fancied going wild swimming.'

'Yeah. Me too. But you wouldn't want to go swimming in this bit. There are a couple of boats. Water taxis, I think.' She breathed in the fresh air spiced with diesel fumes.

'What else?'

'There's a pigeon walking on the grass and I can see the London Eye. I don't think I'd go on that if you paid me. Way too high! I saw the Shard earlier. There were two guys in a crate cleaning the windows.' She shuddered. 'I wouldn't fancy that much either. And it must be a full-time job. You'd get to the bottom and you'd have to start again. How demoralising.'

'At least you'd never be out of a job.'

'That's true and you wouldn't want to be unemployed in London. Everything costs a fortune. I can hear a busker playing somewhere.' She was in her stride now. 'And just outside the station, I passed a couple of living statues. That's got to be harder work than being a window cleaner. How do they manage not to blink?'

'Aren't they usually "resting actors"?' Phil said.

'I think you might be right. I'm glad that isn't my backup job. Anyway, enough of me. Where are you? You sound like you're walking.'

'I'm on the beach.'

'Studland?' she guessed.

'Nope. Swanage pier. A couple of divers are getting kitted up to go in. I was just chatting to them. Apparently, it's quite interesting diving under the pier. There are lots of fish despite the number of fishermen on the beach.'

'I learned to scuba dive a while back,' she said wistfully. 'At a dive club in Weymouth. We did a lot of dives around Dorset. Tom and I also did a fair bit abroad when we were on holiday. I was really keen for a while.'

'Something else we have in common.' He sounded energised. 'I got my PADI qualification when I was in Greece. We should go some time? We don't have to go out on a boat. We could do a shore dive. There must be loads of places locally. Either near you or near me.'

'Let's chat about it when we meet. When is that by the way?'

'I'm free until four-ish on Sunday. Do you fancy lunch?'

'Definitely. I'm buying. I owe you one for last night.'

'You don't. It was my pleasure.'

That was something else she loved about him. He was totally unconditional.

'I'll come to you if you like,' she offered. It would give them a bit more time if he was dashing off to work.

'Thanks, I'll look forward to it. Go and enjoy London.'

'I will. Thanks. Bye, honey. See you Sunday.'

'With a bit of luck, we'll have something to celebrate.'

Olivia disconnected. She felt warmed. All her earlier self-doubt swept away by Phil's enthusiasm. He believed in her, even when she didn't believe in herself as maybe only another actor could.

They were lucky. They might not be famous yet, but they did get paid work. And they were both good at their day jobs. And they had each other.

The sun came out as she walked. Even the Thames looked less green, more blue. When she passed the living statue again, she winked at him and he winked back. It felt like a very good omen.

6

Another of the things Olivia loved about living in Weymouth was that she could run straight from her front door and be on the beach in minutes. Or, to be more precise, she could be on The Esplanade which fronted Weymouth beach. Running, especially by the sea, was one of her joys. Walking was good too, but you were more accessible when you were walking. People wanted to stop and chat.

Olivia had nothing against chatting to people, but when she wanted to unwind or to think, solitary running was better. You could lose yourself when you were running. It was just you and your breath and your heartbeat and the pounding of your feet on the tarmac. No one disturbed you. It was one of the few times she felt totally peaceful. Especially first thing in the morning. Especially when she was trying not to think about the previous day's audition – she still hadn't heard anything from Clarice.

Dressed in a lightweight tracksuit and running shoes, Olivia clicked her front door shut behind her and headed off at a steady jog. It was a chilly morning. It wasn't yet seven, but it was better to be underdressed at the beginning of a run than too warm, so she wore layers.

She ran along the esplanade past the Rockfish seafood restaurant, past the pizza place and the M&S food hall, with the smell of the sea mixed with the traffic fumes of the cars and buses on the coast road filling her nostrils. The tarmac felt hard beneath the cushioned running shoes. On her right, the blue and white railings separated the prom from the sandy gold beach and the sweeping curve of the coastline. The calls of the seagulls, the barks of excited dogs on the sands and the thrum of traffic were a familiar soundtrack in the background, although Olivia kept one ear out for her phone, just in case Clarice should ring.

Her mobile was tucked in her bumbag, snug against her waist – she'd been tempted to leave it at home in an effort to prove to herself that she wasn't obsessing about Clarice's call, but she hadn't quite had the resolve. Who was she kidding anyway? She *was* obsessing.

She ran past the beautiful old Victorian building that was the Royal Hotel and the garish clock that had been erected in 1888 to commemorate Queen Victoria's jubilee – she bet it hadn't been painted maroon and sky blue then, although apparently it had been garish for its time – and then on around the coast until she was far enough away from home to feel totally free. This route was part of the South West Coast Path that ultimately ended in Poole.

Only when she was a couple of kilometres from home did she slow down a little and let herself reflect back on yesterday. She had done the best she could. She had practised, prepared, researched the role and put everything she had into it, and yesterday she had given it her all. Whether or not she got the part was in the lap of the gods. But just for a moment she let herself dream.

Having a major part on *Casualty* wasn't just 'a nice little earner for a while' – as Clarice had put it – it was a gateway to a dream. She knew it would open doors that until now had been closed. It would mean that at some point in the future she could give up making cakes for a living – or at least pick and choose her clients, which was not something she did now.

It wasn't so much the making cakes that she dreamed of giving up. It was everything else she had to do too. Making cakes for a living wasn't quite as simple as people thought. As well as being a baker and designer, she also had to be office administrator, accountant, manager, marketing and sales assistant, cleaner and delivery girl. When she wasn't baking cakes, she was designing them, shopping for the ingredients and dealing with all the relevant admin. In wedding season, which tended to be mostly in June and July, she could have four wedding cakes a week.

Olivia paused on the coast path and checked her Fitbit. It was time she got back. She'd been running with the wind behind her, which was always deceptive. It would be much tougher on the return journey with the strong sea breeze in her face.

Taking a lungful of the coastal air, she headed for home. She had shedloads of work to do today and it was already nearly eight.

* * *

When she had started Amazing Cakes, Olivia had never imagined she'd spend so many of her Saturday mornings fashioning pink willies out of sugar paste. But naughty cupcakes were eternally popular for hen nights.

Today's willies would have little black bow ties and top hats and they would sit on red heart-shaped seats. The trick was getting the curve right without them falling over. As a hen had once told her, no one wanted a droopy willy on their special night!

After she'd delivered the cupcakes, she planned to take Aunt Dawn a thank you bunch of her favourite flowers – freesias – and maybe a treat for Emmeline and her feathered friends.

There was still no news from Clarice. Olivia swung between two scenarios. The first was that Clarice might not be working as it was Saturday and therefore wouldn't let her know until Monday, in which case there was still hope. The second was that Clarice had already had the 'thanks but no thanks' email and hadn't forwarded it as there would be no urgency.

Olivia sometimes had phone calls and emails out of hours from Clarice, but she didn't think she'd ever had one on a Saturday. She spent a tense ten minutes on her phone looking back through historical emails to check and couldn't find any that had been sent on a Saturday. Which gave her hope. But surely Clarice would tell her if she knew one way or the other. Because she would also know how important it was. Except that it would be small fry to Clarice.

Since her run, Olivia hadn't dare let her phone out of her sight just in case she missed a call, which had already resulted in her almost losing it down the loo. Brilliant. A dead phone. That was all she needed.

When it rang at just after eleven and the word, Mum, flashed up on the screen, Olivia took a break to answer it. At least she had the kind of phone that let her know if another call was trying to get through.

Besides, her parents weren't hugely regular correspondents – they tended to have the attitude, 'you know where we are if you need us' and whenever she phoned them, they'd always answer instantly, even if they were totally distracted with history and ancient rocks. It would be nice to have a chat.

'Hello, love. Just phoning for a quick catch-up.' Her mother sounded her usual bright, cheery self. 'Nothing exciting to report unless you count cataloguing Neolithic fertility symbols. Which is what your father's doing, as we speak. What are you up to?'

'Um.' Olivia glanced at the seven completed male appendages lined up on her worktop and she was tempted to say she was doing something similar, but decided against it. 'Icing cupcakes,' she said instead.

'How lovely and wholesome. So you're keeping busy then?'

'Always.'

'How did the audition go?'

She was touched that her mother had remembered. Her parents had been known to forget birthdays and other special occasions when they were totally immersed in a dig. 'It went great. I haven't heard anything yet though.'

'Fingers crossed then.' Was she being ultra-sensitive or was there the faintest of sighs in Mum's voice? It was no secret that her parents thought she should forget about acting and focus on Amazing Cakes. Although how much more focused she could get she wasn't sure.

'Is your sister all right? She didn't answer when I called?'

'I think so. I expect she's working.'

'And I suspect your aunt is knee-deep in vintage clothes today, isn't she?'

'I suspect you're right.'

'I'd better get back to it then, darling. You will phone and tell us if you get the part.'

'I will, Mum.'

If I get the part, everyone in Weymouth will know because I'll be singing it from the rooftops.

'Toodle-pip.'

'Toodle-pip,' Olivia echoed, smiling, but her mum had already gone.

* * *

By midday, Olivia had finished the cupcakes, boxed them and put them in her van without mishap, to her very great relief. She wasn't sure if she could face having to remake twenty-four willies.

The forecasters had been right and despite the fact it was still only the first week of March, the earlier chilliness had given way to a warm and springlike day. Apparently, it was going to be even warmer tomorrow.

She delivered the cupcakes to a delighted hen at a house on the other side of town and called in to the supermarket on her way back to stock up on ingredients for the coming week and get some flowers and some treats for hens of the feathered variety to take to Aunt Dawn's.

She had a wedding cake appointment with a couple on Monday, which would include a tasting session, and she was making a sponge for an eightieth birthday party on Tuesday, ready for Wednesday. Eric, a widower, was a regular client and a cheeky old git – his words not hers. When they'd first discussed his birthday cake, he'd said that what he'd really like was for a gorgeous scantily clad woman to leap out of his cake, but presuming Olivia couldn't arrange that, would it be possible to have a gorgeous, scantily clad woman on the top?

Olivia had told him it was definitely possible, but was he sure that was appropriate as he'd have his daughter and all his grand-children and great-grandchildren at the party? He'd looked disconsolate for a few moments but had agreed with her and in the end, he'd settled on an open-top red Mercedes with a model of himself, complete with white hair, beard and a flat cap, sitting in the driver's seat.

'It's the closest I'm ever going to get,' he had said with a wink.

Olivia was looking forward to making it. She liked Eric.

Just before lunch, she let herself in to Vintage Views with an armful of flowers and some low-fat cheese, which was one of the few treats Aunt Dawn allowed her chickens to be fed. They'd probably quite like the flowers too, given half a chance.

The door of the shop jangled as it shut behind her and she saw that her aunt was dealing with a customer. A smartly dressed older woman who was looking through a rail of flapper dresses from the twenties.

'How quickly could you source the others?' she asked as Olivia walked towards the counter and then busied herself looking at a display of hats so as not to interrupt.

'You tell me your deadline and I'll deliver the day before,' Dawn told her. She smiled across at her niece. 'Hello, darling, that was good timing. I don't think you've met Jennifer Mount, have you? She works for the costume department on Channel Four.' She turned back to her customer. 'My niece, Olivia Lambert's, an actress.'

'Good to meet you,' Olivia said politely.

Aunt Dawn never missed a trick. Vintage Views regularly supplied clothes for period dramas and her aunt often introduced her to people connected with the productions. Who knew, one day she might well meet someone who was in a position to give her a job. If she still needed one and wasn't too busy being a stroppy consultant on *Casualty*. Fingers crossed!

She wished she could think of something else but her audition, as the three of them made small talk. Then finally Jennifer Mount left and Aunt Dawn came and hugged her. She was wearing the polka dot skirt again, this time with a rather beautiful vintage cream silk blouse, and she smelled of roses and lavender. It was her signature scent and to Olivia it was the smell of love.

'Are those flowers for me? You shouldn't have.'

'I absolutely should. You got me out of a huge hole yesterday, not to mention staying up half the night the day before, and I'm eternally grateful. You must be tired out.'

'Does it show?' The older woman rubbed her eyes.

'No,' Olivia said loyally.

'Good. Let's grab some lunch, shall we? I'll put the Closed sign up. I won't ask you if you've had any news yet because I'm sure you'd have already told me.'

Ten minutes later, armed with a plate of cheese sandwiches and some cubed cheese for the hens, they let themselves out of the fire exit and went down into the secret garden. The door itself wasn't to the secret garden, but like the wardrobe to Narnia, it was the portal to it and Aunt Dawn had disguised the portal so well that it was as though the two now merged.

Aunt Dawn's garden never failed to take Olivia's breath away. It wasn't just the fact that it felt like stepping into an oasis of peace, it was just so unexpected to go out of a fire exit and into a space filled with the fragrance of flowers and herbs.

Immediately beyond the door, there was a metal terrace encircled by iron railings. Strung from these were hanging baskets of herbs. Blooming at the moment were rosemary, thyme, sage, chives and mint. On the coldest nights, Dawn brought the more frost-prone baskets in, but they were all flourishing at the moment. It was a warm March. There was also a tub of purple and white pansies and another of daffodils, which were just beginning to stick their yellow heads out into spring. There were pots of other things not yet awake, but they would be soon.

The fire escape's metal steps led down into the garden itself, but even the steps weren't the ugly functional things they could have been. Aunt Dawn had painted them white and every third or so step had been stencilled with a pattern of sunflowers. Olivia remembered long-ago summer days when her aunt had started the trend. They'd begun with a step close to the ground. Her aunt, mindful of safety had never let her help with the ones higher up, but slowly, week by week, they'd been done too.

The garden itself wasn't a huge area, but it had been divided by decking and artfully placed trellises, entwined with clematis and rambling roses. The most had been made of every inch of space. In one part, there was a lover's bench sitting beneath a rose bower. In another, a swinging chair where Aunt Dawn sometimes sat with a book if she wanted to relax.

There wasn't much grass; the chickens had some, but a lot of the area was either paved, slabbed or decked, and a crazy paving path wound its way to the biggest area of garden in front of the back wall.

The garden could also be accessed via a gate in the wall which ran around it to separate it from its neighbours and also along the back boundary. There was also a door that led into a tiny office and storeroom at the back of the shop, but they rarely went out this way. If they had, Olivia had sometimes thought, it would have been even more like Narnia because they would have had to push past rails of vintage clothes and coats that smelled of age and mothballs.

Close to the back wall, beyond which were two car parking spaces, was the area where Aunt Dawn kept her chickens. The six, sleek and glossy, black-feathered birds that kept her supplied with eggs for baking, were spoilt rotten. They had a state-of-the-art chicken coop. This was comprised of a two storey cedarwood henhouse that was accessed from a ladder below it with loads of space to peck about beneath and the whole ensemble was shored up against fox invasion, although when Aunt Dawn was out and about, they wandered freely at her feet.

'No fox would dare touch my chooks when I'm there.'

That was true. Aunt Dawn was more than a match for the most fearsome of predators, especially if something she loved was at stake.

Olivia had experienced a taste of this when she'd split up with Tom, and Aunt Dawn, who never fell out with anyone, had told him in no uncertain terms what she thought of him when he'd turned up at number five to collect a charger he'd forgotten.

Tom had looked so startled at the onslaught that he'd turned tail and run.

'Just like the coward I suspected he was,' Dawn had said with some satisfaction. 'Let him go and buy another charger.'

It was towards the hen coop that they were headed and the hens were already crowding against the wire. Her aunt unlatched a door and opened it and they poured out, clucking and cooing in anticipation of a treat. They flocked around the two women and her aunt threw a handful of seed across their grassy area to distract them. Then she and Olivia settled themselves at the pretty wrought-iron table for two that sat in a little lunchtime suntrap.

Most of the hens were now pecking idly in a flower border, but one of them was determined to elicit more treats and was jumping up at Aunt Dawn's chair almost as if she was a determined dog after a biscuit.

'Is that Emmeline?' Olivia asked. She couldn't distinguish one hen from another. They all looked the same to her.

'No, it's Greta. She's the youngest – you can see her comb and wattles are still a little on the pale side. They get a deeper shade of red when they start to mature. She's the youngest, but she's also the bravest,' Dawn added and glanced at the hen with affection.

'Greta Thunberg,' Olivia guessed.

'Correct. What else could I call her?' There was a pause. 'So – how are you feeling?'

'Anxious – even though I'm trying not to be. Clarice hasn't emailed – I'd thought she might have done by now.'

'Maybe they haven't got in touch with her yet. It is the weekend.'

'I know. And I need to stop stressing. Mum phoned this morning. I was quite surprised. She doesn't usually remember stuff like auditions – you didn't remind her, did you? She texted to say good luck too while I was on the train.'

'When have I ever had to remind my sister about important dates.' Dawn's eyes were wide and guileless. It was a rhetorical question. They both knew she did it regularly. Although both sisters had a foot in the past – Olivia's mother was obsessed with fossils and her aunt with vintage clothes – her aunt was the more grounded.

'I knew it. I knew she wouldn't have remembered. But it was nice to hear from her. Apparently, Dad was cataloguing some ancient fertility symbols or something.'

'Lucky dad.'

After a moment's hesitation, Olivia told her about the sugar paste willies because she knew her aunt would find it amusing and they both laughed.

Aunt Dawn was a widow. Uncle Simon had died of a heart attack in August 1999, just before the millennium, when Olivia had been seventeen.

Olivia had loved him to bits. She remembered him being very clever but with an acute sense of fun. He'd adored his nieces and they'd adored him, so some of the light and fun had gone out of the family when he'd gone.

He and her aunt had been together since they were teenagers and Dawn had always referred to him as her soulmate. In the years since his death, encouraged by her family, Dawn had occasionally dated, but none of them had got past the friendship stage and Aunt Dawn had said that she was perfectly happy that they hadn't.

Olivia knew there was still a photograph of Simon on her aunt's bedside table. It was in a gold frame, a photo of a smiling man against the backdrop of a beach somewhere.

Olivia worried sometimes that her aunt didn't have anyone in her life, but when the subject occasionally came up, she insisted that she was fine as she was and if it happened it happened.

By the time they'd eaten the cheese sandwiches and fed the hens their cubed cheese treats, Olivia was feeling relaxed again. It was amazing what forty-five minutes of chat and sunshine could do.

She left Vintage Views feeling optimistic once more. As everyone kept telling her, it was still early days. And it was the weekend. Her audition had been good. She'd done the best she could do. It was all in the lap of the gods.

7

On Sunday, Olivia woke up with the same lovely feeling of optimism which had carried her through the previous afternoon and evening. There had still been no news from Clarice, but she had, with Phil's help, now convinced herself that nothing much happened at weekends. There would definitely be news tomorrow.

On the plus side, she woke up to another enquiry from one of the hens who must have been at last night's party and had seen the cupcakes she'd made. The hen, whose name was Poppy, had sent a close-up photo of a cupcake willy with the message,

I'm getting married in September – could you do these for my hen night please?

Olivia hoped that she felt the same when she'd sobered up. The text had been sent at 3.15 a.m. and had been followed by a dozen emojis of laughing faces and three emojis of cartoon willies with little bowler hats. Where on earth had she got those from?

Getting texts and pictures from strangers who'd seen her cakes, thankfully most of them weren't close-ups of willies, happened a lot. Much of Olivia's work came from recommendations. After the first year, she'd barely needed to advertise. Although she did have a website and a Facebook page, both with galleries which she updated regularly with the cakes she was most proud of – very often they were the quirky, unusual ones.

In the past, she'd also done the big trade shows like Cake International in Birmingham. She didn't do these any more either. There just wasn't time to do everything. As it was, she sometimes felt as though she was caught between two worlds – acting and cake creation – and both of them had ravenous appetites for her time.

She answered the hen night cupcake enquiry with a link to her website that would take the prospective client straight to her gallery and said she'd be happy to discuss it further.

It was interesting how hen-night cakes had become ruder and ruder lately. She still did hearts and L Plate cupcakes for her more romantic hens. But lots of ladies, these days, wanted sugar paste mouldings of male appendages. Or sugar paste figures in suggestive poses. She'd told Phil about it once and he'd laughed.

'I know. We have hen and stag nights at The Bluebell sometimes. The women are much ruder than the men.'

The Bluebell, which it was known as by the locals, was one of Dorset's most renowned hotels. Perched high up on a headland overlooking Studland Bay, it was named after the bluebell woods in its extensive grounds. There was even a decommissioned lighthouse, Phil had said, that made up part of the fabulous accommodation. The lighthouse was listed as one of the UK's top ten unique places to stay. Not long after they'd met, during rehearsals for *Hamlet*, he had invited Olivia to the hotel for afternoon tea. It was clear he was proud of the place that employed him as its maître d' and Olivia had been curious to see it.

'This place was refurbished by an eccentric multimillionaire,' Phil told Olivia as they got out of the car on the day of their afternoon tea and she looked up at the white art deco-style building. 'Caroline Rawlinson made her fortune as a concert pianist and The Bluebell was her retirement project. She wanted to create a hotel where people could come to fulfil their dreams – so with the help of her niece, Kate Rawlinson, who now owns the place, she designed and created several purpose-built rooms. We have writing rooms where would-be novelists can write their bestsellers.' Phil mimed a pen and paper, although Olivia was pretty sure most novelists used a computer keyboard, these days. 'If you're a budding Picasso, you can use an art room. There's a recording studio for musicians who've an urge to record a hit single. We even have a vintage Steinway grand piano.' His eyes shone as he spoke. 'Or if your dream is just to take a break from the madness of the world for a while you can do that too.'

'Wow,' she'd said, as they walked round to the main entrance. 'That is an amazing concept.'

'Isn't it?' He'd gestured her to go ahead of him into reception.

She'd thought the hotel might be snobby, as high-end establishments could sometimes be, but The Bluebell managed to combine luxury with a lovely friendly atmosphere. The foyer smelled of air freshener – a mix of coconut and vanilla. There was an oak floor and a wide staircase just past the reception desk, which was where they were headed.

Over the desk was a plaque that Phil took great pride in pointing out – *We're here to help you make your dreams come true.*

The young receptionist, who had English rose colouring and was very pretty, had greeted them politely and said to Phil,

'Would you like me to take you in for your table reservation, sir?' She gave him a cheeky grin. 'Or can you find your own way?'

'I think we can manage, thanks, Zoe. Can I introduce Olivia?'

'He never stops going on about you,' Zoe said, dropping all pretence at professionalism. 'It's great to put a face to a name.'

They were all smiling as Olivia and Phil strolled in to the restaurant where a waiter who addressed Phil as boss, showed them to a window table.

Olivia had looked out at a terrace dotted with tables, beyond which lawns stretched down to a low fence that bordered the garden. 'What a fantastic position,' she said. 'I'm guessing the South West Coast Path is behind that fence?'

'Yep. If it was a bit warmer, we could have sat outside.'

'Can I get you guys a drink while you look at the menu?' the waiter asked.

'We're here for one of Mr B's famous afternoon teas, but yes, why not?' Phil glanced at Olivia.

'Diet Coke for me please.'

'I'll have the same, thanks Sam.'

'Is Mr B the chef's nickname?' Olivia had asked when Sam had disappeared again.

'It's what everyone calls him,' Phil said. 'Basically, he's a paranoid conspiracy theorist who thinks the world is out to get him and that someone might steal his identity if anyone knows his real name. Eccentric is an understatement.'

'He sounds interesting. Will I get to meet him?'

'I don't think he's here today.' Phil had sounded relieved.

Sam had arrived back with a tray. Their cokes came with slices of frozen orange floating in the top and fat white straws decorated with tiny bluebells.

'Thanks,' Phil said, picking up his glass and clinking it against Olivia's. 'Here's looking forward to the best afternoon tea in the county. Mr B may be a bit weird, but everyone makes allowances because he's a first-class chef.'

Olivia put the straw to her lips to take a sip of her Coke. Or at least that's what she planned to do. It seemed that no matter how hard she sucked, no Coke was forthcoming. She had adjusted the straw, frowning. Then she realised that Phil seemed to be having the same problem.

He'd gone a bit red in the face from the effort of sucking. Then suddenly he whipped the straw out of his drink, studied it, said something under his breath that sounded like, 'imbecile,' and shoved back his chair. 'Excuse me a minute.' He'd leaped to his feet and strode across the restaurant, although not in the direction of the kitchens.

Olivia had watched in amazement as he headed for a table not far from them where a man was reading a newspaper held up high so that his face was completely obscured. The newspaper appeared to be shaking.

Phil hurled the straw at him. 'I suppose you think that's flaming funny.'

The man, who had short dark hair, jumped to his feet and only then did Olivia notice he was wearing the trademark checked trousers and white top of a chef.

'It was mildly amusing. Yes. But it had nothing to do with me. I've been sitting right here ever since you arrived.'

'I could get you sacked. I'm a customer.' Olivia saw Phil's lips twitch.

'No you couldn't.' The chef picked up the straw and studied it. 'Looks like a faulty batch to me.' He gave a Cheshire cat grin. 'I'm on a break, but don't mind me. I'll get you a replacement straw, sir. And one for the lady?' He'd glanced in Olivia's direction and tilted his head in a question.

She pulled her straw out of her Coke and gave it a closer inspection. One end had been neatly melded together.

She nodded towards Mr B and he said something that sounded like, 'Watercress-gate,' to Phil, which made Phil snort with laughter.

'Does Mr B often play tricks on the guests?' she'd asked him when he got back to the table, still frowning.

'No. It's just me.' Phil sat back down and picked up his napkin. 'I didn't think he was in today or I'd have been more on my guard.' He reached across and picked up the straw she'd taken from her Coke. 'He must have glued the end shut. Fairly amateur for Mr B. I'd have expected him to come up with something more sophisticated than that. Not that he's ever admitted to any of the stunts he's pulled. He's always got an alibi. I think that's the bit he's best at.'

'Are you saying this happens often?'

'Quite often. It means there's never a dull moment at work.'

'But don't you mind?'

His lips had quirked. 'OK – I should confess it's not exactly one-sided.'

'Watercress-gate?' she asked, catching on.

Phil waved a hand. 'Yeah. That was one of mine. I impersonated our watercress suppliers. I told Mr B that due to a health and safety issue, One Stop Watercress needed to recall all of the watercress they'd supplied that week as it was contaminated with mercury and might well be lethal.' His eyes sparked with mirth at the memory. 'I timed it perfectly. He'd made watercress soup for dinner – it's his speciality – and he was running around the dining room whipping away bowls of the stuff from bemused diners. Hugely entertaining.'

'How long did you let him do that?' Olivia had asked in horrified fascination.

'Oh, not too long. Not enough for anyone to get upset and complain to Clara, the manager. Just enough time for a couple of the diners to think he was a total fruit loop. Which he is.' He paused. 'The best bit was that the group were from Toastmasters International. And they made watercress their topic for the live presentations at the end of their stay. Mr B had to put up with watercress health and safety jokes for an entire fortnight.'

'It sounds as though you and Mr B are very well matched.'

'No. I've definitely got the edge.' He glanced up as Mr B arrived with the replacement straws. 'Not up to your usual standard,' he said.

The chef tilted his head. Olivia saw he too was trying not to smile. 'It's a great pleasure to meet you,' he said to Olivia, giving her the slightest bow and holding out his hand. 'I've heard a lot about you. All of it good.'

Close up, he was very tall and thin with dark hair and frown lines that made him look older than she guessed he was.

'It's a pity Olivia can't say the same about you,' Phil said and Mr B looked delighted.

'Better to be notorious than dull,' he'd said, before giving both of them another little nod and heading, straight-backed, towards the kitchen. 'Enjoy your afternoon tea.'

'He won't do anything to that, will he?' Olivia said to Phil in alarm when the chef was out of earshot.

'No, don't worry. He's done for today. He wouldn't do anything unprofessional anyway. There's a line. And he only did the straws because it's quiet in here. He must be bored.'

* * *

They'd had the most delicious afternoon tea Olivia had ever tasted, with tiny cream cheese and smoked salmon sandwiches, miniature home-made quiches, followed by brownies dusted with edible gold glitter and Victoria sponge cupcakes with marzipan bluebells. The cakes were great, even by Olivia's exacting standards.

When they'd finished, Phil had offered to give Olivia a full tour of The Bluebell.

'Are you sure that's OK? Your boss won't mind?'

'Clara is incredibly forward-thinking. She sees everyone who looks around as a potential client. Besides, she's not here,' he said, as he showed her the purpose-built rooms and one gorgeous boutique bedroom that wasn't in use. 'If Clara was here, then Mr B wouldn't have been loitering in the restaurant waiting to see how his straw trick had panned out. Come on, I'll show you the lighthouse.'

He took her out of a back door of the hotel and across a patch of grass, past what looked like a kitchen garden, towards the vanilla-coloured lighthouse, which wasn't tall as lighthouses went, but still impressive enough.

'Once a guy climbed up the outside to propose to his sweetheart,' Phil told her. 'Clara hired a professional climber who brought the safety ropes and gave him some pointers.'

'Wow!' Olivia gasped. 'What did she say? Or he?'

'It was definitely a she and I'm not sure,' Phil said, changing the subject quickly. 'But the point is he did it because it was his dream and that's what we cater for. That's why we're here. The Bluebell has a wedding licence. So you can also get married here and spend your first night in the lighthouse honeymoon suite. No one's in it today, so I can give you a quick tour if you like?'

He'd let them in the main door and they'd climbed up the spiral staircase of the lighthouse, pausing briefly on a small passing place to let a chambermaid come down.

At the top of the stairs, they'd stood in a circular room that was flooded with light and Olivia caught her breath. The room was stunning. Bespoke circular furniture, clearly designed for the place, made it cosy and timeless and the uninterrupted view over what had been a sparkling blue sea on that day was spectacular.

'People hire it out for anniversaries and special occasions,' Phil told her. 'It's not just for honeymoons.'

'How the other half live,' she'd said. 'It's gorgeous.'

'I haven't shown you the best bit yet.' He'd grabbed her hand and for a heart-stopping moment she thought he'd been going to show her the bedroom, which looked as though it must be up at the top of another little spiral staircase that led off this room.

At the time of their visit, it had been so early in their relationship that she hadn't yet seen Phil's own bedroom. He'd been the perfect gentleman in that respect, telling her there was no hurry and they didn't need to rush things. It was one of the things she'd really liked about him. It had been so soon after Tom and she didn't want to jump straight into a rebound relationship.

But Phil hadn't shown her the lighthouse bedroom. He'd beckoned her downstairs again. They'd stepped out into the sunshine of the day once more, where he'd turned to her, his eyes alight.

'Now I'm going to show you the other reason that this is the perfect place for me to work,' he'd said. 'Step this way.'

A few minutes later, they'd been standing in a small but perfect amphitheatre that could seat maybe thirty or forty people and reminded Olivia of the Minack Theatre in Cornwall.

'Rumour has it,' Phil began and threw open his arms to encompass the theatre, 'that back in the day, Richard Burton himself performed here.'

Olivia had widened her eyes in mock disbelief and he'd said, 'I know. I was doubtful myself, but no one's ever told us different – and it's printed in the brochure, so it must be true.'

As they'd stood, hand in hand in the sunlit amphitheatre with seagulls circling over the cliffs and the freshness of sea air in their lungs, anything had seemed possible.

Olivia hadn't been to The Bluebell since, but she'd loved Phil's dedication to the place.

The buzz of her phone interrupted Olivia's daydreams and she reached for it absent-mindedly, knocking it onto the kitchen floor. Fortunately, it had fallen face up so it didn't break.

For a brief moment, she'd suspected a message from Clarice – she hadn't banished it from her mind that much then.

It was actually a text from Phil.

Morning, lovely. Looking forward to lunch. I've got a plan.

Sounds nice. I'll aim to be at yours for midday.

She got a smiley faced emoji back. Phil wasn't a verbose kind of guy, either face to face or when he was messaging. On first impressions he could come across as a little stern. If she hadn't known about the ongoing pranks crusade between him and Mr B, she might have thought him to be lacking in humour, but this was clearly not the case. The more Phil had told her about the 'vendetta' between the two men, which had apparently been going on for years and could get quite elaborate, the more she had laughed.

Like many actors Phil was quite shy. He once confessed that he was much more comfortable showing his emotions on stage than he was in real life. Olivia wasn't sure whether this was insecurity or just introversion – but one thing she was sure about was that, with the exception of her Aunt Dawn, Phil was the only person she'd ever met who instinctively got her.

8

She was about to set off for Phil's when she noticed a missed call from Ruby.

There was no message, so Olivia phoned her sister back and got the number busy tone.

She sent a text:

Sorry I missed you. Just off to see Phil. Chat later?

There was also a message from Hannah.

How was the audition? Do I have a famous bestie?

Olivia texted back:

Not yet. Watch this space.

She got a smiley faced emoji back.

There was no reply from Ruby, so Olivia took that as a yes to her 'chat later' and she headed for Swanage.

Like her, Phil lived in a mid-terrace two-bedroom house, but Brancombe was very different to Weymouth. More residential housing estate than harbourside community, Phil didn't know his neighbours and didn't want to.

'I'm hardly ever here anyway,' he'd told Olivia. 'It was the first house the rental agency had that fitted the bill. Reasonable rent and somewhere to get my head down at night.'

Olivia had rolled her eyes.

That was something they definitely didn't have in common. She'd bought out Tom's half of number five last year when they'd split and she loved it.

OK, so it wasn't her dream home – that would definitely be bigger and less hemmed in by other people and probably even closer to the sea. A house on a clifftop with a huge garden big enough for children to grow up in would have been perfect. But number five would do nicely for now. Unless she made it big on the small screen, or possibly hooked up with a millionaire, she couldn't see the clifftop dream house ever becoming a reality.

She drew up outside Phil's house behind his old blue Ford Focus. Phil earned a half decent salary at The Bluebell, and sometimes she wondered what he spent his money on. Not cars, that was for sure. The Ford Focus was getting on for ten years old.

Tom had been well off. She gave a little shiver. He had also, as it turned out, been flaky and unreliable with no integrity. Thankfully he was no longer in the country. A mutual friend had told her that Tom had got a new job – still in sales and had moved to Spain at the end of last year.

Olivia had been relieved because it had meant there was no chance of bumping into him unexpectedly. The informative friend had also said that Tom had a new girlfriend, but she wasn't sure if she'd gone to Spain with him or not.

Annoyed with herself for even thinking about him, Olivia put

Tom out of her mind. She had already wasted far too much of her life on Tom.

Her phone pinged with a text just as she got to Phil's front door and rang the bell. They hadn't yet got to the stage of having keys for each other's houses.

The text was from Ruby, answering her earlier message.

Yes please to the chat. I could really use your advice.

Another surprise. Ruby rarely, if ever, asked for advice. She was one of those ultra-confident people who soared through life.

Olivia's hand hesitated over her sister's number. Maybe she should phone her back now. But she and Phil only had a few hours as it was, before he'd be leaving for work. She didn't want to eat into their time. Was that selfish?

It probably wasn't urgent. It was most likely about cakes. That was the only thing she imagined she could possibly give Ruby advice on.

The front door opened and the decision was taken out of her hands.

'Hey, honey.' Phil bent to kiss her. He was barefoot and his black hair was unruly. He was one of those guys who looked even sexier when he was a little tousled.

Her heart gave a flip and all thoughts of Tom vanished like mist in the morning sun.

She stepped inside and followed him back along his hall to his galley kitchen.

'I haven't just got up,' he said. 'In case you were wondering. I've been busy.'

'Busy doing what?' she asked, almost tripping over a wicker basket that was just inside the kitchen door.

'Packing a picnic. Sorry. I should have warned you it was

there,' he added, as she stepped round the basket more gingerly. 'I thought it would be fun to eat outside for a change, as it's such a nice day.'

It was true it was. The weather forecasters had been right about it being a blazing weekend.

'What's in it?' She knelt down and lifted the lid which was attached to the basket by a couple of old-fashioned leather straps. Inside, tucked into the lid in special holders, were a couple of plates, two knives and forks and two glasses. In the basket itself, which had a red checked inner lining, were several tinfoil-wrapped packages.

'Salmon and rocket sandwiches, mini quiches and a selection of cheese,' Phil said. 'And there may be some strawberry shortbread.'

'That sounds brilliant. I didn't know you were such a romantic.'

'The strawberry shortbreads are from Mr B. They're an apology for a little argument we had.'

'What did you argue about?'

'He thought it would be entertaining to replace all the money in the restaurant till with peanuts,' Phil said.

'Peanuts?' She swallowed the urge to laugh because he didn't sound amused.

'Yes, the till was updated recently with a modern one and it's the kind that pings out really quickly when you press a button. So there I was, getting the delivery guy from the brewery some cash for an order and I find myself being snowballed with peanuts. They went bloody everywhere. The guy from the brewery – who's a bit of a Jack the Lad – thought it was hilarious. He was choking with laughter when he realised what was going on. And Mr B was howling like a hyena. I could hear him even though he was on the other side of the room. Out of hitting distance.'

'That is quite funny, you have to admit.'

'Yeah, his timing is impeccable.' Now she could see the hint of a smile. 'I'll give him that.'

'And I assume you'd done nothing to provoke the peanut prank?' She shot him a suspicious look.

'As if,' Phil said in a voice of such guilelessness that Olivia knew he was lying through his teeth. 'What?' He caught her gaze and raised his eyebrows innocently. 'OK he may have been getting his own back for the exploding birthday cake.'

'The what?' She shrieked with laughter. 'Oh, do tell.'

'It was a balloon that we'd covered in icing and decorated for his birthday – I never thought he'd go for it. But he didn't think I had anything to do with it because I was off work at the time. To be fair, I didn't have that much to do with it. I just gave a couple of temporary waitresses the idea – and they did all the legwork. They thought it was hilarious. They videoed the whole thing for posterity. And for me, of course.' Phil's eyes lit up with amusement. 'You should have seen his face. It was priceless. He jumped about two foot in the air, sacked both waitresses on the spot and then ranted about health and safety and giving people heart attacks for about ten minutes.'

'He might have a point. And what about the poor waitresses?'

'He hasn't got a heart condition. A black heart maybe.' Phil chuckled. 'Don't worry. It was the waitresses' last day anyway. So no harm done.'

'Until the peanuts.'

'Yes, he left it just long enough for me to think he wasn't going to retaliate. Then he sprung it on me. Sprung being the operative word. Fortunately, it wasn't a customer who witnessed it, just the brewery guy, who will never let me hear the end of it. He mentions it every time he comes in and the entire staff think it's funny to make nut jokes at my expense. Egged on by Mr B, naturally. It was starting to wear a bit thin and we ended up having a row about it. For which Mr B apologised.'

Olivia looked at the strawberry shortbreads suspiciously.

'Do you think he's put anything in them? Should we be worried?'

'No. That would be way too obvious.' He gave her a lopsided grin. 'Besides, it's my turn, not his. We do have this kind of code of honour.'

Olivia decided that, nevertheless, she'd treat the shortbreads with extreme caution.

She grabbed hold of the picnic basket handles and lifted. 'Wow, it's heavy.'

'I know. It was heavy before I put anything in it. We may need to have a picnic quite close to the car.'

'Where are we going anyway?'

He shook his head. He refused to tell her, even when they were in the car.

'You'll have to wait and see,' he said peaceably as he drove out of Brancombe, towards Corfe Castle. 'I think you'll like it.'

Olivia guessed it wasn't the coast, although she supposed they might have been heading for Kimmeridge Bay. Dorset was full of sheltered little coves with sandy beaches and the occasional cave once used by long-ago smugglers.

They passed the turn-off for Kimmeridge, so not there either then. Olivia gave up trying to guess and just enjoyed the scenery, which was a mixture of fields and woodland and, of course, what remained of Corfe Castle, which stood high up on a hill dominating the skyline. The towering dark grey slabs of stone were still pretty impressive even in ruins. Below the castle, the town of Corfe nestled, all Purbeck stone and incredibly picturesque. Maybe they were going to Corfe Castle. She dismissed that idea.

Lugging the picnic basket up the steep path to the top would have been hard work.

They passed Corfe Castle too and then Phil turned off just before Wareham and went across a cattle grid. There were fields dotted with horses and the occasional sheep on either side of them now and about ten minutes later he pulled up into a layby.

They appeared to be in the middle of nowhere, but then she spotted a path that led off into the distance.

'Can you manage that little rucksack?' Phil asked her as they got out of the car. 'It's quite light. It's just got a ground sheet in.'

'You are organised. I'm impressed.'

'I try. It shouldn't be too damp, but you never know. Best to be prepared.'

He picked up the picnic basket and she followed him along a track that ran parallel to the road.

'This is Hartland Moor,' he told her as they walked. 'I've been coming here since I was a kid. It's really peaceful. Even in the height of summer, it doesn't get that busy.'

She felt suddenly really privileged. He didn't talk about his background much. She knew fragments of his story – that he was an only child, and that when his father was in his early forties, he had died of a heart attack. In typical Phil fashion, he had glossed over the details of that, saying it was a long time ago. But he'd blinked several times when he'd told her and he'd looked so sad that Olivia had grabbed hold of his hand and squeezed it tight.

Phil's mother was a Lancashire lass. She'd met his father when she'd been on holiday in Swanage and when they'd got married, she had moved down to be with him. Phil had been brought up in Swanage. Then, when his dad had died, his mother had moved back to Lancashire to be closer to her mum and two sisters. But Phil had stayed in the area he knew and loved.

He didn't see his mother and aunts very often these days.

'We get on OK, but she has her life and I have mine,' he'd told Olivia. 'And hers is very rooted in her village. She's not averse to the south, but she has a phobia of public transport and she doesn't drive. So, if I want to see her, I have to go back up there.'

Olivia wondered if it was either or both of those things that had made him so independent.

'This place is beautiful,' she said now, looking around her at the heathland as they walked and breathing in the scents of gorse and fresh air and the underlay of spring newness that was everywhere. 'Are we going to a particular spot?'

'Oh yes.'

After they'd been walking about five minutes, he turned off the track, which a little while later opened up into a large clearing dominated by a circular pool which must have been about ten metres across.

There were a few gorse bushes straggling around the perimeter and some convenient mounds and it was on one of these that Phil put down the picnic basket with a sigh of relief.

'This is it. Our very own, utterly private picnic spot. Not many people know about this.'

He sounded enormously pleased with himself and she nodded in delight. The pool wasn't even visible from the main track. You'd never know it was there unless you knew exactly where to turn off.

'You know you said you fancied trying wild swimming?' Phil said, as she tipped the groundsheet out of the rucksack and discovered it was rolled up with a couple of towels. 'Well, now's your chance.'

'Before lunch or after?'

Phil shrugged off his jacket and began to unpeel his T-shirt. 'I reckon before.'

'I don't suppose you've got any swimmies in that rucksack?'

Olivia asked lightly, not expecting there would be, but interested to see his reaction.

'Do wild swimmers need costumes?' He lifted one eyebrow in a challenge and they both smiled.

'OK,' she said. 'Last one in gets the picnic laid out.'

9

He raced ahead of her as she knew he would and Olivia looped her hair up into a scrunchy and followed him in more cautiously. The water was freezing and there was a mix of silty clay underfoot, which felt squishy between her toes, but thankfully not too many stones, she discovered, when they had splashed out into the middle, shrieking and gasping at the temperature. They laughed even more when they realised it didn't get more than waist deep even in the very middle of the pool.

'Have you swum in here before?' she called when they were a metre or so away from each other.

'Yeah, but it was deeper then. Mind you, I think I was only about ten.' He turned round, managing, in typical gentlemanly Phil style, not to stare at her breasts.

She splashed him, which made him yell, and then swam away before he could retaliate. Swimming fast was the only way to cope with the cold, but it was amazing how freeing it was, swimming without clothes beneath the sky, even if it was in a pond in the middle of nowhere in water that wasn't very deep.

Or maybe it was because of these things that it was so freeing.

For a few moments, Olivia rolled over and floated on her back and looked up into a sky that was patterned with white clouds. It was incredibly peaceful. There were no traffic sounds. All she could hear was birdsong and the sounds of a faint breeze rustling the leaves on the trees. Sunlight reflected off the water and tiny flies skittered and danced just above the surface. Olivia breathed in the scents of the outdoors – faintly brackish water, fresh air and the new growth of forest fauna that surrounded the pool – and she knew she would always remember this moment.

Phil swam across to her. He had a splodge of silt on his cheek. 'What do you think? Was this a good idea?'

'It was an excellent idea. I love it. Although actually, when I said wild swimming, I was thinking of somewhere less muddy. Like the sea,' she teased.

'I thought mud was supposed to be good for your skin.'

'This is true. You can pay a fortune for certain types of mud. I'm not so sure about it being good for your hair.' Most of hers had escaped from its hastily tied knot and was fanned out in the dark water.

'We can go in the sea next time.'

'It's a deal.'

They didn't stay in very long. It was way too cold. Phil went ahead of her back onto the bank where the picnic basket was and brought a towel down to the edge of the pool. 'Thanks.'

She felt as though her entire body was tingling. Every inch of her skin felt invigorated and alive. They dried themselves off and got dressed. Then Olivia shook out the picnic blanket and was amused when a couple of peanuts fell out on the ground.

Phil tutted good-naturedly. 'I've been finding flaming peanuts everywhere since the till stunt.'

'I bet.' She smiled at him. 'Thank you for this. I think that's one of the most exhilarating things I've ever done.'

'And we haven't even been scuba diving yet. Do you have any of the kit?'

'I do as it happens. It's in my shed.' She had learned with Tom. It had been one of his fleeting passions. In typical Tom fashion, he'd gone overboard and bought top-of-the-range kit, before they'd even qualified, along with membership of a dive club. They'd gone several times in Weymouth, but then he'd lost interest. She'd gone a few more times with Hannah, who was also a keen scuba diver, but then when Hannah moved to Cornwall, Olivia had stopped going too. 'How about you?' she asked Phil. 'Do you have the kit?'

'No, although I've got a mate with a boat who dives regularly. He'd loan me some stuff, I'm sure.'

'How long ago did you qualify?'

'Five years. I didn't do a lot. It was one of those things I thought might be handy for my CV. Not that there's a great deal of call for actors who can scuba dive.'

She laughed. 'No.'

As they ate the picnic, they talked about where they could go. Swanage Pier sounded pretty safe. But there were also a few prime spots near her.

'There's a little cove on Portland Bill where I've done a shore dive a few times,' she told him. 'That's pretty popular.'

'We could go there.'

'Maybe we should go on a refresher course first. Just to make sure we can remember how to do it.'

'That's not a bad plan.'

'I'll haul out my kit and check it over. Some of it will need servicing,' she said.

He smiled in the sunshine and she tilted her face up to the sky, loving the feeling of being outdoors surrounded by birdsong.

They stayed for another hour, soaking up the spring sunshine and chatting. They saw no one else. Not even a dogwalker disturbed the peace. It was one of those fabulous days, Olivia thought, when nothing could go wrong.

As Phil drove them back to his house where they showered and changed, she was reminded of an old Lou Reed song, 'Perfect Day'. That's what today had been. A perfect, timeless day, even though they were bounded by Phil having to fly off to The Blue-bell for work at four. Maybe this was what had made it all the more precious.

* * *

She forgot all about Ruby's text until she had waved Phil off and was sitting in her van about to make the journey back to Weymouth.

She toyed with the idea of phoning her back, but she didn't have Bluetooth in her van so that would have meant sitting outside Phil's house for the duration of the call. She would be virtually driving past Ruby's house anyway, so she may as well pop by and see her.

Ruby didn't live with anyone and she'd split up with her last boyfriend – Olivia thought his name had been Scott – a few weeks earlier. They hadn't been together long – they'd only met just before Christmas – and Ruby hadn't said much about the split, other than he hadn't been what she'd thought he was. She hadn't sounded particularly upset.

The bottom line, Olivia thought, was that Ruby wasn't as interested in dating as she was in art. Her world and her social life revolved around it. Scott had probably been someone on the fringes of her world.

Ruby was a social butterfly and loved schmoozing people,

which was a huge part of her job and probably one of the reasons she was so successful.

Olivia imagined that one day, when she was ready, her sister would settle down with some guy who would be the yin to her yang. He would appear out of the blue and sweep her off her feet. But so far, he hadn't materialised. Ruby may love people en masse, but she'd told Olivia after a slightly tipsy meal just before Christmas, that she'd never been in love.

Maybe that's what Ruby wanted to talk about. A new man.

Olivia hoped so.

* * *

Twenty-five minutes, later she pulled into Ruby's drive. Her house on the outskirts of Weymouth was lovely, but it wouldn't have been Olivia's choice. For a start, it wasn't on a clifftop and it had no sea views, although it wasn't hemmed in by neighbours. It was a four-bedroom detached with a Tudor-style façade and a gravel frontage on which you could park several cars and it overlooked fields.

Ruby's black SUV was outside, Olivia noticed, which meant she was probably in. She parked beside it and crunched her way across the gravel to the front door.

The bell chimed somewhere inside the house and a few moments later the door opened and she was face to face with her sister.

It was immediately obvious that something was wrong. Ruby wasn't her usual immaculate self. She was wearing an old brown teddy bear onesie. Her fair hair was unbrushed and were those tearstains? Olivia's compassion radar twanged madly.

'Are you OK?' The question was superfluous. Clearly Ruby was far from OK.

'No. Not really. I only opened the door because it was you.'

'Is it OK to come in? I know I should have phoned you to check, but I was passing and I was a bit worried.' She was more than a bit worried now. She felt a wash of guilt. Why hadn't she phoned earlier? She'd thought it was odd that Ruby should need her advice.

'It's fine. Come in. Excuse the mess.' Ruby led her past a couple of huge canvases that were stacked against the wall in her large high-ceilinged hall, through to her country farmhouse kitchen, which was all solid oak cupboards with a breakfast island in the middle. The drop-down pendant light over the breakfast island shone on an open laptop, which was surrounded by paperwork. Her sister had clearly been working.

'What's wrong, honey?' It was messier than usual in here too. Dirty cups littered the worktop and there was an open packet of digestives on a plate. Alarm bells were jangling furiously in Olivia's head. Ruby wasn't messy. If anything, she was a bit of a tidy freak.

Her sister pulled out the stool where she'd obviously been sitting and gestured to Olivia to join her. 'I've got a major problem,' she said without preamble. 'And I'm really not sure what to do.' She closed her eyes and rested her head in her hands, elbows propped on the breakfast island.

Olivia was suddenly terrified. She had never seen Ruby like this – so defeated.

'You're not ill, are you?'

'I'm not ill. No.'

Ruby gave a deep sigh and moved a pile of paperwork to one side. Beneath it was an oblong box, but it took a few moments for Olivia to register what it was. A pregnancy test. Oh my goodness, that was the very last thing she'd been expecting.

'You think you might be pregnant?' she asked softly.

'I don't think. I know.' Ruby undid the box and drew out its contents and Olivia realised it was already open. The pregnancy tester had been used. Its pink line underlined what Ruby said next. 'I'm definitely pregnant. No doubt about it. This is the second test I've done.'

10

Olivia couldn't have been more shocked if Ruby had told her she was giving up the art world. Ruby was the least maternal person she knew. Having kids wasn't on her agenda. It never had been, and by the look of her tear-stained face, that much hadn't changed.

Olivia got up and hugged her sister tightly. 'Oh honey. I didn't even know you were seeing anyone.'

'I'm not.' She put up her hands in a little gesture of defence. 'I mean I was – obviously. It's not a divine conception. Far from it. Oh my God, sis. I'm in so much trouble. I don't know where to start.'

'I'll put the kettle on.'

Making and sipping the chamomile tea that Ruby always drank was soothing.

'Come on, let's go and sit in the lounge,' Olivia carried their mugs through. 'We can talk properly.'

A few moments later, they were installed on one of the big old sofas that lined the room in an L shape, facing an inglenook fireplace over which a painting of a nude in a gilt frame hung. There were pieces of art everywhere in Ruby's home, much of it by artists Olivia hadn't heard of but who were hugely acclaimed.

One of the reasons Ruby had bought this house was because there was a loft conversion that the previous owners had used as an office. It had Velux windows in the roof and Ruby had declared it the perfect studio when she'd first seen it because the light was amazing. Not that she had done much painting of her own since she'd moved in. She was too busy buying and selling other people's and the loft had become a storage facility.

The sisters were both workaholics and Olivia had hardly seen Ruby lately. She felt guilty. She should have tried harder to keep in touch with her sister's life. Ruby looked ever so tired as she cupped the mug of chamomile in both hands and sipped it. She also looked more vulnerable than Olivia had even seen her.

After a few seconds, she began to speak in a slightly calmer voice. 'I'm only just pregnant, I think. So, I do have options.'

'Lots of options,' Olivia agreed. Her head was still spinning slightly. She hated seeing her sister so distressed.

'I'm always so careful,' Ruby began slowly. 'You know how Mum terrified the living daylights out of us when we were younger about getting pregnant. Besides, I'd gone back on the pill when I met Scott. I hadn't been seeing anyone for a while before that.'

Olivia nodded.

'But I do remember I had a tummy bug just before Christmas. I probably didn't even tell you. It was so fleeting. I didn't think it would matter. But clearly it did.' She shook her head. 'So I didn't think too much of it when I missed my period. I'm always a bit erratic, but when I missed another one, I thought I'd take a test. Just to check, you know. That was last night. I was so shocked when it came up positive. I did another one this morning, just to be sure. I've been worrying myself sick ever since.'

Olivia squeezed her sister's hand and felt guiltier than ever. 'I'm sorry I wasn't here for you sooner.'

'Don't be daft. You're here now. You're the first person I've told.'

There was a little silence and the big old clock on the mantle-piece ticked and Olivia racked her brains to think of something positive to say. She didn't want to mention termination. Despite her strong views on not wanting kids, Ruby had equally strong views about the sanctity of life. She was firmly against euthanasia, abortion and capital punishment. When she was at art college, she'd been chair of the debating society and had led a debate that had almost ended in fisticuffs between herself and another girl, who said it should be individual choice, not laws, that defined moral issues.

'Would it help if you talked to Scott?' Olivia asked. 'I know you've split up, but this is actually his problem as well, isn't it? If that's the right word.' She faltered. It felt so wrong to be referring to a pregnancy – something she wanted so much – as a problem. But that was clearly how Ruby saw it.

Ruby looked at her with tear-filled eyes. 'This must be crappy for you. I know how you feel about being a mum. I wish I felt the same. Maybe I will one day. But I don't right now. In fact, that's the only thing I am sure about. I definitely don't want Scott's baby.' She sighed. 'There's something I haven't told you.' She took another sip of her chamomile and clinked the mug back onto the coffee table. 'One of the reasons Scott and I split up was because I found out he was married. I didn't have a clue, obviously, when we got together. He wasn't wearing a ring. He was always around. It wasn't the kind of situation where he kept making excuses not to meet and wouldn't let me go to his house, or so I thought, given that it's not his house after all. I went there to help him hang a painting. That's how we met. There was no sign that a woman lived there. I didn't suspect a thing.'

'So how...?'

'He was sneaky. It turned out it wasn't even his house. It was his brother's place. Scott and his "unmentioned" wife...' she mimed the inverted commas, 'actually lived somewhere else. His wife works abroad a lot – she was away in November and December. Out of sight, out of mind. So sneaky Scott decided to have a bit of extramarital fun in her absence. She came back in the new year. Which was when I found out. To say I was mad would be an understatement.'

'Honey, why didn't you tell me before?'

'To be honest, I felt such an idiot, Liv. That I'd been conned. Not to mention ashamed. Scott was so casual and "what's your problem?" about the whole thing too. He said that he and Marianne – that's her name – had an open relationship and it wasn't a big deal. Yada, yada. Once I'd got over the shock, I just wanted to put the whole thing behind me as soon as possible and move on. It wasn't as though it was the love affair of the century or anything anyway.'

'What an absolute Grade A wanker. And how absolutely shitty for you.'

'It was. I should have told you. But...' She spread her hands. 'Like me, you're really busy. It wasn't as thought there was anything you could have done.'

'I still would have been there for you.'

'I know. Like I said, it was mostly me feeling like a fool. But now this has happened. I don't know what to do.'

'Are you going to tell him?'

'I don't even know that. I probably should. But I don't know if he ever told his wife about us – despite all the "open relationship" stuff. For all I know, that could have been one massive lie too. Being as so much of the other stuff he told me was.'

'True.' Olivia's head was beginning to hurt. Goodness knew what Ruby's was doing. Her sister was looking at her as though she expected her to come up with a magic solution. 'Well,' she began cautiously. 'I suppose whether you tell him, partly depends on what you want to do. I take it you still feel the same way you always have about terminations?'

'I think so.' Ruby stared down at her interlinked fingers. 'Although it does feel weird being here. I never in a million years thought I'd end up making a mistake.'

'In which case, I guess you could either keep the baby.' Ruby was already shaking her head. 'Or consider adoption.'

'Adoption is the decision I keep coming back to.' Ruby sighed. 'Although I'm not sure how I'm going to explain that one away to everyone in our family. I don't think Mum would be very keen. I mean, I know she doesn't bang on about being a granny like some mums do, but I also can't see her happily waving goodbye to her first – and possibly only – grandchild.'

Olivia felt a stab of pain that was almost physical at the same moment as Ruby clapped her hand over her mouth.

'Liv, I'm sorry. That came out wrong. I know how much you want children.'

'But I'm not getting any younger. I know.' Olivia had kept her voice as casual as she could but knew she hadn't quite pulled it off. Ruby still looked stricken.

'It's a pity you can't adopt this one.'

For one wild second, Olivia's heart leapt at the idea of adopting her sister's baby, but her head told her it was a bad idea. Babies weren't commodities sisters could swap between them like bags or tops. She couldn't adopt and bring up her niece or nephew. There were too many emotional entanglements. It wouldn't work. She changed the subject before it could go any further down this emotional rollercoaster of a road.

'Have you eaten?' she asked Ruby. It was just coming up to 6 p.m.

'No, but I'm not hungry. My stomach churns every time I think of food. Morning sickness is a misnomer. They should call it all day sickness.' She gave a weak smile. At least she was looking a little less panicked now. It must have helped to share her secret, even though they hadn't made any decisions. 'You must be hungry though,' Ruby went on. 'I could make some cheese on toast. Or do you have to get back? Are you supposed to be somewhere?'

'No. I was just on my way home and no I'm not hungry. Phil and I had a picnic at lunchtime.'

'I'm sorry. I'm holding you up.'

'You're not, honey. I can stay over if you like. If you need moral support, I mean.'

'Would you?'

'Of course.'

* * *

It had been a long time since she'd stayed over at her sister's, Olivia thought when they finally went up to bed. They'd always got on well enough, but they didn't live in each other's pockets. Their lives had run along parallel lines when they'd first left home and in the last few years they had diverged even more sharply. Ruby spent a lot of time in London or travelling around far-flung parts of the country seeing clients and visiting exhibitions, and Olivia was immersed in either acting or cake making. There weren't that many occasions when they were in the same place at the same time. Christmases and family birthdays and the odd celebration were probably the only times they saw each other for extended periods.

Olivia regretted this a little now as she put on the nightshirt she'd borrowed, which smelled of lemon fabric softener, and lay in her sister's luxurious guest-room bed, which was all feather duvet and sumptuous Egyptian cotton bedding.

One wall of the guest bedroom was dominated by a painting of a forest in a huge gilt frame and Olivia lay in bed, looking at it. It was so true to life; she half expected to hear birdsong or see a squirrel skittering through the branches of the trees.

She closed her eyes. She regretted that Ruby had gone through such heartbreak so recently without saying a word. Although Ruby had insisted that she hadn't been heartbroken. 'I didn't love him,' she'd acknowledged. 'He was very charming and pretty hot, but the more I got to know him, the more I realised we didn't have much in common. I think I'd have called things off even if I hadn't found out he had a wife.'

Olivia had hugged her tightly.

By the time they'd gone to bed, Ruby had been looking a lot happier. This was partly because they now had a plan. Ruby was going to phone Scott in the morning and arrange a time to see him. She didn't imagine for a second he would want to claim his paternal rights, but she would also tell him she planned to put the baby up for adoption.

'Just having a plan and being able to see a way forward has made me feel so much better,' she'd said quietly. 'Thanks so much, sis.'

The last thing Olivia thought of as she dropped off to sleep was the perfect day she'd had with Phil. It was a shame it had ended with such a bombshell.

* * *

In the morning when Olivia got downstairs, she found that Ruby was already up and sitting at her laptop, even though it was barely seven.

'Workaholism must run in our family,' she murmured. 'Would you like tea?'

'I'm just doing some emails. And yes please.' Ruby stopped tapping. 'Thanks for staying over and thanks for listening. I'm sorry it's all been about me. You're all right, aren't you?'

'I'm very good, honey, thanks.' Olivia realised with surprise that she hadn't thought about the *Casualty* audition once since she'd rocked up last night. It was true what Aunt Dawn said, 'If you want to forget your own worries, just focus on someone else's.'

'What?' Ruby asked suspiciously.

'It's nothing much. I'm just waiting for the results of an audition. Quite an important one. If I get it, I'll be filming in Cardiff for the next six months.'

'Wow. That's brilliant. When will you know?'

'Today, hopefully.'

Ruby held up crossed fingers. 'If there's any justice, you'll get it. Will your man understand? Won't that mean you'll hardly get to see him.'

'It's not that far to drive. I'll just have to cut back on the cake making. And yes, I think he will. He's an actor, isn't he?'

'Of course. I'd forgotten that.' She closed the lid of her laptop and got off the stool. 'We must see more of each other. We must make an effort. I mean – if we can fit it around our work and stuff.' She tailed off.

'We will. I told you, I'm planning to help you through this. You're not on your own. And you've got a plan.'

'I have. I'm going to phone Scott as soon as he gets to work.' She checked the time on the kitchen clock. 'Which won't be for a couple of hours or so. I won't tell him on the phone. I think it's better if I do that face to face.' She stuck out her chin determinedly. 'Just because he has no integrity whatsoever, it doesn't mean I have to follow suit.'

As Olivia looked at her little sister's resolute face, she felt a surge of love for her. 'I'm proud of you, honey. And I'm going to be here for you every step of the way. Cardiff or no Cardiff.'

'Thanks, sis.' Ruby still looked worried, but she'd recovered some of her usual fire. 'Don't tell Mum will you.'

'Of course I won't.'

11

Olivia was hopeless at keeping secrets. It was just as well their parents were in the Outer Hebrides, she thought, and not likely to rock up any time soon. Especially as Ruby was now giving her a running commentary on every step of the unfolding events.

It turned out that Ruby's prediction of Scott's reaction was spot on. They had met on Monday evening after work.

'You should have seen his face,' Ruby had relayed back to Olivia on the phone, later the same evening. 'It would have been comical if it wasn't so bloody tragic. He actually accused me of making it up in order to get money out of him – like I would need his money. I earn four times what he does.' Her voice was contemptuous. 'Then he offered me money not to tell his wife. So much for them having an open marriage. I hadn't planned to tell his wife. But I felt so insulted he thought I might I was almost tempted.'

Olivia knew she wouldn't. Ruby, for all of her sharp business acumen and easy come, easy go attitude to relationships, didn't have a cruel bone in her body.

'I won't, of course,' Ruby had confirmed ten seconds later. 'It's not her fault she's married to a devious coward.'

'No. That's true.'

There was a part of Olivia that wondered whether the oblivious wife had a right to know that her husband had fathered a child who would end up being adopted and one day, in the far distant future, might want to track down his biological father. That was a ticking bomb waiting to explode, if ever she'd heard of one.

But she decided it was not her place to say this. It had to be Ruby's call.

It was also going to be a tough secret to keep from Aunt Dawn. But it was one that must be kept. Their aunt may have felt morally bound to tell their mother and then Ruby would have faced the barrage of their parents' questions and reactions.

'I'm obviously going to have to tell them all at some point,' Ruby had said. 'But I need some time to get my head around it all first.'

Fortunately, Aunt Dawn was busy with the shop and when Olivia spoke to her, a little after she'd spoken to Ruby, it was a relief to know her aunt attributed her slightly subdued manner to the fact that she hadn't yet heard anything about her audition.

This was partly true. As Tuesday passed too and there was still no word from Clarice, Olivia's heart sank lower and lower. She was tempted to phone the agency and ask, but she knew it was pointless. If there was news, Clarice would tell her. So presumably there wasn't and, in the acting profession, no news was bad news. She had an eightieth birthday cake to get on with too.

She also had a good chat with Hannah when she phoned for a catch-up. 'No news yet, I'm sad to say.'

'I will keep everything crossed for you,' Hannah said. 'Let me know what happens.'

Hannah was well acquainted with the difficulties of making a living from one's dream job. She was a freelance journalist and she also wrote novels in her spare time, but so far, she hadn't managed to attract a big enough publisher to jack in her day job.

'How's the writing going?' Olivia asked.

'Slowly,' Hannah said with a sigh. 'It's really hard work writing in my spare time when I do it all day as well. But I did have a bite for a YA book a couple of weeks ago. I've sent them the whole thing.'

'I'll keep everything crossed for you too. How's Truro? How's your mum?'

'Truro's lovely. Mum's just – well, Mum. Demanding as ever. She seems to have a job for me about twice a week. They're always tiny, like changing light bulbs, but also urgent – even though I've asked her to save them up. I sometimes wish I'd stayed in Weymouth. On the plus side, I've joined a diving club – have you done that lately?'

'Funny you should ask that.' Olivia told her about her discussions with Phil. 'We're planning to go some time.'

'Brilliant. Another thing you have in common.' They talked about having things in common with partners for a bit longer before the conversation came to a natural close.

'Don't give up hope on the publisher,' Olivia said just before they disconnected.

'Ditto on the audition.'

* * *

Phil reiterated this when they chatted on Wednesday morning. 'Maybe there's been some glitch in the system, honey,' he said.

'Thanks,' she whispered, even though she could tell from his hesitancy that even he didn't really believe that. Phil was no fool.

Wednesday lunchtime, Olivia caught up with some admin and then busied herself checking Eric's cake, which she had iced the day before. The red sugar paste Mercedes with the sugar paste model of Eric, complete with white hair and beard, had come out even better than she'd hoped. The old man was going to be thrilled. She couldn't wait to see his face. Presuming she got it there in one piece.

This was another cake she would be delivering personally. Eric lived alone in sheltered accommodation and he wasn't very mobile. As she was lifting the cake carefully into its box, her phone buzzed. Olivia glanced at the display and her heart jumped into her mouth. It was Clarice. For one awful moment the cake wobbled in her grip and Olivia put it back on the worktop swiftly.

Now the moment of truth was finally here, she felt as though the world had gone into slow motion.

Calm down, she told herself. *Deep breaths.* She didn't want to answer the phone with a panicked yelp. She wanted to sound cool and professional and not as though she hadn't let her mobile out of her sight for more than a second since Friday. It wasn't as though she wasn't used to disappointment. It happened all the time in the acting business.

The phone was still ringing. If she didn't answer it soon, Clarice might give up. Olivia touched the green button.

She had planned to say a bright, 'Good morning,' as though she didn't have a care in the world, but it came out as a squeaky, 'Hi.'

'Olivia?' Her agent's brusque voice held a question.

'Yes. Sorry, it's me.'

'Apologies for taking so long to get back to you. I'm afraid they've only just got back to me...'

The whole world stopped. Olivia held her breath. The figurine of Eric looked as though he was grinning up at her, egging her on. His smiley face triumphant. The clock on the wall had stopped at midday. Both hands pointed to twelve. It wasn't even ticking. Had it actually stopped?

'But I'm afraid it's a no,' Clarice went on. 'For what it's worth, I think they've made the wrong decision. Apparently, there was only a whisker between you. Better luck next time.'

'Right. I see. Thank you for letting me know.' Olivia felt as though she were repeating a line, parrot fashion. A line of a script before she'd put in the emotion. Her voice sounded so blank and far away.

'Sorry it's not better news. I'm sure I'll have something else for you soon. Bye for now.'

'OK. Bye.' Olivia could hardly speak, but Clarice had already gone. She wasn't the type to rake over the ashes. Opportunities came and went. If you got rejected, you picked yourself up, dusted yourself down and tried again. That was how the business worked.

Olivia put her phone back on the worktop. The world had gone back to normal speed. It was now two minutes past midday. One hundred and twenty seconds was all it had taken to bring her world crashing down. Even Eric didn't look as though he was smiling any more. His mouth had a definite downturn. Maybe she should adjust that.

She reached out towards the figurine and realised that her fingers were shaking too much to be careful. Maybe she would leave it. The last thing she needed now was to ruin this cake and have to start over.

She sat at her wooden kitchen table and blinked away tears.

On her fridge was a magnet which said, *If you can't stand the heat, get out of the kitchen.* It had been a present from Aunt Dawn. The irony had appealed to them both. But in that moment its real meaning hit her hard.

How many more times could she put herself through this? How many more times could she allow herself to hope that this time it would happen? This time she would be picked. The door to fame that had been so tantalisingly ajar felt as though it had just slammed with brutal force in her face.

There were only two people in the world who would totally get this. The first was Phil because he'd been there so many times himself and the second was Aunt Dawn. But she would be busy in the shop.

Olivia phoned Phil and he answered within three rings.

'Hey you. How's it going?'

'It was a no.' She was trying to sound casual but she was aware she hadn't succeeded. Her voice shook slightly as she added, 'They went for the other actress.'

'Ah.' A beat. 'I'm so sorry. What are you doing? Would you like some company?'

'Thanks, but no, I've got a cake delivery. Then I need to go to the wholesalers. Are you working tonight?'

'I am, but I could maybe swap shifts?'

'No, it's fine, Phil.' She was touched that he'd offered. 'But let's save the shift swapping for emergencies or celebrations. I wouldn't be much company tonight and I'm pretty busy. We're meeting tomorrow, aren't we?'

'Yeah, I hope so. Is that still OK?'

'It's great. See you then.'

'Keep your chin up, honey. Don't let the bastards grind you down.'

'I won't.' Olivia sniffed and swiped a stray tear from her cheek.

She hadn't wanted to blub but it was impossible to hide her pain completely.

They said their goodbyes and Olivia hoped Phil hadn't noticed her tears. She allowed herself another five minutes of self-pity, running once more through all of the dreams she'd had of being on prime-time television. Of Mum and Dad being able to tell their friends. 'That's our daughter, that is.' Of Aunt Dawn's smiley pride. Of Ruby's pleased-as-punch delight – 'I always knew you'd do it.' Of Phil's pleasure – he would have got it most of all.

Then, she wiped her face, refixed the metaphorical lid firmly back on the top of her box of dreams and busied herself taking Eric's cake in its real box out to her van. At least she managed to get that there safely without any mishaps.

Was it only six days ago that she had dropped Arabella's cake making this very same journey?

She remembered how touched she'd been when Aunt Dawn and Phil had rallied round, supporting her, helping to make another cake up into the early hours of the morning. All so that she could get to the audition.

So much for that.

If you can't stand the heat, get out of the kitchen, she reminded herself as she locked up her front door and headed for Eric's.

* * *

Eric lived in one of the more run-down parts of Weymouth. Flat 1B was on the ground floor of the sheltered housing block and she parked in the communal car park, breathing in the scents of diesel fumes from the nearby main road, mixed with the straggle of spring flowers that someone had planted in the border. She could hear the shouts of children from the primary school a couple of doors up. It must be break time.

As she walked across to the entrance of the flats, her mood dipped again. She had always been the kind of person who thought that things happened for a reason, but she was struggling to find a reason for the events of the last twenty-four hours. Her sister was having the baby that Olivia had always wanted – a baby that would be given away and brought up by strangers, and would never know it had a lovely, warm, if slightly eccentric birth family. And the part that even her agent said was perfect for her would be played by another actress. Olivia had googled her when she'd got home from the audition and discovered that she'd been in the business less time than Olivia. She had less experience and she was also younger, despite the fact that the script called for a woman in her late thirties, early forties. She was thirty-four. Olivia would have killed for a break like that at thirty-four.

It all seemed so unfair. When would it be her turn? Maybe never. Maybe she should do what she knew her parents secretly wanted and give up her acting dreams and focus on Amazing Cakes. Maybe she should start trying for a baby – just in case that proved to be difficult too.

What was she thinking? She didn't even know if Phil wanted a family. Phil was absolutely lovely. But he'd never once mentioned children. They needed to talk about it. They needed to talk about their future and how they both saw it unfolding. Things had moved on from when they'd first got together. They'd got closer, but what if this was as close as he ever wanted to be – meeting up a couple of times a week to do lovely things like the picnic on Sunday. What if that's all he wanted? She was assuming it wasn't, but she didn't actually know. What if he was another Tom? She needed to find out.

She blinked away the crowding thoughts and rang Eric's

buzzer. A few seconds later, he buzzed her in.

He looked even more doddery than the last time they'd met – which had only been a month or so ago when she'd called round to discuss the design for this cake. He was leaning on his Zimmer frame and puffing slightly as he let her into his front door. He was also smiling broadly.

'Good afternoon, doll. Did you see any curtains twitching?'

He'd confessed, the last time she'd come over, that he loved the thought of his neighbours speculating about the identity of the 'young hottie' (his words not hers) who came calling. 'They love to gossip,' he'd added with a wink.

'I didn't see a soul,' Olivia told him. 'Which is probably just as well.' She gestured towards the box. 'They might have worked out that I'm just a cake delivery girl and not your secret girlfriend.'

'I guess you're right.' Eric gave an exaggerated mock sigh. 'If only I was twenty years younger.'

'Thirty,' she told him, trying not to smile.

'All right. All right. Don't rob an old man of all of his dreams.' A beat while he caught his breath. 'Let's have a look at this masterpiece then.'

Once in the kitchen, she put the box carefully on the worktop and lifted the lid. Eric shuffled closer and peered in to see.

For a second, Olivia held her breath. What if he didn't like it? What if it wasn't quite how he'd imagined it would be? Or he didn't like the image of himself? What if he didn't see himself as she had? She had enough disappointment swirling round in her head already. She didn't think she could deal with his as well.

Then, to her huge relief, the skin around Eric's eyes crinkled up until his whole face was a picture of delight. 'That's cracking, that is. You've done me proud. You really have.'

He looked so thrilled that she felt the warmth swelling her heart. At least she was good at something.

'I'm really pleased you like it.'

'I do.' He adjusted his glasses and reached to touch the little figurine. 'Don't I look dapper. I'm made up. Really, I am. Made up.'

He tried to give her an extra tenner as a tip, which she refused. She knew he couldn't afford it. Eric lived in the shabbiest of clothes. His slippers were threadbare and she was pretty sure he eked out his pension by keeping the heating low. It was never that warm in the flat.

She was just leaving a very pleased old man when she spotted the recycling bin by the door. 'Shall I take this out for you?'

'If you would, doll, ta.'

'Enjoy your party,' she said, as she picked it up.

'Ta. I'm looking forward to it. Can't wait to see my Vanessa's face when she sees your cake.' Vanessa was his daughter.

'Get her to take a photo for posterity,' she told him.

'Don't you worry. I will.'

Outside, just before Olivia put his bag into the big black communal recycling bin, she sneaked a peek. She'd been right about him eking out his pension. In the white plastic bin liner were sixteen baked bean tins, all neatly washed out, each with its lid, not the easy-to-open ring-pull kind, tucked inside.

She caught her breath before swallowing an enormous lump in her throat. Here was an old man, unable to walk without his Zimmer frame, and clearly without a pot to pee in. He must have saved up for weeks to afford that cake, even with the discount she'd given him but not told him about. Yet he still found plenty to smile about. And here was she, half his age, feeling desperately sad because her life wasn't working out as she'd hoped.

She straightened her shoulders. 'Get a grip,' she told herself. 'If Eric can make the best of life with no money and the bulk of his years behind him, then I'm damn sure you can do it too!'

12

This was a sentiment she shared with Phil the following evening when she went to his and he agreed with her wholeheartedly.

'You are so right. When life brings you lemons...' he said and spread his hands for her to fill in the blank.

'Make lemonade,' she said resolutely.

'Or find someone who has a bottle of tequila,' he amended, as he went to his cupboard and produced one.

'I thought it was limes with tequila.'

'I've got limes,' he added, laughing at her surprise. 'And salt. I thought we could knock back a couple of tequilas and set the world to rights. Or at least the acting world. Being positive is all very well, but there's no reason why we shouldn't have a good old rant too.'

'What a superb idea.' Her heart lifted in gratitude that he understood so well what would help.

He tapped his nose. 'I occasionally have them.'

Five minutes later, they were installed in his lounge on a squashy sofa in front of a low glass coffee table. On the table was a wooden chopping board on which was a row of neatly sliced lime halves, a little pot of salt with a miniature teaspoon – who knew Phil would have such things in his bachelor pad? – two shot glasses and, of course, the bottle of tequila.

'So, is it salt first or lime?' Olivia asked him.

'Watch me.' He poured out two shots, sprinkled some salt on his clenched right fist, then touched it to his lips, downed the shot and sucked on the lime.

Olivia followed suit. The salt bit was OK. The tequila left a burning trail down her throat and the lime made her screw up her face. An assault on her tastebuds which screamed in outrage. But it got much easier after the first one.

For the next hour, they drank tequila and ranted about the vagaries and unpredictability of the acting world.

This slowly got more pointed.

'Bloody actresses barely out of drama school creaming off the best jobs,' Olivia said.

'Yeah.' They downed a tequila each.

'And who are younger...'

'Yeah.' Another one.

'And prettier...'

'Not a chance,' Phil objected, blowing her a kiss.

'The casting director was probably her cousin.'

'Yeah.' They downed a couple more.

'At this rate, we'll be as fissed as parts – hissed – pissed,' Olivia said, hamming it up.

They both collapsed with laughter and Olivia knocked over the tequila bottle, which fortunately had the cap on.

'It's medicinal,' Phil said, pouring them another.

'Yeah... Yeah.' She said it twice for good measure, although she noticed that they had actually slowed down a bit. Which was probably sensible, even though she planned to stay at his and neither of them had to get up hugely early the following day. She didn't cope as well with drinking too much as she once had, and she was slightly out of practice.

They ate some cheese and biscuits she'd brought with her in an effort to soak up some of the alcohol. And to a certain degree it worked.

Olivia considered confiding in Phil about Ruby's unplanned pregnancy, but loyalty stopped her. Not even their own family knew yet and it certainly wasn't her secret to share. Instead, she leaned across and kissed him. 'Thanks, Phil. I know that was probably really childish, but I feel so much better now.'

'Good.' His gorgeous dark eyes held hers and she felt a rush of warmth for him.

It was on the tip of her tongue to say, 'I love you.' But she stopped herself just in time. She didn't want to say it when she was three sheets to the wind. He'd think it was the drink talking.

There was a drawn-out moment when neither of them spoke. He blinked. His eyelashes were too long for a guy's. Suddenly all she wanted was to be in his bed with his arms around her.

'We should have an early night,' she said.

'Sounds good to me.'

Then, because she felt so unravelled, so unguarded and definitely slightly drunk, she said on impulse. 'Phil, can I ask you a question?'

'Go ahead.'

'Do you want to have kids?'

He blinked a couple more times and then brought up his cupped hand to his mouth. It was a gesture she knew so well. It was what he did when he was uncertain and trying to think of an answer.

Oh my God. So he didn't. And he must know she did and he was trying to think of a way to say he didn't without letting her down. She shouldn't have said that. She shouldn't have asked him when she didn't want to know the answer – not if it was no, anyway. The thin knife of reality pierced the rosy haze of her inebriation.

'Sorry,' she said quickly. 'Forget I said that. That was a mistake.' She scrambled to her feet. 'I should really get going. I...' She swayed slightly.

'What?' Phil said, looking up at her in bemusement. He was still sprawled on the settee.

'Maybe I should go home.'

'You can't drive. You're way too drunk.'

That was true.

'I thought we were going to bed.' He looked puzzled, as well he might. 'Have I missed something.'

'I need the loo.' She could feel her face burning as she fled.

Upstairs in his bathroom, she locked the door, splashed water on her face, which didn't make her feel any less drunk or light-headed or embarrassed, and sat on the closed lid of the loo seat.

Why had she asked him about kids? Yes, it was a discussion they should have, but not when they were both half-cut. Still, at least she knew now, didn't she? If he'd been on the same wavelength as she was, he'd have said something like, 'Sure, I'd love them.' Or even, 'Sure, someday I'd love them.' Or maybe even a joke, such as, 'Shall we start now?' But he hadn't said any of these things. He'd just put his hand over his mouth and looked like a cornered rat.

Olivia cleaned her teeth with the toothbrush she kept at his and then she flushed the chain and went out onto the landing.

Phil was coming up the stairs now. His tall figure blocking out the landing light. He looked concerned. 'Hey, honey. Are you OK?'

Deciding that this was an occasion when it was least said soonest mended, she went into his arms. 'Yes, I'm fine. I'm sorry. I felt a bit sick. I feel better now.'

He studied her face. And she knew he wasn't sure whether to believe her. But then he obviously thought better of pursuing it. 'That's good. Are you ready for bed?'

'I am. Absolutely.'

Neither of them said anything else about what had happened downstairs. They snuggled up in his warm bed and he spooned against her, but neither of them instigated lovemaking and the last thought Olivia had as she fell asleep was that maybe he was worried that she might have had plans to start a family without his consent.

That night, she had strange tangled dreams in which Phil was the father of Ruby's baby and instead of adoption they had put the baby for sale on eBay, but there was no reserve and however high she bid, she couldn't win because the price just kept going up and up.

It was a relief to wake up and find that it was just a dream.

The other half of the bed was empty and then she heard the sound of feet on the stairs and Phil came in bearing two mugs of tea, one of which he put on her bedside table.

'Good morning, sleepyhead. How are you feeling?'

She sat up in bed. 'Not exactly bright-eyed and bushy-tailed but better than I probably deserve.'

'Good.'

'How about you?'

'I'm good, thanks.' Phil rarely got hangovers and he looked exactly the same as he did every other morning.

'What time is it?' she said, suddenly panicking. 'I've got a cake to make.'

'Relax, it's not eight yet.' He took his mug around to the other side of the bed. 'That tequila is strong stuff – the end of last night is a blur.'

'Yeah, same,' she said, wondering whether that was true or if he'd just said that to shut down the conversation about children. Either way, they didn't mention it again. They slipped into their morning routines, Olivia cleaned her teeth, took two paracetamols to ward off the beginning of a headache, but she had a vague feeling of disappointment that they had unfinished business between them, and the relaxed camaraderie of the previous evening was gone.

Phil was working at The Bluebell the coming weekend. He'd also had some voiceover work that had come in. He had a loose agreement with an agency who contacted him periodically when they had a client he could work with – they were usually radio adverts, which Phil liked because he was great at accents and the money was good.

Occasionally, he got asked to do audiobooks too. This involved him going up to a recording studio in Bristol. Narrating books can be more stressful than people realise. Olivia had never done it, but Phil had explained that it involved sitting in a cubicle with a headset on, sipping orange juice to stop your mouth clicking and reading from a screen while an editor was in the room next door. If you made a mistake – or if they deemed you'd made a mistake – you had to go back to the beginning of the line. It required a lot of concentration and it could be slow. Even a short book could take two or three days. But it was very well paid, so Phil didn't turn them down.

Olivia was relieved they wouldn't see each other much for the next few days. She wanted some time to regroup and to think things through. His reaction to the having kids question had rocked her even more, perhaps, than she'd expected it to.

* * *

Aunt Dawn was lovely about her failed audition. She didn't offer tequila, for which Olivia was grateful. She gave Olivia a hug when she called by to tell her the news and said, 'I'm sure it's no reflection on you, darling. As your agent said, there will be something better out there, waiting for you.'

'I hope so,' Olivia said.

Aunt Dawn had also given her two boxes of eggs. 'The girls are laying well. It must be the warm spring we're having.'

Olivia had gone home feeling happier. Every time she had seriously thought about packing in acting, something else had come up. And Aunt Dawn was right. There might well be something better around the corner.

The one advantage of being an older woman – thirty-nine was ancient in the acting business – was that directors tended to want you for your acting skills, not the way you looked. She'd had loads of call-backs in the past year. One or two of them had come off. Her CV was slowly building. She might not have had her big break yet but she was certainly learning a lot, she told herself.

Hannah was lovely and sympathetic too, although she'd had better news. The publisher had asked for some rewrites, which was a big step in the right direction, but there was still a tough road ahead. Nothing was ever certain in the publishing industry.

In typical Hannah fashion, she was probably playing it down, Olivia decided, as she wished her luck.

Her parents sent a text which said:

Commiserations, darling. We're coming back at Easter. Let's have a
big family knees-up then.

They sent the same text to Ruby, minus the commiserations.

Ruby was equally sympathetic about the audition when they
spoke on the phone. 'It sounds as though it was a very close
thing,' she said. 'But I am sorry. I know how much you wanted it.'

'There will be other opportunities,' Olivia replied, as stoically
as she could. She was starting to believe that too. The only other
option was to give up, but she had no intention of doing that. Not
yet. The trouble with this business was that there was always a
glimmer of hope.

'Stay positive,' Ruby said.

'Talking of staying positive, how are you doing?' Olivia asked.

'I'm OK. I've been looking into things regarding adoption. I've
found out that my first port of call is social services. I've decided
not to contact them until I've had my first scan.'

'When is that?'

'They can do it between twelve and fourteen weeks. I'm pretty
sure I got pregnant the first week of January, so that takes us into
the week after Easter.'

'Would you like me to come with you?'

'Yes please.' She hesitated. 'I have a dilemma. Should I say
anything to Mum and Dad when they come back for Easter. Or
should I wait until after the first scan? I don't know what to do,
Liv.'

She sounded vulnerable and Olivia wished they weren't
having this conversation on the phone so she could give her
a hug.

'I don't know. But we've got another three weeks before Good
Friday. So you don't have to decide just yet.'

'Thank you.' She paused. 'I know it's really selfish, but in some ways, I'm relieved you're not dashing off to Cardiff. I don't think I could do this without you.'

Olivia felt warmed. It would have been brilliant to get that role but maybe things did happen for a reason. She felt closer to her sister than she'd done for years. Every cloud has a silver lining.

13

The three weeks before Easter, which was at the beginning of April this year, flashed by in a blur of cake baking, visits to Auntie Dawn and snatched phone conversations with Phil. These were usually at night, when they were both in bed, exchanging trivia about their day and – it seemed to Olivia – carefully avoiding any references to either their future or the subject of whether or not they wanted a family. He hadn't mentioned it and she wasn't going to, not until she'd had time to totally think everything through.

Olivia fitted in as many runs as she could. She loved this time of year. She went early in the morning or after she'd finished for the day, depending on her workload. Sometimes she ran by the sea. Or sometimes along footpaths, lined with bright yellow celandine that looked for all the world like small yellow stars growing on either side of the path. Daffodils grew in clumps alongside them and golden forsythia flecked the hedges, so it didn't matter if it was dusk, because it felt as though she was running through a corridor of sunshine.

Olivia was beginning to think that Ruby had been right.

Would she really have been able to be there as much for her sister if she'd been driving off to Cardiff three days a week? She suspected she'd have fitted it in somehow, but it was nice to have the time for leisurely chats on the phone and not to feel that she should have been somewhere else learning a script. There was always a bright side.

The Outer Hebrides dig wasn't finished. Their parents were coming back the day before Good Friday and heading back again to the dig on the following Tuesday. Their house was still rented out, so they were staying with Ruby who had the most room.

The plan was that they would all get together for a roast dinner at Ruby's late afternoon on Good Friday. The get-together included Aunt Dawn, and Phil too, as he'd got daytime on Good Friday off.

For the rest of the Easter weekend, there were no set arrangements. Their parents might be obsessed and meticulous when it came to archaeology, but when it came to their spare time neither of them was big on plans.

'We know you'll want to see your Phil in between his shifts,' her mother had said. 'So don't worry too much about us. No doubt your sister won't want to stop working too long either – so we don't expect you to drop everything to accommodate us.'

Phil was working most of Easter at The Bluebell – they had some big musical gathering, which involved two choirs and an orchestra who were practising for a *Britain's Got Talent* audition.

'Hopefully they'll have some talent,' Phil had joked to Olivia. 'It's going to be noisy. Good job we're up on a cliff and haven't got any neighbours.'

Ruby had asked Olivia if she'd go over on the Thursday evening to give her some moral support.

'I'm a bit scared that Mum's going to take one look at me and then guess I'm pregnant,' she'd confided.

Indeed, the first thing Ruby did when Olivia arrived was lift up her top to bare her tummy.

'Do I look pregnant?' She turned sideways on. 'I mean, I know I'm not showing really yet. But do you think she'll be able to tell – you know, with a mother's instinct?' She winced and touched her abdomen.

'Are you OK?' Olivia frowned. 'Are you in pain?'

Ruby shook her head. 'Not pain exactly, but I have been getting the odd little niggle. I think that's normal. I asked Dr Google and then I ended up on this post on Mumsnet. As far as I can see, practically anything is normal in early pregnancy. As long as it's not full-on agony or bleeding. I'm probably imagining it.

Olivia didn't think her sister looked that well, but she insisted she was fine.

'I'm just stressed,' she replied. 'And I'm still throwing up. It's not surprising I look crap. Anyone looks crap when they're throwing up all the time. How women can look blooming is beyond me.'

'I expect the blooming comes later,' Olivia said.

'Hope so. At least I'm nearly done with the first trimester. Apparently, the sickness gets better after that.'

Half an hour later, they'd finished peeling potatoes and topping and tailing sprouts and slicing carrots for the Good Friday dinner and were sitting in Ruby's kitchen at the breakfast island.

'So have you decided what to do about telling them?' Olivia glanced at the clock. It was seven thirty. There was only an hour or so before their parents were due to arrive.

'I don't know. But I'm not telling them tonight. I don't think it would be fair to spring it on them when they're both tired.

'Good point.'

They would definitely be tired. It was quite a journey however you did it, involving a ferry, a flight and a train. They had also refused an offer to be collected from Weymouth train station, insisting they would get a taxi as they didn't know exactly what time they'd be back.

'I've got all weekend to tell them,' Ruby said, waving a hand casually, which didn't fool Olivia for an instant. Her sister looked as though she might snap under the slightest pressure. 'I think I might just wait until the time feels right.'

'Good idea. I'll leave it to you, honey. But I'm in your corner. However it pans out.'

* * *

As it turned out, their parents didn't arrive until just before ten – there had been a few delays. They looked tired but really pleased to be there.

'So sorry we're later than we thought,' Mum said, coming into the house in a flurry of long white mac and carrier bags and fresh night air mixed with the Lancôme scent she always wore.

Dad followed more slowly, carrying a bulky overnight bag. 'You girls haven't waited up especially, I hope?'

'It's ten o'clock, not midnight, Dad,' Ruby pointed out. 'So, no, we haven't.'

His eyes crinkled up in warmth. 'I forget you're all grown up now.'

'With our own houses and cars and everything,' Olivia joined in with the banter. 'Sorry it was a tricky journey. You should have let one of us pick you up.'

'And do some poor Uber driver out of a job?' He shot her an indignant look. 'Not a chance, Bean.' Bean was the nickname her parents had given Olivia even before she had a name. It had filled the gap before they'd settled on Olivia and it had stuck.

They retired to the lounge and sat on the two sofas, Ruby and their mother on one and Olivia and their father on another. There were hugs and hot drinks, which included hot chocolate for Marie and a swift whisky nightcap for James – he only ever drank alcohol as a nightcap. Ruby and Olivia had chamomile tea.

'I don't know how you can drink that stuff,' Marie said, shaking her head. 'It always smells like hay to me.'

Then ensued a discussion about the best thing to drink before bed and the eventual conclusion that it was probably nothing if you didn't want to get up in the middle of the night.

The carrier bags her mother had been carrying contained gifts, which turned out to be a Highland cow chopping board for Olivia and some Highland shortbread for Ruby, as well as Highland themed handmade Easter eggs for everyone. 'We got a set of Highland place mats for your aunt too,' she told them, her eyes eager. 'They're nice, aren't they?'

'I see a theme emerging,' Ruby said. 'I didn't think you liked gift shops.'

'It was attached to the Taigh Chearsabhagh Museum and Arts Centre. Your father fancied a visit.'

'Fabulous place,' Dad said. 'Over a thousand artefacts. I'd tell you about them, but your mother's made me promise not to talk shop. At least not for the first hour.'

Everyone tutted affectionately or rolled their eyes.

Seeing their parents always made Olivia feel like a child again. She wondered if it was always like that, however old you got. Maybe it was because they never seemed to look any different.

Mum's fair hair didn't show the grey and she lived in dark leggings and oversized sweatshirts, which she swapped for Tshirts in the summer. It was sometimes hard to believe Mum and Aunt Dawn were sisters. The only thing they had in common, fashion wise, was that they both lived in comfy shoes.

Dad looked the same as he always did. He lived in round-necked, lambswool jumpers which he wore over a shirt, adding a tie if the occasion ever demanded it. Tonight's jumper was olive green.

It was lovely to see them, though. Especially as they looked so happy. She loved that they were so wrapped up in their professions and not like Hannah's mother, who didn't work and who'd had empty nest syndrome from the day Hannah left for college. Hannah felt responsible for making sure she was OK all the time, and duty-bound to see her every Christmas, Easter and family birthday – maybe that was the reason she didn't want children, Olivia thought idly. It was definitely the reason she'd moved away from Weymouth. Olivia missed having her around, too.

'You're quiet, Bean.' Her father's voice interrupted her thoughts. 'I was sorry to hear about the gig. Bit of a kick in the teeth, that one.'

'Thanks, Dad. It's just one of those things.'

'You could try nobbling the other girl. That would fix it, wouldn't it?' he smiled.

'Yeah, but I might get arrested.'

He patted her shoulder and shifted on the sofa. 'Keep your chin up. I've never liked *Casualty* anyway. Now, *Holby City* – that's a different matter.'

'They're dramas about the same hospital, though. Just different shifts.'

'Are they?' He looked amazed.

She never could tell how much he hammed things up. James Lambert was the archetypal mad professor. He spent most of his life with his nose buried in the ancient past, only occasionally coming up for gasps of air before disappearing again. He found the modern world difficult to understand and he didn't like it much. There would come a time, he was fond of telling people, when he would give up on it altogether and retire to the past, where he would spend his days amongst dusty books and old bones.

'Mum said you were cataloguing fertility symbols,' Olivia asked him. 'How's that going?'

'It's not as much fun as it sounds.' He winked. 'Although you can learn a lot about indigenous people by how they viewed the whole subject of procreation...' And he was off.

Olivia zoned out – once Dad was on his favourite subject, the past, he could talk for hours – and sneaked a glance at her mother and sister, who were immersed in conversation on the other sofa, in case Ruby needed her help.

But Ruby looked fine. From the odd word she could hear, it sounded as though they were talking about a Banksy that Ruby had just put up for auction for a client.

'How much?' their mother said now. 'Good grief. That's crazy money.'

Olivia tried to suppress a yawn and then realised she hadn't been very successful when her father said, 'Sorry – I'm boring you.'

'You're not, Dad. I'm just tired.'

'Of course you are, Bean, you work too hard. And there's me blathering on. It's time for bed.' He drained his whisky and called across to his wife. 'I think I'm going to turn in, love. I'm bushed.'

Marie nodded. 'Yes, I'm coming now. We can have a proper chinwag tomorrow.' She beamed around at them all. 'It's lovely to catch up with my girls.'

A few moments later, they were gone, although their presence and their mother's trademark Lancôme scent lingered in the room.

Olivia shut the lounge door and looked at her sister. 'Are you OK?'

'I'm good.' Ruby blinked, but then her eyes filled with tears.

Olivia was beside her in an instant. 'Sweetie, it's going to be OK.'

'Is it? I feel so guilty. They're going to be so disappointed in me.'

'Don't be daft.' Olivia hugged her. 'They'd never be disappointed with you. They love you to bits.'

'They won't agree with what I'm doing. I know they won't.'

Olivia could feel the slight shuddering of Ruby's shoulders and she realised she was crying.

'You're tired out, that's all,' she said softly. 'Things always seem worse at night-time.'

'Have you said anything to Aunt Dawn?'

'No. I told you I wouldn't.'

'Yes, but you two are so close.'

'It's your secret, not mine. I haven't told another living soul. Not even Phil.'

'Thank you.'

'Let's go to bed. It's nearly midnight. It will all seem better in the morning.'

Olivia hoped she was right as she followed her sister up the wide, thick carpeted staircase to bed. It was true what she'd just said. Their parents were understanding and they did love their daughters to bits. And they were open-minded. But adoption was big and it was permanent. If she was truthful, she had no idea how they'd react when they heard Ruby's news.

14

To her surprise, Olivia overslept. She must have been more tired than she'd realised. When she woke up, sunlight was streaming through the gaps in the blinds which she couldn't have closed properly. Even the forest painting on the wall looked sunlit. It was nearly nine.

She showered quickly in the en suite bathroom, cleaned her teeth, put on the minimum of make-up and went downstairs.

She could hear the clattering of plates before she reached the kitchen and she could smell bacon frying – that would be Dad – he might be old-fashioned in some ways, but he loved a cooked breakfast and he would be wielding the frying pan.

She could also hear laughter. So, Ruby couldn't have told them yet then. Maybe she would decide against it this weekend. Maybe she would decide against the whole adoption idea. Olivia was praying that she would. She loved the idea of having a niece or nephew. Who knew, that might be the closest to having a family she ever got.

Her heart gave a thump of pain. Of course it wouldn't, she berated herself.

She resolved to talk to Phil as soon as Easter was over.

Another peal of laughter greeted her as she opened the kitchen door. Maybe putting off important conversations ran in the family, she thought.

Mum and Ruby were perched on stools at the breakfast island – the laptop had been cleared away for once. Dad was at the hob, waving a spatula around, as she'd predicted.

'I told you the smell of bacon would get her out of bed,' he announced, beaming from ear to ear. 'And here she is.'

'Good afternoon,' her mother quipped.

'Ignore them,' Ruby replied. 'I said you were tired and could lay in as long as you wanted.'

Ruby looked a lot happier than she had the previous day. That was a relief.

'I've done you a full English,' Dad said. 'You girls could both do with fattening up.'

'Not true in my case,' Ruby said. 'It's Olivia who never puts on a pound. I don't know how you do it, being surrounded by cakes all day.'

'Running helps a lot,' Olivia replied. 'And wild swimming.'

'Wild swimming? Does that mean you go in naked?' Mum looked interested.

'No, it means you go in wild places,' Olivia told her, deciding not to mention that she and Phil had done that very thing at Hartland Moor. 'Although apparently there is a nudist beach at Studland, not far from where Phil lives, if you and Dad fancy skinny-dipping, Mum.'

'We certainly do not.' She gave an exaggerated shudder. 'Do we, James?'

'No, love. Absolutely not!' He winked at Olivia, and as he dished up, there was a scraping of stool legs and general murmurs of appreciation as they got stuck into the business of breakfast.

At the end of it, Ruby jumped up to clear the plates.

'I'll do it,' Olivia said.

They did it together; Olivia stacked the dishwasher and Ruby washed the pots and pans, while their parents joked about having to come and stay more often if they were going to get waited on hand and foot.

When the sisters finally had a moment on their own, Ruby said, 'I don't think I'm going to tell them today. They're so happy, aren't they. Once I tell them, that's going to be the only topic of conversation there is.'

Olivia agreed, knowing it was true.

'Shall we just enjoy Easter with them?' Ruby said.

'It's your call, honey. Like I said, I'm in your corner whatever you do.'

'Anyway, I'm thinking that I should probably have the scan first, make sure everything's OK.'

'Are you feeling all right now? Have you had any more of those niggles you mentioned?'

'No. I had a bit of a pain in my shoulder last night, but I'm pretty sure that was indigestion. You know what it's like when you're paranoid about something. Lately, every tiny ache and pain in my body has sparked me off into thinking there's something wrong. I don't think there is.'

'The scan's on Tuesday, isn't it?'

'Yes. 3 p.m. Are you still OK to come with me?'

'Of course I am.' Olivia hesitated.

'What?' Ruby looked at her sharply.

'They're going back up to the other end of Scotland on Tuesday. Won't you have to tell them on the phone if you wait until after the scan?'

'I know.' Ruby dropped her gaze. 'I'm a coward, aren't I?' She bit her lip. 'I just want us all to have a nice Easter.' She stopped talking abruptly as their mother came back into the kitchen.

'Is there anything I can do, girls? It doesn't feel right sitting doing nothing.'

'Dad seems to be managing OK,' Olivia smiled.

'No change there,' Ruby quipped.

'He did cook the breakfast,' their mother said. 'At least let me peel the potatoes or do the sprouts or something. It will give me a chance to catch up on all your gossip. It's not often I get the chance to have both my girls in one place.'

'We did most of it last night,' Ruby told her. 'If you want to do something, you can make another pot of coffee. We're having roast beef by the way. That's your favourite, isn't it?'

'You know it is, lovely girl.' She hugged her younger daughter and then turned to Olivia. 'Isn't your sister lovely and thoughtful?'

'Absolutely,' Olivia agreed.

'So what have I missed?' Marie asked, putting on the kettle and turning back to them. 'What mischief have you two been up to that you can't tell me about in front of your father? How are things going with the gorgeous Phil? Is he still wowing audiences with that wonderful Shakespearean voice?'

'He's been really busy for the last couple of weeks. In between his shifts, he's been recording an audiobook. It's a biography of some historian. I thought Dad might be interested in it. It will be something for them to chat about over dinner.'

'Fine plan.' She turned back to her younger daughter. 'How about you? Are you dating anyone, darling? Or is life in the art world too hectic?'

'I'm happily single,' Ruby told her. 'There's no one in my life at the moment.'

'So I can't rely on you to give me a grandchild then?'

'No, you can't.' Ruby's face closed down and their mother obviously picked up on the tension because she said, 'It's all right, darling. I'm only teasing.'

Olivia saw Ruby's forced smile and the angst in her eyes, which she interpreted perfectly. Ruby didn't want this lovely, chilled-out time to change, but it would. It would change forever once their parents knew about her news.

* * *

Aunt Dawn was the first one to turn up for dinner. They were sitting down at five and she arrived just after three. Olivia went to let her in.

'I'm sorry to be so early,' she announced as she walked through to the kitchen, smelling beautifully of roses and lavender, and wearing a gorgeous blue checked, off-the-shoulder, vintage dress. 'I couldn't wait to see you all. Wow, something smells divine in here. Is there anything I can do to help?'

There was more shedding of coats and gifts. Aunt Dawn handed over a bottle of wine, some non-alcoholic fizz for anyone not drinking, and a bag that held a Tupperware container and two cardboard ones.

'There are two shop-bought cheesecakes, because, frankly, I can't make them any better. But I did bring you a home-made dessert as well.'

Ruby pounced on it. 'Ooh, Queen of Puddings, you angel. I love that. Your meringue is to die for.'

'I brought you a dozen eggs as well,' Aunt Dawn said. 'The girls are laying well. And, of course, some chocolate ones.'

'You can come more often,' Ruby said, diving into the bag and retrieving a clutch of very flash-looking Easter eggs – the type in transparent cases so you could see how gorgeous they were. They definitely hadn't come from a supermarket.

An hour after Aunt Dawn had come, Phil arrived too. He'd brought bottles of wine and some soft drinks which he added to their collection. He'd also brought Ruby, as host, a big box of her favourite after-dinner mints, which Olivia had tipped him off about, and more Easter eggs for everyone.

He complimented all the females on their appearance and looked totally relaxed in Ruby's house.

'Good to see you,' James said, pumping his hand. 'I was beginning to feel distinctly outnumbered.'

Phil was great with her family, Olivia thought, watching with pleasure, despite the fact she knew he wasn't a big fan of social gatherings. He'd met her parents, Aunt Dawn and Ruby at Christmas and they'd all got on like a house on fire. Phil was personable and very good at making people feel at ease. It was why he was so good at his job. She hoped he wasn't putting on an act here though.

It was very hard to read Phil. Sometimes she thought that the closer they got, the harder it became. But there was still so much she didn't know about him. He was very self-contained. She had never seen him get really angry or rage or cry or look out of control. Except on stage – and then, of course, he was acting.

They'd talked about that once and he'd said, 'I know. I don't do it on purpose. I just don't find it very easy showing emotion. It's much easier on stage. It's... I don't know – more channelled, I guess. And liberating.'

Olivia knew what he meant by liberating. She felt like that too. When she was in front of a camera, she felt as though she was free. Totally free to express her emotions fully without worrying about anyone else. Maybe that was why acting was so

cathartic – because it gives you the opportunity to do that. She'd
heard writers say the same thing about writing.

She caught Phil's eye across the room; he held her gaze for a
moment and she felt reassured. She relaxed as he made small
talk with her father, complimented Ruby on the gorgeous house –
he'd never been to Ruby's before – and asked after Aunt Dawn's
hens. Then he kept them entertained with tales of April Fools'
pranks that went on in kitchens. Apparently, this year, someone –
by which he meant himself - had put green food colouring in all
the milk in The Bluebell's fridges.

'It backfired a bit because Mr B, our chef, made a green rice
pudding and put it on the menu as a kid's special and the kids all
loved it.'

This was a side of Phil she didn't see very often, Olivia
thought, looking at him with affection. His ability to laugh at
himself.

Mr B often came out on top when it came to pranks, it
seemed. Luckily, her partner was good-hearted enough not to
bear him any lasting resentment. She had a feeling that beneath
it all the two men were quite good friends.

'This must feel like a busman's holiday to him,' Ruby whispered to Olivia when they escaped, just before dinner, to check
everything was ready on the dining table. Ruby had a separate
dining room, which came into its own on family occasions. A
long wooden table in a pastel cream-painted room with an
inglenook fireplace. 'I'm glad you're with him. I like him much
better than Tom.' She moved a fork. 'I mean, don't get me wrong.
I liked your Tom well enough. But I didn't like the way he messed
you around. He should have been straight with you a lot sooner
than he was. And he didn't have Phil's sense of humour. Your
Phil's quite dry, isn't he? When I first met him, I thought he was
too serious for you, but it's just his initial manner.'

'Very perceptive,' Olivia said.

There was a pause. Olivia was about to fill it with trivia when Ruby asked the inevitable next question.

'I take it that he wants a family, does he? Or is it too early to ask him that kind of thing? How long have you been seeing him now?'

'It's not far off a year.'

'Wow. That's flown. I didn't realise it was that long. Do you think he's the one you'll settle down with for ever and ever? You have told him you want six kids, haven't you?'

'Seven at least,' Olivia teased, feeling a little tinge of longing despite her attempts to make a joke of it. 'No, I thought I'd leave that a bit longer. I don't want to send him running for the hills.'

A cough at the door alerted them to Phil's presence.

Olivia felt her face burn. How long had he been standing there?'

He looked from one to the other. 'I wondered if there was anything I could do to help?'

'Not at the moment. But thanks.' Ruby disappeared out of the dining room, leaving Phil and Olivia alone, and for a few moments there was an awkward silence.

They both rushed to fill it.

'Thanks for asking—'

'I hope my—'

She gestured for him to go first. 'I was only going to say, thank you for asking me here today,' he said. 'Are you sure I'm not intruding? I didn't realise it was just family.' He looked a bit flushed too. It was quite hot. Ruby always had the heating too high.

'Of course you're not intruding. Mum and Dad both wanted you to come. Are you OK?'

'I'm good. I like your family. I've told you that.' He hesitated. 'What were you going to say?'

She'd been going to say she hoped they weren't too much for him, but that suddenly felt disloyal. So she just shrugged. 'I forget. Nothing important.'

She hadn't yet met Phil's mother. In the eleven months they'd been dating, Phil had only visited her a couple of times too. The first time had been on her birthday, at the beginning of November, and the second, at Christmas.

The first time he'd gone up to Lancashire for a weekend when Olivia had been rushed off her feet, icing what had seemed like endless Christmas cakes for clients. The second time he'd just gone for a night and a day. They hadn't put it into words at the time, but Olivia had known that it was probably too soon for him to be taking her up to meet his mother. They'd still been dealing with the slowly unfolding realisation that they really liked each other. That this might not be a flash-in-the-pan thing, borne out of the closeness of doing live theatre together.

Ruby came back into the dining room. 'I'm just about to dish up,' she said, glancing from Phil to Olivia with a slightly questioning expression which made Olivia wonder what she was thinking, but it was gone almost as soon as it had appeared. Olivia put it out of her head.

* * *

Dinner was a riot. It was filled with chatter and laughter and everyone talking at once. If Phil had heard what Olivia had said about wanting to have seven children, he certainly didn't seem to have reacted to it. He was the only one who wasn't drinking wine. When Ruby had invited him to the dinner, she'd also said he was welcome to stay over too if he liked. But when Olivia had passed this on, he'd said he'd rather get back.

Olivia hadn't been surprised. He was working for the rest of the weekend, so it made sense that he'd want to spend some time on his own. Phil often said he needed to be in his mancave, which, roughly translated, meant that he wanted to hole up and watch YouTube. He spent so much time around people, that he needed to recharge. Olivia liked that about him. No one could ever accuse Phil of being needy or controlling. When it came to acting, he was as happy to work as a team, spending all his spare time with people, as she was, but he was also happy to spend long periods alone.

It was just before ten when he finally got up to go. They had finished dinner and had all tried more than one dessert, followed by coffees and mints, and Olivia was feeling comfortably stuffed.

'I should make tracks,' Phil said, catching her eye. 'I've got a lot on tomorrow.'

'I'll come and see you out.'

As he said his thank yous and goodbyes, Olivia could feel her mother's approving gaze.

In the hall, when it was just the two of them, he put his arms around her. 'I've had a lovely time. Thanks for inviting me.'

She looked into his dark eyes, but before she could say anything else, he beat her to it, 'Do you really want seven kids?'

So he had heard, after all.

'Um no. But maybe one or two?' she hedged, emboldened by the wine. 'How about you?'

'I've always thought I'd have a family one day.' His voice was light, but his eyes had darkened a bit as he pushed her gently away. The atmosphere was suddenly strained.

Olivia forced composure, even though there was a part of her mind that had flown straight back to Tom. That was pretty much the exact same phrase that he'd used. He'd also said it in the same non-committal tone of voice. He had also pushed her away. It was like déjà vu.

She wanted to add something else – to question Phil. But this wasn't the time and it definitely wasn't the place. She had an image of herself being that needy, desperate, biological-clock-ticking woman she'd always felt slightly sorry for and suddenly all she wanted to do was escape.

'Night, Phil,' she said, forcing herself to harden her voice.

'Night, Olivia. We'll catch up next week, yeah?'

She nodded and then he took a step back and her heart ached as she closed the door.

15

Olivia and Aunt Dawn both headed back in their separate cars early on Saturday. Aunt Dawn left first thing because she had a shop to open and Olivia left around lunchtime because she had a tasting-session appointment with a woman who wanted a cake for her upcoming hen night.

As she kissed Ruby goodbye, her sister said, 'I'll see you Tuesday then,' while her eyes said, 'Don't judge me.'

Olivia hugged her, knowing she was hardly in a position to judge anybody. Ruby wasn't the only one who had trouble with difficult conversations. Phil had been his usual lovely self on the phone this morning when he'd called to say could she please pass on his thanks to Ruby for the lovely meal. He had also apologised that they wouldn't see each other for a while as he'd be full on at work over the busy Easter break. Olivia already knew this – he was being maître d' for the musicians and he'd missed a few shifts lately to do the audiobook so he was on catch-up – yet somehow it still felt like a rebuff.

She put it out of her head as she drove to her appointment with a quick stop off at hers to pick up the cake samples.

The woman who wanted a cake for her hen night was called Sarah-Louise Miller. Olivia had expected someone older because of the name, but the woman who opened the door of the terraced house to her was young and bubbly.

'Come in. I'm so excited. I think I've decided what I want, but I can't wait to try the cake. I hope you don't mind, but I've asked my bridesmaids to join us.'

'Of course I don't mind.' This was fairly common practice.

Olivia followed Sarah-Louise along a narrow hall that opened out into a surprisingly large kitchen, where three other women – two who must have been in their early twenties and an older one – were chattering around a table. The conversation stopped when they saw her and their faces became expectant.

Olivia put her bag of samples, and the brochures with the various options, on the table. There was much giggling as she showed them the naughty cupcake range and then some oohs and ahs as she went on to the more romantic ones with red sugar paste hearts on the top.

There were a lot of appreciative mmms as they tried the slivers of cake she'd brought as samples. Chocolate, vanilla and lemon sponge. She also did more exotic flavours, but most brides wanted one of these mainstream flavours.

She'd expected Sarah-Louise to choose something from the naughty cupcake range, but she didn't. She went for the ones in the romantic range.

'It's good to know that romance is not dead,' Olivia told her client as she made a note of the order and took a deposit.

'Oh, it definitely isn't,' Sarah-Louise said enthusiastically. 'I think it's possible to meet your soulmate and to get married and stay with them for life.' Her pretty face went pink. 'I love Andrew more than anything and I know he feels the same. I think we're going to stay the course.' She cleared her throat. 'My grandparents were the same age as us when they got married and they've just celebrated their diamond wedding anniversary.'

'That's amazing,' Olivia said, feeling warmth stealing up through her.

The older bridesmaid, who was called Marianne, Sarah-Louise's elder sister, let her out of the front door. 'Is it OK to have a quick word? Out of earshot of Sarah-Louise.'

'Absolutely.'

Marianne fell into step beside her as Olivia walked back to the spot where she'd parked her van.

'I didn't want to say anything in front of Sarah-Louise for obvious reasons, but I wouldn't mind a cake for my divorce party. I've got a few ideas. It could feature me breaking out of a cage.' She hesitated. 'Or maybe it could involve a picture of my adulterous ex with his head in a dustbin. I've seen that one done. Or even a cake with an axe through the middle, separating me from him.' She was clearly warming to her theme. 'I once saw a cake where the guilty party had his head cut right off and there were red chocolate-button drops of blood all down the side. That one also ended badly – not that I think there's any such thing as a good divorce... Although we did have fun eating the chocolate buttons.' She put her head on one side and looked at Olivia thoughtfully. 'Could you do something like that?'

'I certainly could.' Solemn-faced, Olivia gave her a card. So much for her theory that romance was alive and well then. Although this wasn't the first divorce cake she'd made, sadly.

'It hasn't put me off getting married again,' Marianne added idly. 'I think it's definitely possible to find a soulmate.'

'You do?' Olivia said, surprised.

'Oh yes, it's just that mine wasn't Scott – the two-timing bastard thought I didn't know he'd been playing around for months. I don't blame the women – he used to take them to his brother's house and pretend that's where he lived – he lied to them and he lied to me, but he's going to pay through the nose for it now. My cousin's a solicitor and we are going to wipe the floor with Scott.'

Olivia had bells ringing in her head. Oh my goodness, what were the chances of her bumping into the wife of the man who'd got Ruby pregnant? She bit her lip, aware that Marianne was still speaking.

'I'd risk it again,' she added with a glint in her eye. In fact, I've already got my eye on someone else.'

Olivia couldn't think of a suitable reply. 'I'll look forward to hearing from you then,' she said quickly and made her escape.

* * *

She told Ruby about it on Tuesday afternoon when she picked her up to take her for the scan, more to take her mind off things than anything else. Ruby had looked quite anxious when she'd got in the car.

'I'm glad the scumbag's getting his comeuppance,' Ruby said, narrowing her eyes. 'He might think twice about two-timing in future.'

'That's exactly what I thought.'

For a while, there was silence and then Ruby gave a deep sigh. 'I wish—' she said and broke off.

'Tell me what you wish,' Olivia gently encouraged.

'I wish things were different. I wish I'd had the guts to tell Mum and Dad before they went back. I wish I was looking forward to today instead of dreading it because it's going to make it all real. I wish I was a normal excited mum-to-be. I wish everything was different.'

'Could things be different?' Olivia kept her voice as neutral as possible. She didn't want to say anything that would put even more pressure on her sister. But it was really hard.

'I don't see how. I can't keep this baby. I can't be a single parent. I just can't.'

Olivia bit her lip. 'Let's just get today done, sweetie. See how you feel then.'

She couldn't imagine her sister could fail to be moved by seeing her baby's heartbeat on the screen. She had thought about that moment so many times. She had visualised herself and Tom with their gaze fixed on a monitor, watching the miracle of technology that allowed you to see another human growing inside you... It had never happened, of course, and she'd closed down that dream when they'd split up.

She really wanted to be here by Ruby's side, but she knew that today was going to be odd for her too.

'I guess I didn't bargain for the hormones,' Ruby went on. 'I feel as though a million little maternal hormones are whizzing around my body, making me feel broody. I suppose that's nature, isn't it.'

'I suppose it is.'

Olivia pulled into the hospital car park, found a space, and the two sisters walked across to the main entrance. It was one of those breezy spring days where everything felt fresh and new and full of hope, and Olivia hated seeing Ruby look so sad. But she couldn't think of a single thing to say that would help, so she just squeezed her fingers.

A short time later, Ruby was laying on an examination bed with her tummy bared while a radiographer smeared a jelly-like substance on it and moved the scanner into place. 'In just a moment we should be able to hear baby's heartbeat,' she said brightly.

They all concentrated on the screen and then there it was, the soft boom boom boom of another heartbeat in the room.

For a second, it was impossible to look anywhere other than at the miracle that was taking place on the screen. The rhythmic beating and the outline of the foetus. Then Olivia stole a glance at her sister's face.

Ruby's eyes were round with wonder and she'd stopped breathing. Olivia knew in that moment that there was no way on earth Ruby was going to be able to give this baby up. She blinked back tears.

'Do you know what sex the baby is?' Ruby asked.

'Not yet, my love. It's a little early. But we should be able to get that on your next scan. How have you been feeling?'

'A few twinges and quite sick. Is that normal?'

'I'd say so. Everything looks absolutely fine.'

Half an hour later, they were back in the car park once more.

'What would you like to do?' Olivia asked. 'Straight back home or somewhere else?'

'Do you think we could go to Pebble Beach,' Ruby asked. 'And walk for a little while.'

'Of course we can.'

* * *

Pebble Beach was actually the name they used for 'Chesil Beach, one of Dorset's most famous landmarks. But no-one in their family had used its correct name for years. At least not when they were referencing it to each other. When Ruby was little, she hadn't been able to pronounce Chesil and had always said pebble instead. The name had stuck and was now part of their family's own unique language.

Chesil Beach was actually a very long shingle spit connecting

Portland Bill to West Bay. According to the history books – and to their parents, obviously both experts on the subject – there was strong evidence to suggest it may once have been two beaches. Apparently, there were different geological characteristics on the Portland Bill to West Bay part than there were on the West Bay to Abbotsbury part.

The beach itself was made up of a towering bank of shingle and was only accessible in certain places by car thanks to the huge lagoon that separated it from the mainland. Fleet Lagoon was quite something in its own right. It was a thirteen-kilometre stretch of water that was an absolute haven for nature and famous for the Abbotsbury swans. Both Chesil Beach and Fleet Lagoon were part of the World Heritage Jurassic Coast.

But to Olivia and Ruby, 'Pebble' Beach was just part of their childhood and Olivia knew exactly which bit of it her sister wanted to walk on – the Portland end, on the causeway, which was the only road that connected Weymouth to the Isle of Portland. They had gone there a lot when they were children. Olivia had vivid memories of scrambling over the shingle, which shifted away beneath their feet, making it impossible to walk. More often than not, they would be hoisted onto their parents' shoulders or they'd never have got anywhere at all.

She drove past the Ferrybridge pub, onto the causeway. Sometimes when she was feeling energetic, she ran along the causeway to the Isle of Portland itself. There was a footpath on the left-hand side of the road and a pavement on the right. The sea was on both sides, but on the right, it was obscured by the bank of shingle that was Chesil Beach so she preferred running on the left.

If Olivia was feeling really energetic, she ran up to the top of Portland Bill, but that didn't happen very often because it was a flaming long way uphill, and it seemed like an endlessly steep climb. Although, she had to admit, the view from the top was stunning. There were two lighthouses up there. There had been two lighthouses since 1716 and the original ones had operated as a pair to guide ships between Portland Race and the Shambles sandbank. Judging by the number of shipwrecks out in the bay, they hadn't always succeeded. Only the taller of the two lighthouses was still in operation today, although Olivia thought that both were open to visitors.

A cough from beside her jolted her back into the present as she drew into the car park next to Fleet Lagoon.

'Are you OK, Rubes?'

'Yes. I'm fine,' her sister said quietly as they got out of the car.

It was always windy at Chesil. Today, on the left-hand side of the causeway, the kiteboarders were out in force. Their bright sails – scarlet, black and gold – dotted the sky, and their boards skimmed across the sea at top speed.

'They must be bonkers,' Ruby said, glancing across at them. 'Have you ever tried that?'

'No,' Olivia replied, following her gaze and feeling the wind tugging at her ponytail and chilling her ears. 'I had enough trouble with windsurfing. Apparently, with kiteboarding, you can end up several feet in the air.'

'Mad buggers,' Ruby said.

They headed towards the wooden footbridge that crossed Fleet Lagoon and onto the beach. There were carved wooden birds on the plank handrails each side, that blended so well into the light pine you could easily have missed them, but Olivia loved the fact that someone had gone to the trouble of hewing them out of the wood.

Today, the lagoon either side of the footbridge was rippled with tiny wavelets from the wind because it was relatively sheltered in the dip. It would be a different story when they crossed the bank of shingle to the open sea beyond.

Climbing up was like walking on a moving shingle platform, because with every step you took, the pebbles shifted away beneath your feet as the ground reformed. Good job they were both wearing trainers. Olivia wondered if Ruby had planned to come here after the hospital. She wasn't usually a trainers kind of girl.

There were a few people dotted about. In the distance was a man with a dog and a couple holding hands further away. Olivia was surprised it wasn't busier, but then again, there were more hospitable beaches than this one, where walking wouldn't make your calves ache madly after a few minutes. This was a wild beach, untamed and majestic, despite the National Trust plaque by the footbridge. If you wanted a white sandy haven for sunbathers you didn't come to Chesil. On the other side of the shingle bank, down by the shoreline, sat a couple of intrepid fishermen with their lines.

The roar of the sea increased as the sisters approached the water's edge. Evidently, this beach had been created from storm waves rolling in from the Atlantic and elbowing their way up the English Channel and it was very easy to believe that on a day like today.

The pebbles dipped sharply towards the tideline, but the great, green-grey waves roared uphill as if it were no effort at all and smashed down onto the shingle with an amplified shushing sound that put Olivia in mind of a thousand giants shushing someone who'd dared to speak during a theatre performance, both performed and watched, by giants.

A turbulent white foam spread out across the pebbles in a great froth of lacework before being sucked back down again into the ravenous sea.

'It's so powerful, isn't it,' Ruby said, raising her voice as they paused to watch the waves.

'Incredible,' Olivia agreed, breathing in the fresh untainted air and feeling the spits of froth on her face as she glanced out across the heaving grey-green mass towards the horizon. Just above the sharp, dark edge, where the sea met the sky, there was a line of silver cloud.

'Do you remember the picnics we had here?' Ruby asked, looking out to sea.

'How could I forget. It was always freezing and blowing a hooley.'

'Yes, and Dad used to bang on about it being the best place to come for a beach picnic because there was no sand to get in your sandwiches.'

Olivia laughed. 'And we used to beg for soft white sand to lie on.'

'They were never big fans of soft white sand, were they?' Ruby grimaced and bent to pick up a pebble. 'They wanted rocks, rocks and more rocks. Fossils to find, history to uncover.'

'I know! Not like other families who were quite happy to just go to a nice gentle beach and lie on a deckchair with an ice cream.'

'Tell me about it. I dreamed of deckchairs.' Ruby skimmed the pebble into the sea and it bounced through a swell of water and sank. 'I used to envy my mates who had normal parents. Ones who just lay on deckchairs and read newspapers and stuff. Even if they did get sand in their flaming sandwiches. I used to long for parents who were normal and not obsessed with the past.' She sighed. 'Did you ever feel like that, Liv? Did you ever wish we had a dad who worked nine till five at the office and wore a suit, and a mum who stayed home and cooked stuff? Is that why you spent so much time at Aunt Dawn's learning to bake?'

Olivia hesitated. There was definitely some truth in that, although she'd always defined it slightly differently. She'd always thought she spent all her spare time with Aunt Dawn because she was the only member of the family who really understood her.

She glanced at her sister. 'I thought you loved all that stuff. You always seemed really happy, marching off after Dad with your bucket and putting stones in it and catching spider crabs. I thought it was just me who wasn't so keen.'

Ruby picked up a handful of pebbles this time and skimmed another one into the sea.

'I thought it was the only way to get on Dad's radar. I was trying to get his attention. One of my most enduring memories of childhood is of Dad striding away from me. All I could ever see was his back – you remember how he always wore those stupid woollen jumpers, even on the beach.'

'He still does,' Olivia murmured. 'They're probably the same ones!'

A ghost of a smile flickered in her sister's eyes. 'I'd be scrambling after him, trying to catch up, and he'd be shouting over his shoulder, "Hey, Rubes, check this out. A dinosaur once lived on this beach." She skimmed another pebble and this one hit the sea right and bounced twice before disappearing into the swell. 'I went through a phase of really hating dinosaurs.'

'Wow. I had no idea you felt like that.'

'Well, I did. In some ways, doing a degree in modern art was a way of rebelling against them too. It was about the furthest I could get from the past. I felt mean for thinking it,' Ruby said, turning towards her. 'And, I suppose it kind of backfired, because they were fine with me studying art – they didn't care if it was modern. They were always so massively supportive.'

That was true. It had been the same when Olivia had said she wanted to go to drama school. They hadn't tried to talk her into doing something academic or more likely to lead to a steady career. Although Mum had been – and still was – very approving of Amazing Cakes.

'They've always wanted us to be happy,' Olivia said gently.

'Yes, I know.' Ruby dropped the last pebble back onto the beach and it hit its fellows with a little clunk. 'And don't get me wrong, I'm not saying I wasn't happy. In many ways, we had a totally idyllic childhood, didn't we?' She looked back at the sea. 'Growing up by the coast. Spending so much time outside. Living in a nice house.' Ruby paused. 'But one of the reasons I've never wanted children is because I didn't want them to grow up feeling the same way I did; knowing that their parents would be so immersed in their careers that they could only ever play second fiddle. And that's how it would be, Liv. Because I can't imagine giving up art. Especially if I was a single parent and needed to support us. Which would be the case, wouldn't it...?' She cupped her hands over her abdomen and shivered. '...If I kept this little one.'

Olivia saw the tears hovering in her sister's eyes and she finally understood why she was so conflicted. She was afraid she was too much like their workaholic parents. She was afraid that she wouldn't be a good enough mother.

'Hey,' she said. 'It doesn't have to be like that.' But even as she spoke, she could feel both a deep sense of identification with her sister and an overwhelming compassion, because she knew Ruby was right. Both sisters were like that. They both took after their parents. 'Come on. Let's walk for a while. You look as though you need warming up.'

'Are you sure you're not in a hurry to get back?'

'No, I'm not. I cleared this afternoon to be with you. I have nothing to get back for and Phil's working.' And even if she hadn't cleared it, she would have cancelled everything and carried on listening to Ruby, Olivia thought, as they crunched side by side along the shifting shoreline.

Because she had a feeling this was the most important conversation they would ever have. It would affect all of their futures and it struck her how ironic it was that it was a conversation about the past that had the power to change the future.

16

For a little while, neither of them said anything else as they trudged across the pebbles, and Olivia thought that, shingle or sand, there wasn't much that was more cathartic than walking by the sea. The endless thunder of the waves crashing and the hissing sizzle of the surf as it retreated once more back down the steep slope. The calling of the gulls. The crunch of their footsteps, the smell of drying seaweed and fresh air, the vast emptiness of the sky, even if it was getting ever more grey. It had just started to spit with rain but neither of them was in a hurry to go back yet.

It was Ruby who started up the conversation again.

'You thought I might change my mind, didn't you, when I had the scan? About the adoption, I mean.'

'I hoped you might. Why? Have you changed your mind?' she asked carefully.

'I think I may have been changing my mind for a while. Mother Nature's an amazing thing – mother being the operative word. I didn't bargain for all those pregnancy hormones swirling about. They'd kicked off all sorts of maternal stuff. Did I tell you I bought a painting of the virgin and child last week at an auction? It's an artist who I like, but it's not one of his best works. I paid way over the odds for it.'

'Maybe it'll come into fashion in the future.' In her heart she knew this was about much more than just a painting.

'It bloody well better.' She glanced at Olivia. 'I'm scared though, Liv. I don't know how I'm going to cope with being a single parent. I can't be in two places at once; I can't be looking after a baby and also be working. I haven't got that kind of job. And if I employ a nanny, then my child will grow up knowing they came second and then they'll end up hating me.'

'I'm here. I can help you. I'd love to help you.' She hesitated. 'Could you take a break – I don't know, for a year or two, maybe, and see how it goes.'

Ruby was already shaking her head. 'Financially, maybe yes. But I love my job. What if I resented my baby because of it? They would know. Just like I knew that Mum and Dad always wanted to be someplace else. The trouble is, Liv. I could see that happening. History repeating itself – me running after Dad's back, only this time it would be my child chasing after mine. I don't know, maybe it wouldn't. That's what I would have thought before I actually got pregnant. Since then, it feels as though my entire head's been rearranged... I'm sorry. I'm not making much sense, am I?'

'You're making perfect sense. And whatever you decide, you wouldn't be on your own.' Olivia could feel a warmth creeping up through her at what seemed like the very real prospect that Ruby might change her mind about adoption.

Ruby stopped walking for a moment and looked at her properly. 'That's the thing though, isn't it? I would be on my own. Mum and Dad will always be on a dig somewhere. You'll be off being famous on TV. Auntie Dawn will be holed up amongst the mothballs. The baby's father would be in, "I don't give a shit" land. I don't think I could cope.'

Olivia shook her head. 'I know it would be a struggle, but I don't think it would be like that. We would rally round. I can take time off and help you. So would Aunt Dawn – you know how fond she is of little ones. I think Mum and Dad would surprise you too.'

'Do you really?' Ruby's eyes were bright with tears and the sea breeze had whipped roses onto her cheeks. She sniffed. 'Honestly, Liv, I can't think straight at all at the moment. I feel as though some alien's got the controls of my mind.' She clapped her hand over her mouth. 'That sounds terrible. I don't mean my baby's an alien.'

'Honey, it's going to be OK.' Olivia stepped forward, the shingle shifting under her feet, and hugged her. 'I know it's going to be a struggle. But it could be wonderful too.'

'Do you really think so?' She paused. 'I wish it was happening to you.'

'So do I,' Olivia said and they both smiled and then laughed and Olivia was glad they were outside, next to the vastness of the sea, because it was as though their surroundings were absorbing much of their emotion. Otherwise, they might have sobbed instead.

They began to walk again. It was hard work, walking on the deep shingle, being buffeted by the salt breeze. Olivia wasn't surprised when Ruby said, 'Shall we head back. This is killing my legs.'

They didn't speak much on the return journey, but when they were back at the car and out of the buffeting wind, Ruby said, 'Can I ask you a question?'

'Of course.'

'If you had a choice of being a really famous actress or being a mum, but you could only do one or the other, what would you pick?'

Olivia hesitated. 'I honestly don't know,' she said, which surprised her, because she'd always thought she'd say, 'being a mum', no matter what. But right now, she was no longer sure. 'I think maybe it would depend on the circumstances,' she added. 'Shall we head home or did you want to go anywhere else? Are you feeling any better?'

'Much. At least I've made a decision.'

'And what's that?' Olivia said, holding her breath, even though she was almost sure she knew the answer.

'I'm going to ring Mum and Dad tonight and tell them. And I'm not giving up bump here, even though right now he or she is more of a molehill than a bump.'

Olivia swallowed hard as a huge swathe of relief and pleasure swept through her. 'I'm really pleased to hear that. So – do you mind if I take the opportunity to introduce myself?'

'Be my guest,' Ruby said, halting and putting her hands on her hips and sticking out her tummy as far as she could.

Olivia stretched out a hand. 'Hello, bump. This is your Auntie Olivia speaking. Now I don't want you to be giving your mum any trouble. No kicking, no thumping and no more stressing her out. You understand.'

She looked back up into her sister's face and saw such a look of tenderness that her throat closed with emotion.

Ruby swiped a tear from her cheek, but her voice was bright when she spoke. 'I'm willing to lay bets that won't be the last time you two have that conversation.'

* * *

Olivia spent the rest of the evening on tenterhooks, wondering whether she was going to get a call from either Ruby saying she was having second thoughts or their mother reacting to the news. Neither happened.

She was actually on her morning run the next day when Marie called. Her phone was on silent so she didn't see the missed call until she got back and had stepped, with a sigh of relief, over her threshold. Her run had been hard work today. Probably because they'd spent so much time walking on the shingle yesterday.

She showered, dressed for the day ahead – mostly baking today – and phoned her mother back.

'I am so excited,' were her mother's first words. 'Your sister is very naughty. Why on earth didn't she tell us at the weekend? We could have celebrated properly.'

So, Ruby hadn't mentioned her adoption plans then. Olivia could understand that. Thank goodness that was no longer on the table. 'I think she wanted to just check everything was OK first,' Olivia said diplomatically. 'You know, with the scan.'

'I would've loved to have been there for that. But, never mind, I'm going to be at the next one. Wild horses wouldn't keep me away. Scans are so different these days. In my day, it was just a little blob of something on a black and white picture, but now you can get 3D and video and all sorts, can't you?' She didn't pause for breath, so Olivia didn't reply.

In fact, for the next few minutes Olivia couldn't get a word in edgeways. She couldn't remember hearing her mother so excited about anything, other than a new artefact, for years.

'Your dad's made up too. He hasn't stopped talking about it. I've never seen him so excited...'

Olivia let her mother's chatter wash over her. It was good that she was so pleased. That was one less thing for Ruby to worry about.

Her ears didn't prick up again until her mother said, 'We'll come back to help, of course. Ruby isn't going to be able to cope on her own. And we'll make sure that waster of a father does the right thing. Wife or no wife, it's his responsibility to support her – financially, if nothing else.'

'Mum, I'm not sure that's a good idea. I don't think Ruby wants us to interfere.'

'It's not interfering. It's common decency.'

There was no sense in arguing with her mother when she was in this mood. 'What do you mean you're going to come back to help?' she said, deciding a diversion was called for.

'Exactly what I say. We won't do any more digs. Or at least I won't. Your father will, of course.'

Olivia gasped. Blimey, she hadn't expected that her mother would give up her life's work, even if she did have a grandchild. How amazing.

Another call flashed up on her screen and she saw Ruby's name. Poor Ruby had, no doubt, been subjected to a similar onslaught. 'Mum, sorry, I have to go. Can I call you back later?'

'Of course you can, love. Sorry. I'm going on.'

'You're allowed. But can we speak later?'

'Course we can. Toodle-pip.'

Olivia disconnected and answered Ruby's call. The first words out of her sister's mouth were, 'Oh My God – Mum's gone into super hyper mode. I think I should have kept it a secret until the birth.'

'That might have been tricky.'

'Not if they were still in Scotland. What possessed me?' Ruby's cheerful voice belied her words.

'She's just been on to me,' Olivia told her. 'She sounded super excited. And really pleased.'

'And she's giving up being away on digs. I would never have thought – in a million years – that she'd do that.' There was a lightness in her voice that hadn't been there the previous day. 'But I need to persuade Dad not to go anywhere near Scott. How do I do that?'

'Don't tell him where he lives,' Olivia suggested. 'Or, better still, tell him he's working abroad or something. He'll calm down. He's bound to be pissed off. He loves you.'

'I know.' Ruby paused. 'He was all choked up when I spoke to him. I wasn't really expecting that. I was expecting him to change the subject back to fertility signs and ancient artefacts after thirty seconds, like he usually does.'

'Of course he wouldn't do that,' Olivia said gently. 'He's going to be a grandad. It's big news.'

'Did Mum tell you she's planning to stop work and help me?'

'She did mention that. Yes.'

'She's offered to take care of the baby three days a week, more if I like, so I can carry on working. I don't think I could cope with that. Not that I don't appreciate it, obviously.' She was beginning to sound stressed again. 'I'm sorry, Liv. I don't mean to dump all this on you. I'm holding you up.'

'You're not. It's fine. And it will settle down – give it a few days. They're bound to be overexcited to start with.'

'Yes, that's true.' There was a little silence and then Ruby added, 'Thank you. I know we don't live in each other's pockets and we tend to get on with our own lives, but I really do appreciate you. Thank you for coming with me yesterday. I know that couldn't have been easy for you either.' She paused. 'Thank you for everything. Just thank you.'

Olivia could hear the huskiness in her voice. 'You don't need to thank me. I'm your big sister.'

'I know. But—'

'No buts. And yes, before you ask, I will babysit – think of me as your backup babysitter. I want to be part of my niece or nephew's life.'

'Thank you,' Ruby said again, more steadily this time.

When they disconnected, Olivia felt warmed through and through. It was true what Ruby had said, they didn't live in each other's pockets, but she felt very close to Ruby at this moment. Odd how her sister's pregnancy could bring them together. Her mind flicked back to what they'd talked about on the beach.

Olivia had different memories of their childhood to those Ruby did, although it was true that she'd always known their parents were a close-knit couple, tightly wrapped up in each other and their work, and that she and Ruby were slightly outside of this. It had never bothered her. It had been normal.

Just as gravitating towards Aunt Dawn had been normal because they were so alike and because she had always known that Aunt Dawn loved her totally and unconditionally in a way that she didn't feel her parents quite did. But she had never put these feelings into words. She had never really even acknowledged them until now.

The conversation with Ruby had shone a light on one thing, that was certain. Olivia now knew why she hadn't yet plucked up the courage to sit Phil down and have a proper grown-up conversation about his views on having a family. It was because if he said that he definitely didn't want one, as Tom had done, it would mean the end for them. And she didn't want it to be the end. It was wonderful being with Phil. It was wonderful being with someone to whom she never had to justify her dreams of having a full-time acting career. It was wonderful not having to apologise for the amount of time she spent learning scripts, or the endless hours she couldn't see him because she also had to make her day job pay. She couldn't bear it if he turned out to be another Tom. But she knew they had to talk about the future. Just in case they didn't have one.

17

As predicted, Aunt Dawn was also thrilled to hear Ruby's news. She invited both of her nieces to join her for what she called 'a celebratory tea' on Thursday evening.

Olivia arrived first and she and Aunt Dawn were now putting things on trays ready to carry them out into the secret garden. It was such a fabulous evening that they'd decided to eat outside.

'That quiche looks amazing. Is it home-made?' Olivia asked.

'Actually, darling, it's from the deli. They do the most amazing Blue Vinny one, but I had a feeling blue cheese isn't recommended for pregnant women, so I got a ham one.' She picked up the tray. 'Can you get the Colman's mustard from the fridge please?'

'Of course I can.'

As well as the quiche, there were jacket potatoes, salad, which included tiny sweet cherry tomatoes on the vine, and, of course, hard-boiled eggs – there were always eggs in Aunt Dawn's teas.

'I've made a Victoria sponge – that's your sister's favourite, isn't it?'

'Yes.' Olivia got the mustard and they went outside.

As they were negotiating the steps down to the garden, her phone pinged with a text.

When they reached the suntrap table, she put the tray down and read it.

'Ah,' she said to her aunt, who was already transferring things from the tray to the table. 'That's Ruby. She's stuck on a call with a client in New York. She'll be a bit late.'

'Good,' said Aunt Dawn.

'Good?' she questioned, glancing at her.

'Yes, good. Because I want to talk to you.'

'OK. What about?'

'Let's sit down a minute. The jackets can stay in the oven and keep warm.'

So they sat at the pretty wrought-iron table amidst the pots of sweetly scented spring flowers, peonies and freesias, with the evening sun on their faces. The hens in the corner of the garden clucked hopefully and surged towards the wire of their run but gave up looking so interested when no food seemed to be forthcoming.

'I wanted to talk about how you feel, my darling. About the baby. I'm guessing it was as much a surprise to you as it was to Ruby.'

'Yes.' Olivia felt suddenly exposed and vulnerable.

'And you wouldn't be human if you didn't have mixed emotions. When you want one so much yourself, I mean.'

Olivia could feel her aunt's gaze, but she didn't look up. 'I'm really happy for her, of course I am. But yes, I did wish it was me. Does that make me a bad person?'

'Oh, my darling, no. Of course it doesn't. You'd have to be a robot not to feel anything.'

Olivia felt a tear run down her face. Aunt Dawn was the one person in the world who she could have this conversation with, because although Ruby totally understood it and they'd touched on it at Pebble Beach, it wouldn't have felt right to cry for herself in front of Ruby. Besides, she knew if she'd started, she might never have stopped.

She heard the scrape of iron chair legs on the paved terrace as her aunt moved towards her and then the light touch of her hand.

'Olivia, darling, your turn will come.'

'Will it? After all Mum's dire warnings when we were teenagers, I've never thought either of us would get pregnant by accident. Ruby didn't either, but it just happened. It sneaked under the radar, like Mum said it did with her. But I've always wanted to do it the right way round. I've always had this dream of being with the man I love and of us planning it together – painting the nursery, buying booties. All of those bad clichés.'

Now she'd started, the words poured out of her unstoppably.

'I thought Tom and I would be together always, I just coasted along, secure in the knowledge that we'd get married, have kids, live happily ever after. But I was so wrong about that. I was so shellshocked from Tom reneging on everything we'd always planned for, that I didn't even really notice Phil. He barely registered on my radar. Then by the time I realised that actually we were so much better suited than Tom and I had ever been, we'd gone past the point of having the 'do you want kids' conversation. And now it's too late because I'm in love with him.' She sniffed and took the monogrammed, vintage handkerchief her aunt was offering.

'Darling. Slow down a minute.' Aunt Dawn put a gentle hand on her arm. 'Does Phil know you're in love with him? And has he actually said he doesn't want children?'

'No, he doesn't know – I've never told him and – well, no, he hasn't said he doesn't want children either in so many words. But

I've got the impression lately, that he's no more interested in having a family than Tom ever was.'

'But you haven't had a direct conversation with him?'

Olivia blew her nose and shook her head. 'Not yet. No.'

'Then you must. It's the fairest thing for both of you. And then you'll know.'

'I've been too much of a coward.'

'You have never been a coward. It's perfectly natural to want to hold on to the people we love. Does he love you?'

Olivia sighed. 'That's something else we've never discussed, or what kind of relationship we're having. When we started seeing each other, we decided we'd keep it light. Because I'd just split up with Tom, and Phil was tied up with that dating show thing. And I know things have moved on for both of us, but we've never talked about it. Men don't, do they?'

Aunt Dawn shook her head. 'Not generally, no.'

'It never seems to be the right time. The thing is, Aunt Dawn, I think he's utterly gorgeous and we're totally right together, but if he never wants a family, then that's going to end. And I don't think I could bear it if it did.' She broke off to blow her nose again. 'I'm probably not making much sense.'

'You're making perfect sense. To go back to something you said earlier, I think it's very seldom that life happens in the right order. Some people would tell you that there's never a right time to have babies and there's never a right time to die. Coming into the world and leaving the world happen all the time, but it's really hard for us to make plans around these things.' She squeezed Olivia's fingers and Olivia knew she was referring to Uncle Simon and the fact that he'd died so unexpectedly. She rarely talked about him these days.

Olivia hardly dared breathe as her aunt cleared her throat and went on.

'As you know, when I lost Simon, I was about the age you are now. What I don't talk about so much is that we'd been trying for a baby for the eighteen months prior to that. But it hadn't happened. At the time, it was less common to have babies in your mid to late thirties. You were considered older mothers. A woman who got pregnant when she was over thirty-five was known as an elderly primigravida. I remember how just speaking to the GP about it made me feel ancient.'

'I didn't realise you'd been trying for a baby.' Olivia felt a heartbeat of shock. 'I just thought you'd never wanted a family.'

'We'd decided to wait because of Simon's career. We wanted to get established financially. We were nest building. I had a job in the rag trade, but it wasn't that well paid, and he was working as a journalist, which also wasn't so well paid.' Her eyes were far away. 'And you don't know about it because I've never told you. I never even told your mother. Not back then. That was another thing we were more private about in those days. Or at least Simon and I were.' Her voice became a little wistful. 'We both thought I would fall pregnant as soon as I gave up taking the pill. Like your mum did with you and Ruby. We were just beginning to wonder why that hadn't happened. I had literally just had an appointment come through to see a specialist fertility guy when Simon died.'

Olivia gasped. 'Oh my goodness. I had no idea. I'm so sorry.'

'Don't be, darling. It was a very long time ago. But I guess what I'm saying is that it's not very often that life unfolds in the nice, neat order we would like.'

'No.' Olivia's head whirled with this information. She had thought she knew everything there was to know about her aunt and now she felt a mixture of emotions. Surprise mixed with sadness for her. But she also felt really privileged and humbled that Aunt Dawn had confided in her now. 'Thank you so much for telling me. I'm so sorry,' she said again.'

'Don't be. Being so close to you has been a marvellous blessing. I've always felt that if I'd ever had a daughter, I'd have liked her to be exactly like you. And she may not have been. So, I consider myself very lucky.'

There was a little silence filled only by birdsong, the ever-present cries of the seagulls and the distant thrum of traffic trundling across Town Bridge and along the quay road. It was amazing how much the garden walls muted the outside world.

Olivia was about to say something else when the banging of the back gate announced Ruby's arrival and then her sister was coming along the path, laden with plastic carriers.

'I'm so sorry I'm late. I could not get off the phone. That man can talk the hind legs off a donkey.'

Aunt Dawn got up to greet her, but not before she'd touched Olivia's shoulder. 'Don't put that conversation off with Phil too long – hey?'

'I won't. I'll tell him I love him. You're right. It's the only way forward. I'm pretty sure he feels the same about me. And even if he doesn't – well, at least we'll both know where we stand.'

* * *

Phil was working again all weekend. But they had another precious full day together lined up for the following Wednesday. They planned to go walking on the South West Coast Path and talk about going scuba diving. At least that's what Phil thought they were going to be doing. As the day approached, Olivia felt both scared and excited because she knew that Aunt Dawn was right. She needed to be direct with him. It was only fair.

She would risk wearing her heart on her sleeve. No matter

what. And she also needed to tell him how important it was to her to have a family, and if he ran for the hills, then so be it.

She wondered what Aunt Dawn would have done if Simon hadn't died and they had gone down the fertility testing route, but had still not managed to have children. She thought she knew the answer to this already. They would have stayed childless, or maybe they would have tried to adopt. Aunt Dawn wouldn't have left the man who she'd always said was her soulmate. Mind you, they'd been married and established. It was a completely different situation to her and Phil.

Olivia shook her head. When Tom had told her he didn't want a family, she'd been able to walk away. It had hurt badly, but it had been doable. She and Phil may have set out with the idea of no strings and no commitment, but somewhere along the way all that had changed. At least it had for her. Piece by piece, and not entirely voluntarily, she had taken down her 'fear of commitment in case I get hurt' armour and she knew now, with a sudden sharp clarity, that losing Phil would break her heart.

18

The Wednesday of their walk turned out to be an absolutely stunning day. When Olivia looked out of her window, the sky was a cerulean blue and it was warm. The forecasters had been right. It was the third week of April, and so far, it had been the hottest April since records began.

Olivia packed a rucksack. She was taking their lunch – cheese sandwiches and hard-boiled eggs. Emmeline et al were in fine form, Aunt Dawn had said when she'd pressed another dozen eggs on her the previous day.

There was a crunch of anxiety in Olivia's stomach as she packed the rucksack. Poor Phil. He was expecting them to be chatting about having a fun time going scuba diving and she was going to get all heavy and serious about the future.

What if he told her that having a family was not part of his plans and never would be?

'Then, at least you will know.' Aunt Dawn's voice echoed in her head. 'And once you're both armed with the facts you can make a decision about the future.'

Olivia forced her mind away from the dilemma. There was no

point in second guessing it. And it was too beautiful a day for anxiety.

Fortunately, she had plenty of other things to think about. Her phone kept buzzing with texts. A couple were from Ruby about baby-related stuff. They'd all had great fun talking about babies when they'd sat in Aunt Dawn's sunny garden. It was lovely hearing her sister getting excited about the baby. There were also several work ones. The unseasonably warm spring had clearly put everyone in party mode and where there was a party, there was a cake.

But for now, work would have to wait. First, she needed to discuss her relationship with Phil.

* * *

She'd arranged to pick Phil up at ten, so they could make the most of the day, and she arrived outside his house on the dot.

Her heart gave a little leap as he opened the door. He still made her stomach flip and her skin tingle when he touched her. She'd wondered sometimes if it was because they didn't see each other much. Although they spoke frequently on the phone, there were often gaps of several days between their dates. Whatever it was, that honeymoon sensation that new lovers experience hadn't yet waned.

Phil was smiling. He had a fabulous smile, which was all the lovelier because it transformed his face, which could look quite sulky in repose. Phil was the archetypal brooding hero, sexy as hell, but also kind and thoughtful.

Today he was wearing cut-off denim jeans and a dark green vest top which showed off his bronzed muscular shoulders, and he smelled of suntan lotion.

Oh my God, he was gorgeous – and here she was, contemplating walking away – was she mad?

'You OK?' Phil asked, 'You look worried?'

'I'm good,' she said. 'Are you ready?'

'Ready if you are?'

She nodded, knowing she was as ready as she could ever be.

They drove to the National Trust car park at South Beach, which was next to what Phil said was one of the best pubs in Dorset. The Bankes Arms is a sixteenth-century stone building with open fireplaces, wooden floors and mismatched tables and chairs.

Sometimes they stopped in after a walk, for lunch, but it was the kind of place where you couldn't book a table and it tended to fill up very quickly with hikers and families, especially on a warm day. So bringing a picnic was safer.

Phil went and got a ticket for the car and then insisted on carrying the rucksack because the bottled water made it heavier. 'You can carry it back,' he said when she protested. She smiled at him, loving the freedom of walking beside him, along the small country road outside the pub, weighed down by nothing heavier than a bumbag.

Within a few minutes, they were up on Ballard Down which overlooks Studland Bay and Old Harry Rocks – one of the most famous landmarks of the county, if not the country. The rocks are giant chalk stacks that broke away from the cliff, testimony to the power of the sea that had reshaped the coastline for millennia.

Legend had it that Old Harry – the chalk stack furthest out to sea – was named after a famous local pirate, or possibly the devil. Either way, it was a spectacular viewpoint, right on the eastern tip of the Jurassic Coast, and a prime spot for tourists. On a good day, you could see as far away as the Needles – another chalk stack off the Isle of Wight.

Today really was the most perfect day. Far below them, the sea glittered as though there were a million diamonds sprinkled just beneath the surface of the water. Gorse bushes flecked with yellow flowers that smelled sweetly of coconut dotted the path on either side of them. Above their heads, the mournful calls of seagulls filled the skies as they glided on the thermals.

They were walking on what was part of the South West Coast Path – a 630-mile track that stretched from Poole in Dorset to Minehead in Somerset and wound its way along the coastline of Devon and Cornwall. If you loved walking and lived anywhere near it – or even if you lived miles away – the South West Coast Path was the place to go, especially this bit, Olivia always thought, along the Jurassic Coast. Ruby may have grown up hating dinosaurs, but Olivia had been fascinated by the fact that they lived on the doorstep of what their parents called a 'gateway to the past'. Even though she preferred walking in the footsteps of the past, to digging it up.

'You're quiet,' Phil said, when they'd been walking for a while. 'What are you thinking about?'

'I was thinking about coming here when I was small,' she told him truthfully. 'My parents used to say that all of the world's history could be viewed in these rocks. From as far back as 250 million years ago. In the geology of the land, I mean. You could literally walk back through time by looking at the different rocks and fossils.'

'Ah,' Phil said. 'Well, they would know.' A beat. 'The most interesting fact I know about the history of the South West Coast Path is that it came about because of smugglers – or, more specifically, catching them. The coastguards had to walk close to the coves so they could look down into the bays and see what the smugglers were up to.'

'I never knew that.' Olivia looked at him with respect. 'And I've lived here all my life. Did your parents tell you that?'

'No.' He flicked her a smile. 'It's on a brochure at the hotel.'

'Like the fact that Richard Burton once performed in The Bluebell Cliffs amphitheatre,' she teased.

'Yes, but I think the coast path fact is more likely to be true.' He slipped his hand into hers. 'It feels like ages since I've seen you properly. What's been going on in Olivia's world?'

It was the perfect opportunity to stop talking about the past and ask him about the future. He already knew about Ruby's pregnancy – she'd told him on the phone the other day. She decided to bring that up now and then lead into the conversation about their future too. She opened her mouth to speak, but before she could say anything, a woman in red shorts who was coming in the opposite direction flagged them down.

'Excuse me, have you seen a little brown and white dog with a white smudge on his nose. He looks a bit like a Jack Russell?'

'We haven't noticed one, have we?' Phil looked at Olivia and she shook her head.

'No, I hope you find him.'

'He'll turn up – he ran off after a rabbit, I think.' The woman thanked them cheerfully and carried on walking.

'Where were we?' Phil said. 'Ah yes, work. I know you've been mad busy like me. But anything exciting? No news from Clarice about any intriguing auditions?'

'If there was, you'd be the first to know,' she said. 'No. It's been mostly cake making, my end.' They had just reached a part of the track that widened out and a group of hikers were approaching, chattering and laughing. The moment to talk was gone again.

* * *

They stopped for lunch and sat in the shelter of a tufty hillock, away from the cliff top and out of the wind. Phil unpacked the rucksack and Olivia unwrapped sandwiches. They ate them with sips of fizzy water and then Phil took out two Creme Eggs and handed her one. She hadn't noticed him slipping those into the rucksack.

'We'd better eat them before they melt,' he said.

'Oh yes, definitely.' She adored Creme Eggs. He was so thoughtful.

He also produced some brochures.

'I found these in the information rack at The Bluebell. What do you think?'

She looked down at a picture of someone in full scuba gear, underwater, looking directly into the camera beneath a headline that said: Scuba Diving. Beginner or qualified diver – we have the course for you.

She flicked through the details. 'It has been a while since I went diving. It might be nice to brush up on my skills.'

'Me too. I'll book a date. Which would you prefer? Boat or shore dive? These guys do both.'

'It would be nice to go out on a boat, I think. We can do a shore dive by ourselves after that.'

'That's what I thought,' Phil said, laying back on his elbows and looking up at the sky. He gave a little sigh of contentment and shut his eyes.

Olivia's heart was beating madly. She had to say something. The time was now. Aunt Dawn's voice echoed in her ears – '*You need to have a direct conversation with him.*'

'Phil,' she began, wondering how it was possible for her throat to be so dry when she'd just swallowed a mouthful of fizzy water.

'Yes, honey.' Something in her voice must have alerted him, because he half sat up again and looked at her.

'I need to talk to you about something important.'

'Sounds serious.' There was a glint of humour in his eyes. 'I'm all ears.'

'I need to know how you feel about the future.' That sounded heavy even to her. She began again, 'What I mean is that I know, when we met, we said we would keep things light and just have fun, but I think we've moved on. Or at least I think I have.' She paused because he was smiling.

'Me too.' He caught her hand and planted a kiss on the palm. 'I love being with you.'

'I love being with you too.' Her heart was beating very fast. 'But I need to know how you feel about having children.'

There, she had said the words out loud and he hadn't laughed or brushed it off. She was so relieved that he hadn't joked away the comment that for a few seconds she didn't register that he hadn't said anything at all. Or that his face had become more serious.

'Do you not want children?' she asked gently. 'I know it's not something we've ever discussed for one reason or another, but I need to know.'

'Are we having this conversation because of Ruby getting pregnant?' he said, carefully.

'Not really no.' She plucked out a piece of scrubby grass. 'I'm asking because it's really important and... well, I want to know if we're on the same page about this.' She paused again. 'I've never told you the full story about why Tom and I split up.'

'I thought it was because you'd realised you wanted different things from life and then he went off to Spain...' He licked his lips and looked nervous.

'Yes.' She remembered she had told him that. 'He did go off to

Spain. But we split up because Tom had always said that he wanted us to settle down and have a family. And then one day, a long way in to our relationship, he told me he'd changed his mind. He couldn't see himself ever wanting a family at all.'

Phil was nodding. 'That's a pretty shitty thing to do.'

'It hurt,' she said, realising she'd been chewing the grass stalk and was now discarding it. 'Because I do want a family.' She met his steady gaze. 'And I need to know if you do too, Phil.'

In that moment, Olivia felt as though the whole clifftop had stopped to listen to their conversation. The wind had dropped. The sound of the sea far below them was muted. Even the seagulls had hushed their incessant cries, waiting for Phil's reply.

'Hey,' he said, leaning forward and taking her hand again. 'Don't look so worried. I do want kids. I've always hoped I'd have them.'

The world started up again. Olivia could hear a whooshing in her ears. The distant sea combined with the sound of her own thunderous heart. The relief of his answer was totally overwhelming. The sweet coconut scent of gorse was everywhere around them. She'd read somewhere once that gorse was called the kissing plant because you could kiss your sweetheart when it was in bloom and it bloomed in every season.

Slowly the thunderous sound of her heartbeat quietened and she realised that Phil's fingers had closed around hers and that he was speaking again.

'There is a but though, Olivia. Unfortunately, I don't think I can actually have kids...'

19

When she looked back on that conversation later, Olivia realised she hadn't heard much of the rest of it. She knew that he'd begun to talk about blocked tubes and abnormalities, but she hadn't taken it in.

All this time she had worried he might not want children, but that hadn't been the case. It wasn't that he didn't want them – it was that he couldn't have them. Those two little words, 'can't' and 'won't', that sounded so similar but were worlds apart in meaning.

She'd cut the conversation short. The sense of relief she'd felt at the brilliant news he wanted kids, followed by the shock of discovering he couldn't have them, had rocked her. She had covered her devastation with flippancy. 'That's a shame. Enough of that then. We'd better get cracking, hadn't we?'

Phil had looked slightly startled, but he hadn't argued and they'd both scrambled to their feet. He'd repacked the rucksack with the remains of their picnic and the diving brochures and for a long while they'd walked in silence, each of them alone with their thoughts.

Suddenly, all of Phil's throwaway lines made sense and she realised that the reason they hadn't ever had this discussion wasn't just because she'd been afraid to broach the subject but because he had been afraid of discussing it, too.

She remembered that cornered rat look on his face when they'd been drunk on tequila, just after she'd asked him if he'd wanted a family. Then, later on at Ruby's, when he'd said, noncommittally, that he'd always hoped he'd have a couple of kids, one day. She had known on some level that he wasn't being straight with her then. She just hadn't realised why.

What was the point in hoping for a family if you knew you couldn't have one?

* * *

She told Ruby about it on the phone a few days later. She didn't mean to, but it just came up in conversation. This wasn't surprising as it was the only thing in Olivia's head. It kept repeating like a rhyming refrain – '*I can't have kids, can't have kids, can't have kids.*'

'Why would he say he wanted them if he couldn't have them, Rubes?'

'Maybe he meant he could hook up with a woman who had them already,' Ruby said, which wasn't very tactful. 'Get a ready-made family.'

Olivia forgave her the lack of diplomacy because Ruby's head was swimming in pregnancy hormones.

Aunt Dawn had a different take on it. 'If he wants to have them, and it sounds as though he might, then there's still hope. You can adopt, or maybe some medical intervention would help.'

Olivia had got stuck on the word adopt. With it, every one of her dreams of holding her own gorgeously warm, newborn baby in her arms fled away into the ether and she'd felt swamped with despair.

Medical intervention. That was possible though. She wanted to talk to Phil about it – would he mind? Would he be up for being messed about with? She didn't know much about fertility treatment, but Phil was so proud that she was sure he'd hate it – even if it did lead to them having a family.

With hindsight, the best time to have talked about it would have been straight away while they were out on the coast path. Or, at the very latest, a day or two after, when they were both cool and calm and rational, but they hadn't done either. This was partly for practical reasons. Phil had been given some more voice-over work and had been away for a few days. Then, when he'd come back, Olivia had been swamped with work for new orders.

They had met a few times in the couple of weeks after, but neither of them had mentioned that clifftop conversation. His inability to have children was the elephant in the room. It was there every time they met, but it wasn't discussed. She didn't bring it up because she didn't know how to do it diplomatically and he didn't bring it up, she guessed, for the same reasons.

It was now mid-May. The month of Morris dancing, maybugs and the council cutting back the overgrown verges. Work seemed to be the only thing that helped stop her thinking. Making cakes and icing them. Olivia welcomed the total, focused concentration that it took. She immersed herself in her hot little kitchen, which filled up with the scents of spiced fruit, cinnamon and nutmeg, and the sweetness of vanilla, and lemon, sponges.

In between work, she went on long runs, pounding the pavement and the coast path by the sea, letting the soundtrack of nature soothe her whirling thoughts. There was no acting work on the horizon. None of her theatre friends had been in touch lately. She hadn't heard from Clarice either – not even a sniff of an audition, although she had phoned her once on the pretext of asking if Clarice thought she should update her CV.

'Not unless you've got anything substantially new to put on it, no,' Clarice had said in her brusque kindly fashion. 'There's a lot of waiting around in this business. If something comes up, you'll be the first to hear.'

Which Olivia took to mean, 'Stop pestering me. I'll call you if I hear of any jobs for almost-past-their-sell-by date actresses.'

Then something very odd happened. She had a text from Tom.

He sent it late one evening and she didn't see it until the next day because she'd had an early night.

Hey, Olivia, you've been in my thoughts. I'm back from Spain. I wondered if I could pop by and see you? Tom.

When she did finally see it, she had to read it twice. Now that was a blast from the past she hadn't expected. Their parting had been acrimonious and very final and their last communication over a year ago.

For one crazy second, she wondered if she knew another Tom, other than her ex. He must have changed his number because it wasn't the one she'd had on her phone. Then she remembered she'd blocked him.

Her hands sweated and for a few seconds her stomach swirled with anxiety. She might know another Tom, but it was highly unlikely that she knew another one who'd been in Spain. It had to be her ex and his timing was terrible. She felt way too vulnerable. Seeing him – or even speaking to him – was the very last thing she needed right now. She deleted it.

Twenty-four hours later, however, she got another message from him.

How about it, Olivia? A drink for old times' sake.

She deleted that text too. She had no desire whatsoever to see Tom.

Fortunately, she got distracted because she had a voicemail message from Eric.

'Hello, doll.' Eric was the only person she'd ever met who'd called her 'doll'. 'I've got something I want to talk to you about. When can we discuss? I—'

He might have said something else, but he'd taken so long to get that bit out in his slightly wheezy, breathless voice that the time had run out on the voicemail message and he'd been cut off.

Olivia phoned him back. It rang for ages before he answered and she pictured him struggling along the hall on his Zimmer frame.

'How are you?' she asked when he'd got his breath back enough for a conversation.

'Never better, doll. Thanks for asking.'

'I'm very glad to hear that,' she said, pleased, because he sounded so chirpy.

'I need another one of your gorgeous cakes.'

'I assumed it wasn't just a social call.'

'It would be – if I was twenty years younger.'

'Thirty,' she reminded him and he chuckled. 'So, is it for another birthday?' She did some calculations in her head, remembering the baked bean cans, and wondered how little she could get away with charging him. Maybe she could say she had some kind of promotion going on. In fact, that wouldn't be a bad idea. Doing discounts for regular customers was something she'd been toying with for a while.

'It's no one's birthday. It's much more exciting than that. Have a guess.'

'Your granddaughter's getting engaged?'

'Nope. You can have another guess – on the house.'

'You're getting in early to beat the Christmas rush?' She hoped he wasn't going to say that one of his offspring was having a baby or getting one christened. She didn't think she could deal with making any more pink booties or teddy bears at the moment.

'It's not for Christmas. That's enough guesses. I'll tell you.' He paused. She wasn't sure if it was for dramatic effect or because he needed to catch his breath. 'I'm getting married.'

'Um. Wow.' She hadn't seen that one coming. 'Well. Congratulations.'

'Thanks.' He stopped for a moment. 'We haven't been courting very long. But Brenda says at our age, you can't hang about.'

'No. I guess you can't.'

'She calls me her toy boy.'

'There's an age difference then?'

'She's eighty-one and a half.' He chuckled again and it was so infectious that Olivia laughed with him. Not least because it had always amused her that only the very young and the very old referred to ages that were less than a full year.

'So when is the happy event going to take place and what kind of cake would you like me to make for you? Aside from an amazing one, I mean. Were you thinking fruit cake or sponge?'

'Not a hundred per cent sure on that. But we're getting hitched on the twelfth of June. Is that too short notice?'

Olivia gulped. That was less than a month away. 'I'll squeeze you in,' she said, trying not to think of her jam-packed order book. Maybe it was just as well Clarice didn't have any work for her.

'I was hoping you might tootle on over for a proper chat with us both.'

'I'd be delighted,' Olivia said truthfully. 'Where does your fiancée live? And what's her name?'

'It's Brenda and she lives upstairs. Flat 4. She's niftier on her feet than I am.' More heavy breathing. 'So she can pop down anytime.'

'I'll get my diary.'

They fixed a date for Olivia's visit for late the following afternoon.

*   *   *

As she drove to the sheltered housing block for four thirty, Olivia practised the speech she'd prepared.

'At the moment, I'm doing a regular customer discount.' Or maybe, 'You're in luck. I'm doing a customer promotion. Half-price, how does that sound?'

Would he go for that? Eric may be old and doddery, but he was as sharp as a tack. He also had his pride and he'd never go for a deal if he knew she'd created it especially for him. He'd been a market trader when he was younger – she imagined he'd been very good at it, but it wasn't the kind of job that had a pension or sick pay attached. He'd told her once that he was proud of doing what his father, and grandfather, had done before him, even if it had meant working all hours outside in the rain and the cold, which had no doubt hastened the crippling arthritis that plagued him.

She rang the buzzer when she arrived and, as usual, it was a little while before she was buzzed in. Eric's front door opened before she got there and he was standing on the other side of it, beaming. She'd half expected Brenda to have answered it, but there was no sign of her.

'Thanks for coming, doll,' he called over his shoulder as she followed him down the hall. He didn't take her into the kitchen as usual but flung open the lounge door with a flourish. 'Allow me to introduce my fiancée, Brenda.'

A smallish, roundish lady in a pink floral dress sprang up with surprising agility for someone in her eighties. She didn't look too happy for an excited bride-to-be. In fact, she was scowling. 'So, you're the hottie what regularly comes calling.' She looked Olivia up and down and raised her eyebrows. 'My oh my, you're even younger close up.' She folded her arms and peered at Olivia's face. 'Prettier too. I've seen you from my window up above. Fixing your hair before you get to the door. Touching up your lippie. Sweet-talking my fella.'

'Excuse me,' Olivia said, taken aback.

'Primping and preening yourself.' Her eyes narrowed into a cat-like frown. 'No better than you should be. And him a vulnerable old gentleman, completely at yer mercy.'

'Stop it now, B,' Eric said. 'You know what we said. This is no time to get insecure. Not now we're getting wed.'

'Well, you would say that, wouldn't you?' Brenda looked at him and then back at Olivia. 'But I'm not so sure. I mean, you only have to look at her – all airs and graces and fancied up. How do you expect me to feel? How would any normal, nice, upstanding woman feel when confronted with her fella's hussy?'

Olivia blinked, at a loss of how to respond. She was gathering herself to say that there had clearly been some mistake when Brenda took another step forward.

The old lady's face was utterly deadpan. Then it crumpled and Olivia realised with relief that she wasn't about to cry – she was just screwed up with the effort of not laughing, before finally caving in and collapsing with mirth.

'I'm sorry,' Brenda got out between bursts of giggles. 'I can't keep it up. You should see your face. Eric said you'd fall for it. I'm joking. Of course I'm joking, my dear...'

From behind her, there was the sound of snorting and she turned to see that Eric could hardly contain himself. He was suffused with laughter too, bent double and slapping his knees. In between snorts, he managed to get out the words, 'I'm sorry, doll. I just couldn't resist. My Brenda's in am-dram. She's good, isn't she. You believed her there for a minute, didn't you? Go on. Admit it?'

Olivia shook her head. 'You old rogue – and there was me planning to give you a discount. For being such a loyal customer. I'm not so sure I will now.' She arranged her face into a haughty frown. Two could play at this game. 'In fact, I think I might have to put the price up. To make up for you wasting my valuable time. I do have other clients, you know. Clients who understand I'm a businesswoman not a target for ridicule.'

Eric stopped laughing and Brenda stepped forward and held out a petite hand. Gold and silver bangles jostled for space on her wrist. 'I am sorry. Forgive me,' she said in a voice that was much posher than her jealous fiancée one. 'I should have said no. But he told me you'd got a great sense of humour and that you were lovely. And that you'd probably laugh.'

'He was right,' Olivia said, taking her hand and shaking it so that all the bangles jangled merrily. 'It was funny. I'm teasing. I'm very pleased to meet you, Brenda.'

'And I, you.' Brenda's eyes sparkled with fun. 'May I offer you some tea?'

Olivia noticed a tray on a small table, set up with a blue china teapot, three cups and saucers, and a jug of milk. She bet they hadn't come from Eric's cupboard.

'I'm impressed,' she said, sneaking a glance at Eric. 'I usually get a chipped mug in the kitchen.'

Brenda chuckled. 'Typical bachelors. Well, don't you worry, my dear. Standards have gone up considerably since we starting courting.'

Eric came across to her side and put an arm around her shoulder. 'I'm learning.' He rubbed his hands together and looked at Olivia. 'Right then, let's get down to business. Did you bring any samples?'

'Eric Mintern, where are your manners. Let the young lady sit down first,' Brenda admonished.

Eric gave a sigh of satisfaction as Olivia got out her box of samples.

'Do the new improved standards mean there are plates to go with the cups?' she asked idly. 'Or shall we just get crumbs on the carpet?'

The next half-hour was a riot. Plates were produced and they tried the various samples, finally deciding on chocolate sponge cake.

'I know fruit cake is traditional, but neither of us is a particular fan of tradition,' Brenda confided. 'And our families are more sponge eaters, aren't they, Eric?'

'They are,' he confirmed, looking adoringly at Brenda.

In between bites of cake, Olivia learned that Brenda had two sons and four grandchildren. She also learned quite a bit about Brenda's career. It turned out she had spent her entire life in the theatre.

'I was a make-up artist to the stars,' she said. 'I originally wanted to act. I actually went to drama school, but I soon realised that it was much more fun being behind the scenes. Besides, I suffered from severe stage fright. I'd never have made the big time. I wasn't that good really.'

'You had me convinced just now,' Olivia said.

'The training never leaves you. I've been in a few am-dram productions. I usually get cast as a cleaner or someone's stroppy mother. I've been a traffic warden a few times – I must have a stern face.' She giggled. 'Being behind the scenes suited me much better. It was perfect because I could fit it around bringing up my sons.'

Olivia didn't often tell her cake clients about her second career, but she couldn't resist. She found herself confiding in Brenda, and the old lady listened attentively, her eyes softening when Olivia told her about the *Casualty* part she'd missed getting by a whisker.

'Chances are there was someone who knew someone or who was doing someone a favour,' Brenda said. 'There's a lot of that goes on in every profession. The business is no different.'

It turned out she knew Clarice too. Everyone in the business knew Clarice. She'd been an agent for around forty years.

'She has a reputation for being a very good agent,' Brenda said, nodding. 'As well as taking no prisoners. You wouldn't be on her books unless she thought you had something special.'

'Thanks,' Olivia said, touched.

Their chat turned back to weddings. One of Brenda's sons was a local hotelier who was licensed to hold weddings and so they'd get married and have their reception there.

'It'll just be a smallish affair,' Brenda explained. 'A few friends and family and an evening knees-up. We'd love it if you and your partner would join us for the evening do.'

Beside her, Eric was nodding vigorously.

'I'd be delighted,' Olivia said.

Olivia was glad she'd made them the final appointment of the day because in the end she didn't leave until nearly seven.

She drove home with a warmth rising through her. No one could ever say her job was boring. Or that it didn't give her huge job satisfaction. She'd also managed to do them a demon deal on the cake.

Back home, she crossed the car park towards her house. The smell of cardamom and other spices on the evening air was enticing. She was trying to decide whether she could be bothered to make something for tea or whether to give in to temptation and order a curry when she heard the slam of a car door. This was immediately followed by the sound of someone calling her name.

'Olivia.' It came again, along with the sound of hurrying footsteps.

She turned, curiously, and saw the man coming towards her. The dark, close-cropped hair and the long black coat that Olivia had once dubbed his 'hitman's coat' were instantly recognisable. It was her ex, Tom – the man she'd once thought was her soulmate. As he got closer, she saw that his face was anxious.

'Tom,' she said, feeling her heart jump in shock. 'What are you doing here?'

'I sent you a couple of texts, and I called. I wasn't sure if you'd got them.' He drew to a halt in front of her.

'I got your texts. When did you call?'

'Only about an hour ago. I was passing.' He put his hands in his pockets, stared at the ground and then back up at her face. She caught a waft of his familiar expensive aftershave on the evening air, which rocketed her back to the past. 'You didn't answer them.'

'No. To be honest, I didn't think we had anything left to say.'

'I guess I'm not surprised you feel like that.'

'But you still decided to come round.' He looked a little

thinner than when she'd seen him last. Maybe not quite as immaculate as she recalled, and he was bringing back painful memories that she wanted to forget.

'Yes, I, er, hoped that...' She had never heard him so unsure of himself. 'Look, Olivia, I'm sorry. I know I behaved like a knob before and you've got every reason to tell me to do one, but would you just give me five minutes. Please?'

20

It was that word 'please' that swayed her. At least, it was the way he said it. Tom had always been so sure of himself, so confident, yet tonight he sounded unsure, defeated almost before he'd begun. She wondered, fleetingly, if this visit had something to do with his mother.

Olivia had always got on really well with Caroline Boyd. She was a no-nonsense, straight-talking kind of lady with iron-grey hair that matched her iron will. She'd been a headmistress for thirty years at a girls' boarding school. When Olivia and Tom had split up, Caroline Boyd had been bitterly disappointed.

'Oh my dear, I'm so sorry,' she'd told Olivia. 'The silly boy has never known what's good for him. Give him time, if you can possibly bear it. I think he might change his mind.'

Shortly after that conversation, Tom had gone to Spain and then Olivia had met Phil. Even then, she'd kept in touch with Caroline for a while. It had worried her a bit that Tom was so far away because Caroline had never been in very good health. She'd had a couple of heart attacks before she was sixty and she wasn't the kind of lady who ever asked for help. More the kind that was on hand for others and always said she was fine.

But when she'd started getting more involved with Phil, Olivia had let the contact drop. It didn't seem fair to keep Tom's mother hoping for a reconciliation when it clearly wasn't going to happen.

Now, as Olivia let Tom into the house they had both once lived in, the house he had vowed he would never come near again, she really hoped this wasn't bad news about Caroline.

She gestured for him to take a seat at her kitchen table. 'What was it that you wanted to talk about? Is your mum OK?'

Still wearing his coat, Tom sat at the table and looked at her. 'Thanks, Olivia. Mum's fine.' He rested his chin in his hands for a minute and took a deep breath. 'How are you?'

'I'm very well, thanks, Tom. Business is booming. In fact, I'm rushed off my feet, so I really don't have very long to chat.' Now she knew Caroline was OK she just wanted him gone.

'No. Of course. Sorry.'

Blimey – this really was a different Tom to the one she remembered. He'd never been big on apologies either and that was the second time in five minutes he'd said sorry.

'I won't keep you long,' he said. 'Ten minutes, max, I promise.'

She sat down opposite him. 'OK. I'm listening.'

He stared at the table for a few seconds, as though he were gathering himself, and then back up directly at her and she looked into the familiar dark blue of his eyes. It felt so strange sitting here opposite him – as if she'd skipped back in time and had ended up in her old life. Tom had always been what her mother and sister had called a heart-throb – Mum said he'd put her in mind of a younger Pierce Brosnan and Olivia was reminded of that heavily now.

He had definitely lost a bit of weight since she'd last seen him and it suited him. There was more grey in his hair too, but there was something else about him that wasn't so easy to define.

When he spoke again, Olivia realised what it was. Tom had always been confident and he still was, but the underlying edge of arrogance that had never been that far from the surface – well, that seemed to have gone.

'I've really missed you,' he said quietly. 'I realised that when I was in Madrid. I should never have let you go.'

'I think it was the other way round, Tom, wasn't it?' Surely, he wasn't going to rewrite history.

'Yes, OK. Fair comment. But you know what I mean. I should have fought for you.'

'We wanted different things,' she reminded him. 'Fighting wouldn't have helped.'

He clasped his hands on the table in front of him. 'Fighting's the wrong word, you're right. What I mean is that I didn't realise... well, I didn't realise what we had until I let you go. In fact, that's an understatement. Letting you go was the biggest mistake of my life.'

She began to speak and he put up a hand.

'Please. Let me just say what I came to say and then I will get out of your hair, I promise.'

Olivia waited. She could feel a prickle of sweat running down the back of her neck and she realised she hadn't taken off her jacket. Or maybe it was the stress of having him in her kitchen. The unexpectedness of it all.

Tom cleared his throat carefully. 'When I was in Madrid, I had time to do a lot of thinking. I met a family there – Miguel and Nina – they were connected to the company I was working for, a jeweller's. It doesn't matter about the connection. The fact is I had a lot of contact with them and I grew to like them a very great deal and something happened over there that affected me hugely.

Actually, it doesn't really matter what that was either.' He paused. 'I'm probably not making much sense.'

He wasn't, Olivia thought, and he was looking very serious for someone who kept saying things didn't matter. His eyes told her that whatever it was he was trying to get out mattered very much indeed.

She gave him the benefit of the doubt and kept quiet and after a few seconds he continued. 'They have a very different attitude to families over there. I suppose they do in a lot of Europe. I mean, I knew that already in a rational sense. In a cultural sense, if you like. But I guess when I was there, I slowly got to know it in an emotional sense too. But, more importantly, I started to feel it.'

He stopped speaking again and looked at her.

'What I'm trying to say, Olivia, is that I made a mistake about not wanting a family. I do want children. I want them very much. But not just children for children's sake. I want them with you and I came back to ask if you would give me – give us – another chance. Because I think that it was our opposing views on having a family that split us up and... well, that wouldn't be the case now, would it?'

'Wow.' The word slipped out of her mouth before she could stop it.

'Before you answer...' He held up a hand. 'Please just do one thing for me. Don't say no, out of hand. Just tell me you'll think about it. I know it must be a shock, me turning up like this out of the blue. But I had to let you know how I felt.'

'And now you have.'

'Promise me you'll think about it.' He made a move to stand up and she stood up too. A few moments later, they were back at her front door.

'I have to let you know, Tom, that I met someone soon after we split up.'

'I know,' he said. 'He's an actor, isn't he, and he works as a waiter.'

Of course he'd know. Just as she knew he'd gone to Spain with a woman.

'He's a maître d' not a waiter and I love him,' she said, meeting his eyes. 'And yes, we've got a great deal in common.'

'He understands that part of your life better than I ever could. I get that. But he doesn't have a decade of shared history with you, does he?'

'You met someone too,' she reminded him.

'I did. But she wasn't you.' He touched her shoulder – the most tender, the most gentle of touches. 'An actor won't be able to support you like I can. Our children would want for nothing. I've rented a house, just along the coast. It's on a clifftop – the garden runs down to a gate that leads out onto the coast path. It's for sale – I'm renting with a view to buying. It's a perfect place to bring up kids and to invite their grandparents to stay. There's loads of room. Think about it, Olivia. That's all I'm asking.'

And with that, he went. Olivia shut the door and leant against it, realising she was shaking. He had been in her house less than a quarter of an hour and she felt as though he had tipped her world upside down.

It was ludicrous. The whole thing was ludicrous – of course it was. Tom was ancient history. She had got over him a long time ago. Not in a million years would she take him back. It was crazy.

She realised she'd lost her appetite. She felt faintly sick. For a moment, all she wanted was to feel Phil's warm arms around her. To be looking into his level gaze. She contemplated phoning him now, but something stopped her. She needed to process what had just happened. Think things through.

She tried Ruby's number but instantly got an automated message, telling her that her sister was on another call. She disconnected. She couldn't just sit here, feeling like this, all churned up and emotional. Maybe she should phone Aunt Dawn. She resisted doing that for the same reasons that she hadn't phoned Phil.

Olivia glanced at the clock over the cooker. It was 7.45 p.m. Her plan for the rest of the evening had been to grab something quick to eat and chill in front of Netflix with an episode of *Modern Family* or *Ginny & Georgia* or something else that didn't require much concentration.

None of this now appealed. Why was every series in the world about bloody families anyway? Families and babies – always babies. No way could she sit and watch happy families on screen when her own happy family was still a distant dream.

There was still another hour or so of light. Changing quickly into her running kit, Olivia let herself out of the front door again and set off in the direction of Weymouth Quay. Running settled her mind.

She crossed Town Bridge, still with no firm idea of where she was headed, and then realised about five minutes later that she was close to the start of the Rodwell Trail.

The Rodwell Trail had once been part of an old railway track but was now a section of the South West Coast Path. It wasn't a long trail – half an hour or so from beginning to end. It started in Weymouth and ended at Wyke Regis, but it was another of Olivia's favourite places to run and the nearest access to it was only ten minutes or so from her house.

As Olivia ran down the stone steps onto the trail, she had the wonderful sensation that she was leaving behind the noise and the traffic fumes and joining a peaceful oasis of green. Trees and evergreen bushes lined either side of the tarmac path. There was new growth everywhere as spring had emerged in a riot of buds and green shoots. Now and then, between the trees, she saw the almost incandescent blue of bluebells clustered together in a vibrant dusting of colour. They would be gone soon, but right now it was as if they were having one last glorious burst of colour. An encore of bluebells before they bowed out once more until next year.

On one side of the trail, the long back gardens of houses stretched down to the path, and on the other, it was possible to see the navy-blue sea through gaps in the trees. This path never went far from the sea. Olivia could smell its salt freshness as she ran. There weren't many people about – a lad with dreadlocks, on a cycle, passed her and a teenager plugged into earbuds didn't look her way. She relished the freedom of being part of the great outdoors, but also entirely separate from it, in her own little protected bubble.

Olivia didn't pause for breath until she reached the Rodwell Trail exit, by Sandsfoot Gardens; a subtropical garden created by Weymouth Town Council. The gardens overlooked the ruins of Sandsfoot Castle, which in turn overlooked Portland harbour. There wasn't a lot of it left now, but apparently the castle had been built by Henry the Eighth in 1539 to protect his kingdom from foreign invasion.

Then she did pause, because she couldn't resist the walk down through the gardens between the palm trees which stood like sentries on the regimented square lawns that contained regimented square flowerbeds, which right now were bursting with flowers; blue, yellow and white, the various scents of which mingled with those of the sea.

There were railings at the bottom, so there was no direct access to the castle, although you could go down onto the grass and have a closer look if you wished. There were more railings keeping the public out of the potentially dangerous bits. Not quite enough of a deterrent to put off determined teenagers, if the squashed and empty beer cans further in were anything to go by.

Olivia stayed up on the viewpoint, her hands resting on the railings, and looked past the castle, out to the sea which was calm beneath a lilac sky. Had Tom really come to her house and asked her if she'd consider taking him back? The events of the previous hour seemed a bit dreamlike and surreal.

The total arrogance of the man – just turning up out of the blue after more than a year of silence. Except that he hadn't seemed arrogant at all. He'd been a much quieter and gentler Tom than she remembered.

There was absolutely no way she would go back to Tom. For a start, she was totally happy with Phil. She was in love with him. Her hands felt sweaty on the railings. Was she in love with Phil? She had thought that she was – even though neither of them had ever said the words. They had just spent the loveliest year together – Phil was amazing. They had so much in common.

'*I can't have children.*'

The line popped into her head.

Phil was supportive, funny, kind, thoughtful and he got on brilliantly with her family.

'*I can't have children.*'

He was gorgeous, perceptive, and as independent and autonomous as she was.

'*I can't have children.*'

They wanted the same things from life. They were easy together and yet still he made her heart race when they touched. Their honeymoon period felt as new and as fresh as it had on the first day they'd kissed.

'*I can't have children.*'

She wanted to spend her life with Phil.

Did she? Or had it just been a lovely year? An interlude.

'I can't have children.'

She had once planned to spend her life with Tom. She did know that. She had never thought there would be anyone she'd love more than Tom. They'd planned a future together. Then he'd brought down her world when he'd said that he didn't want children. The life that had felt so rock solid and secure had crumbled into ruins, like the castle in front of her, along with all of her future hopes and dreams.

She remembered the gorgeous engagement ring she'd hurled back at him. Her one outburst of pain and anger. It had bounced off his chest and tinged as it hit a radiator and dropped onto the kitchen floor. She remembered how he'd reached quickly to get it, scooping it up and putting it in his pocket, and the disgust she'd felt at his haste.

And now, he'd had the audacity to swing back into her life and promise her everything could be resurrected again. He'd promised her the world. The babies and the big house on the cliffs she'd always dreamed of, where the whole family could come. He knew all the right buttons to press.

Olivia felt an almost physical pain go through her. Tom knew exactly how to hook her back in.

But, oh God, what if it was all true? There had been something about him that had been entirely different. It hadn't just been contrition but genuine regret. She'd seen it in his eyes and she had felt it. Did she still have feelings for him? Before tonight, she'd have said no – definitely not. Phil was the only man for her.

But what if Phil wasn't in her life? For a brief moment, she allowed herself to imagine a scenario where she hadn't met Phil. Would she have been tempted by Tom's offer in these circumstances?

A sea breeze sneaked in under her plait, drying the sweat on her neck and shoulders and she shivered. She'd been standing still too long. She could feel the lactic acid building in her calves. It was time to get moving again.

She retraced her steps back up to the Rodwell Trail. Did she still have feelings for Tom? Even if she did, would she ever be able to fully trust him again? She realised that she had no idea of the answer to either of these questions as she set off in the direction of home.

21

'I can't believe he had the audacity to turn up at your house,' was Ruby's response when Olivia saw her a couple of days later.

It was the weekend and they'd taken to snatching a coffee on a Saturday afternoon if Olivia was out and about, which she often was on Saturdays, either delivering cakes or meeting clients who'd requested tasting sessions.

Right now, Ruby and Olivia were in a Costa Coffee in town because Ruby had plans to go and do some shopping.

Olivia took a sip of her latte. 'He'd texted me a couple of times first. But I didn't answer. I should have known that wouldn't put him off. Tom's never been the type to take no for an answer. That's why he's such a good salesman.' She was still trying to decide whether she felt resentment towards him or forgiveness. She seemed to swing back and forth between the two.

'So, tell me again what he said? Exactly?'

'He said that he'd realised he'd make a mistake about letting me go.'

'Which he didn't,' Ruby corrected. 'You dumped him.'

'Yes. That's what I told him, but anyway, the main thrust of it was that he's realised he does want a family now. Something happened in Spain apparently that made him change his mind. He didn't tell me what.'

'He probably got dumped by the girl he went out there with.' Ruby's eyes flashed with indignation.

'I wondered that too,' Olivia said, 'but, actually, I'm not sure it was that. He mentioned a Spanish family he'd got involved with. I think something happened with them. Anyway, to give him his due, he did seem different. He was quite unsure of himself.'

'I hope you didn't fall for it,' Ruby said gently. 'Remember how much he hurt you before.'

'Yes, I remember it very well.' She paused, drumming her fingers lightly on the table. 'Ruby, do you think I was on the rebound when I met Phil?'

Ruby's face stilled and for a moment she didn't reply. When she did, her voice was considered and thoughtful. 'I did think that maybe you were, but only because you'd been with Tom for such a long time and it was very soon after.' She stirred the ginger tea she'd swapped for chamomile since discovering it helped with morning sickness, and dropped her gaze before meeting Olivia's eyes again. 'But so what if you were on the rebound. That doesn't mean that you and Phil aren't right for each other, does it? Wasn't he seeing someone too when you met?'

'Yes and no. He was involved in that dating show that was being filmed at The Bluebell. He barely knew the woman. I don't think they even got past the flirting stage.'

'Are you and Phil OK?' she asked, giving her a concerned look.

'I think so.'

'I'm sensing a but...' Ruby reached across the table and Olivia felt her fingers rest lightly on hers before her sister went on in her inimitable, straight-to-the-point Ruby style. 'It's the baby thing, isn't it? You and Phil have an uncertain road ahead of you, family wise, and then your ex rocks up saying that he's ready for kids – and all you have to do is say yes and he'll whisk you off to his kiddie-friendly castle and impregnate you. Hang on a minute. Does he know you're seeing Phil?'

'Yes, he does.' Olivia could feel her eyes filling up with tears. Ruby was so spot on in that description.

'Oh honey, no wonder you're questioning everything. Well, if you ask me, that rat Tom has just decided he wants you back because you're happy with someone else and his ego can't handle it. He also knows exactly what to say to get you back. Please don't tell me you're considering it?'

'I'm not. I'm really not.' She wasn't 100 per cent sure this was true. She couldn't deny she'd had moments of doubt. Maybe she was in denial.

'Good. Because if he can hurt you once so absolutely devastatingly, then he can definitely do it again.'

'I know,' Olivia said. 'You are preaching to the converted.'

'Good.' Ruby drained her ginger tea. 'I like Phil. He's lovely.'

'He is lovely.' There was a little pause. Olivia didn't want to tell her sister that she and Phil had come to another stalemate on the having a family front.

But Ruby wasn't stupid. 'What is the score with Phil anyway? Has he looked into having any tests? Why can't he have kids?'

'We haven't talked about it again.' Olivia swallowed. 'I think he might be avoiding me. He's been really busy at work and hasn't had much time. Mind you, he's not the only one.'

Ruby's eyes softened and Olivia felt an unbearable ache. 'Do you think we can change the subject?'

Her sister nodded. The coffee house had become crowded

and a waitress was wiping down a table behind them for a waiting couple.

'Let's talk about you,' Olivia said. 'How are you feeling about everything?' She spread her hands in a question.

'Physically, much better – thanks to ginger tea. It's the one thing I've found that really helps with the morning sickness. And emotionally much better too. I know it's going to be tough being a single parent, but I also know that I can do it. Even if it does mean I have to grow up fast.'

'You've always been grown up,' Olivia said. 'Look at you. You're a massively successful art dealer. You're independent, with a gorgeous house and very little mortgage. You're doing stuff that takes most people decades to achieve.'

'That's not the same as being grown up,' Ruby said. 'It just means I've got the gift of the gab; I've got a good eye for art and I can talk very rich people into parting with huge amounts of their money.'

'Did you sell the virgin mother and baby painting?'

'I did. For a handsome profit.' Her eyes sparkled with merriment.

'Do you ever miss doing the actual painting?' Olivia asked.

'Doing what I'm trained for, you mean?' Ruby's eyes clouded briefly and for a moment Olivia sensed sadness in her.

'Yes, I do actually. Sometimes I feel as though I've got involved with the dirty end of the business. The artist is the only pure one. They're the guys with the soul. The collectors, and in some cases the dealers too, just make obscene amounts of money from a product they don't much care for.' She paused. 'Take that client in New York I was talking to the other day – he's a classic example. Eight years ago, he gave me six million and sent me off to buy paintings for his collection. He didn't even want to see the work. Every single one of those paintings is in storage, packed up and locked in a vault. All he will do is sit and wait for them to go up in value. The only thing he's interested in is the profit he's making.'

'Wow. So you mean people buy great art and don't even put it on the wall?'

'Correct. Although sometimes they will hire pieces out to museums. Or galleries.' She waved a hand. 'Then at least the art is still available for people to see – I much prefer to do that than hide it away.'

'It's a different world,' Olivia said. She had always known it was, but it felt weird sitting here listening to the actual reality of it all.

'Enough of that. I'm beginning to depress myself. What are you up to now?'

'I'm heading home via the supermarket for supplies. Why? What are you up to?'

'Well. This may be spectacularly bad timing and totally tact-less, but I'm about to go to that flash new mum and baby shop in the high street. Do you fancy coming along with me?'

'Of course I do,' Olivia said. 'I can buy him or her a present. I can't think of anything I'd like better.'

Ten minutes later, they were browsing the rails of baby clothes in JoJo Maman Bébé. Ruby held up a pair of navy, giraffe-print baby dungarees. 'Aren't these the cutest things you've ever seen?'

'They are utterly gorgeous,' Olivia said, picking up a Peter Rabbit comfort blanket and touching its softness to her face. 'I remember when you had one of these. It wasn't a rabbit – was it a kangaroo?'

'That's right, it was. I think I kept it until I was about ten, didn't I? I would have kept it longer, but Mum managed to spirit it away. She said it was falling apart. I was really upset when I couldn't find it.'

'Mothers have a lot to answer for.'

'Yes,' Ruby said, unconsciously touching her tummy. She had a little baby bump now. She glanced across at Olivia. 'Are you OK being in here? I mean, really, OK?'

'I'm fine. I really am,' Olivia told her. It was funny, but the initial pangs of envy she'd had when Ruby had told her she was pregnant had morphed into a feeling of huge protectiveness. 'It used to sting quite a bit when I saw a woman my age, or younger, pushing a buggy down the street,' she added, 'or obviously pregnant. I even envied the way they walked. That proud, pregnancy waddle. But weirdly, I don't feel like that with you. Perhaps it's because we're related and I know I'm going to be part of this little one's life. No matter what happens.'

'You certainly are. 'You're going to be my number-one babysitter.'

'I thought that was Mum.'

'OK, my backup babysitter. Because Mum is going to have a lot more time. She's still intent that she's giving up work in October and she's moving back into the house permanently. I'm not sure whether to be grateful or worried.'

'A bit of both, I suspect,' Olivia said as Ruby picked up a duck-embroidered baby sleepsuit and another lemon-coloured romper suit and a little hat. 'Oh my God, here's a kangaroo teether. I have *got* to buy that. It must be fate.'

'And I'm getting the Peter Rabbit comfort blanket,' Olivia said. 'My very first present to my new niece or nephew.'

'I thought that might be a cake,' Ruby said hopefully. 'With a teddy bear made out of chocolate icing like the ones I've seen on your website.'

'You can have one of those as well if you like? Although something tells me that's a present for you, not the little one who won't have any teeth. Unless we're talking when he or she is six months old, are we?'

Ruby had the grace to blush. 'OK, it's for me. But as I'll be breastfeeding, it is kind of for baby too.' She touched her tummy. 'I think it might actually be a girl by the way. I have this feeling.'

A young woman who was in the shop, with a double buggy, glanced across at them. 'I was convinced I was having a girl when I was first expecting,' she said, dropping her gaze to the buggy. 'Look what I ended up with.' She pulled back the hood and Ruby and Olivia moved across for a closer look. 'Twin boys!'

The two babies were asleep and one of them snuffled and stretched out a small fist.

'Gorgeous,' said Ruby.

'Particularly when they're asleep,' said their mother with a fond look at her children.

'I guess all new mums say that,' Olivia murmured.

'And new aunties,' Ruby said when they'd paid for their purchases and were outside again.

They hugged each other briefly before walking back to their respective cars together.

'You're not going to make any rash decisions about Tom, are you?' Ruby asked, just before they went their separate ways.

'No, of course I'm not.'

After Ruby had pulled away in her SUV, Olivia sat for a little while in her car, thinking. On her lap was the Peter Rabbit comfort blanket, still in its bag, wrapped in almond-coloured tissue paper. She undid the tissue paper carefully and held the comfort blanket to her face. It smelled of newness and faux fur.

Just for a second, she imagined the life she would have if she went back to Tom. She saw herself heavily pregnant, pinning an elephant mobile, like the one she'd seen in JoJo Maman Bébé, above a luxury cot in a nursery that she and Tom had chosen.

Just for a second, she imagined herself in the garden of their house on the cliff, pushing a toddler on a swing and hearing her shrieks of delight. A little girl who would totter across the grass, chubby arms outstretched, shouting, 'Mummy, Mummy'.

There was suddenly an ache of longing so fierce in her heart that it doubled Olivia over with pain.

Oh my God, what was she thinking? Surely she wasn't considering going back to Tom. Not even if he could give her a dozen babies. You didn't go out with someone – marry someone, just for what they could give you. You married them because you couldn't live without them. You married them because you loved them desperately. Yes, she had once felt like that about Tom, but it was in the past. All in the past.

In her bag, on the passenger seat, her mobile bleeped with a text. Olivia half expected it to be Tom chasing her up for her answer. He had never been big on patience. But it was Clarice.

Call me when you have a moment. I have something that might be of interest.

Clarice hardly ever got in touch on a Saturday.

Relieved to be diverted from her painful thoughts, Olivia called her and discovered her phone was engaged.

Why did people ask you to call them and then phone someone else?

She tried again several times in the next five minutes with the same result. In the end, she gave up and, gritting her teeth with frustration, she drove to the supermarket.

Clarice's phone was still engaged when Olivia came out and loaded her bags into the back of the van. She was beginning to think there must be something wrong with the line. Then, just before five, she finally got through.

'Ah, Olivia.' Her agent's voice was all sweetness and light. 'Thank you for calling me back. I've got a proposition for you. Just let me find the paperwork.'

22

Olivia listened to the rustle of paperwork on the end of the line and felt as though she would burst with impatience. Then finally Clarice came back to her.

'Right, here we are. I've had a phone call from a casting director from Channel Four. It's another hospital series called *Nightingales*, you may have heard of it, they've done two series, which were well-received, and there will be another one, maybe two. They're looking for a female administrator on the board of governors. Someone who's immensely powerful but also messed up. I think she may be an alcoholic. Shall I email you the script?'

'Is the Pope Catholic!' Olivia said before remembering she was supposed to be professional.

Clarice sniffed. Or it could have been a chuckle. 'They're doing auditions in Bristol a week on Thursday. Start date for filming is October, so they won't be hanging about. What's your availability?'

'No problem for the audition,' Olivia said automatically, thinking about Ruby. 'When in October?'

'They're starting on the fourteenth.'

Olivia gulped. Ruby's due date was the seventeenth.'

'That isn't an issue, is it?' There was a note of concern in Clarice's voice.

'No,' Olivia said quickly. 'That sounds perfect.'

She crossed her fingers mentally. First babies were always late, weren't they?

* * *

Olivia reiterated this old wives' tale about late first babies to Aunt Dawn when she told her the news about the *Nightingales* audition.

Aunt Dawn clapped her hands and jumped up and down on the spot. 'Of course they are, darling. So I'm told. And you haven't agreed to be Ruby's birth partner, have you?'

'No. She says she's not having one. You know how independent my sister is. She said the only thing worse than having a family member kicking about in the delivery room would be having the father there. And that's definitely not going to happen.'

'She hasn't said anything about the father lately. I'm taking it he is still planning to absolve himself from all responsibility, is he?'

'I haven't heard her say anything different,' Olivia admitted.

'Well, I guess time will tell what happens there.'

* * *

Phil was over the moon when Olivia told him her news. Because they'd hardly seen each other lately she had been expecting a slightly cooler reception, but he was as lovely as always.

'That is the best news I've had all week.' And even though

they were only speaking on the phone, she could hear him grinning. 'Well done, honey. You'll get this one.'

'Don't tempt fate.'

'I'm not.' A beat. 'I have every confidence in you. Clearly, so does your agent. You just need to start believing in yourself.'

'Thanks. You always say the right things.' She felt her voice go slightly husky. It was true he did. Phil was unfailingly supportive, her biggest fan. And she was feeling slightly guilty because she hadn't yet told him about Tom's visit. She had told herself this was because it wasn't the sort of thing she wanted to say over the phone and they hadn't seen each other face to face, but she wasn't sure if that was true.

She realised suddenly that he was speaking again.

'I've got some news actually...'

'Oh tell me, tell me. I need some good news. Have you got an exciting job too?'

'No such luck. No. It's about scuba diving. I found the skipper of a dive boat who goes out of Weymouth Harbour and he's happy to take us along. He's the partner of one of the waitresses at The Bluebell. I had a chat with him and he's happy to drop us at a dive site next time he takes a group out. It wouldn't be the private tuition we were thinking of because the instructor already has his quota of beginners, so we'd be doing our own thing. But they won't go deep – fifteen metres max – but I thought it might be quite a good opportunity for us to have a little dip and refresh our memories while there's someone else around. And I've got mates' rates. So it's a cheap way of doing it. What do you think?'

'I'd love it. When is it?'

'That's the even better news. We can go any Sunday morning. We just need to find one when we're both free. And obviously the time will depend on the tides.'

'I'll check my diary.' She grabbed it and looked. 'Not tomorrow. But I'm free for the next two.'

'I can clear a space for one of them. Great. Done. I'll see how he's fixed. And talking of tomorrow, am I seeing you? It seems like ages.'

'Yes, definitely,' Olivia said, feeling ridiculously pleased at the idea of seeing him. 'What shall we do?'

'Let's have lunch at a wonderful little country pub I know.'

* * *

They met at the Rose and Crown, which was midway between them both. It was an upmarket place without being snobby. More countryside pub than coastal one, it had a stag's head on the wall and there were things on the specials board like game soup and breast of pheasant.

As they sat down, Olivia glanced at Phil's face. He looked tired. She knew he'd been working all hours – they both had. Or was he stressed because they still hadn't properly talked?

'I think we should plan a holiday,' she said impulsively. 'What do you reckon? A nice block of time. Just for us.'

'Yeah.' He didn't sound as enthusiastic as she'd hoped. 'It's a bit tricky at work at the moment. Clara hasn't been there much. We tend to cover each other. But yeah – I'll look at the rota. For the next fortnight I haven't got time to blink. I know that.'

He picked up his menu and, feeling slightly deflated, Olivia followed suit.

They both chose chicken and skinny fries and while they waited for it to arrive, they chatted about the role Clarice had called her about.

'*Nightingales* is getting some rave reviews,' Phil said. 'It's got awesome viewing figures and my spies tell me they have the heads-up on at least two more series. Not to mention the fact that they are keen on launching brilliant but less well-known British actors and actresses.'

'That's because we're cheaper,' Olivia said cynically. 'What spies?'

Phil tapped his nose. 'That would be telling.'

They both laughed.

'It seems ages since I've seen you,' she said, looking across at his lovely face and feeling that familiar lurch that never quite went. 'Apart from Clara going AWOL, how are things at the Bluebell?'

'That's what I like about you,' Phil said. 'Your discerning perception and the ability to cut straight to the heart of the matter.

'You do?' Olivia frowned. 'Um...'

'It's OK, I'm teasing, but The Bluebell is actually the source of my intel on *Nightingales*. We had two producers in for dinner the other night and they were talking about it.'

'No way.'

'Yes way.' He looked very pleased with himself. 'Want to know more?'

'Of course I want to know more. Tell me, tell me, tell me...' As she jumped forward in excitement, she accidentally knocked a fork off the table, which skidded across the wooden floor into the path of an oncoming waiter, who looked startled. 'Sorry,' she said.

'No worries, madam. I'll get you another one.' He bent to pick it up and hurried back towards the kitchen. As he opened the connecting door, the scent of roast beef and rosemary wafted into the bar.

'Well...' Phil said, leaning forward. 'If you've finished causing chaos?' His eyes gleamed with humour. 'I'll tell you. Have you ever heard of the actor Simon Caine? I don't think he's any relative of Michael, but he's very up-and-coming. He's just been given a part in the new series for starters... You could be playing opposite him.'

'If I get the part. But yes, I've heard of him. Oh my goodness. Clarice didn't mention him. This audition's going to be even more high stakes than the last one! Now I'm terrified.'

'Don't be. You just have to do your best. Your best is more than good enough.' His dark eyes held hers and she was touched. It was lovely knowing he had so much faith in her. Even if he didn't want to go on holiday just yet. Maybe he did. Maybe he really was just busy. She should probably stop edging around the subject and just dive straight into the matter of their future. After they'd eaten, she would do just that.

The waiter arrived back with their chicken and fries and a replacement fork, and they had just started eating when a shadow fell over their table. Olivia thought it was the waiter back again to ask how they were enjoying their meal. Why did they always do that when you had your mouth full?

But it wasn't the waiter. It was Tom. For a moment, she thought she had slipped into an alternative universe. What was Tom doing here? He was dressed casually – well as casual as it ever got where Tom was concerned – in designer chinos and one of his tailor-made jackets. Olivia caught a waft of his expensive aftershave.

'Greetings,' he said, giving a half nod towards Phil before returning his gaze to Olivia. 'I don't mean to intrude, but I thought it was you when I saw that fork go flying just now. So I took the liberty of coming to say hello.'

Phil looked at him blankly and then shot Olivia a puzzled look.

'Phil, this is Tom. Tom, Phil,' she said, feeling obliged to introduce them and wishing she didn't have to.

Phil put down his knife and fork and wiped his face with a napkin. 'Pleased to meet you, Tom.'

'Likewise,' Tom said. 'Liv and I go back a long way. Always a pleasure to meet her friends.' He was smiling, but it didn't quite reach his eyes.

'Are you here with friends?' Olivia asked, adding pointedly, 'Please don't abandon them on our account.'

Surely even Tom with his rhinoceros hide could read the code for, *Please go away, we're eating and this is a private party*, but unfortunately he didn't seem to be in any particular hurry.

'I'm here with Mum. It's her birthday.' He gestured across the dining area to where a grey-haired smartly dressed woman sat. Caroline. Her face lit up when she saw Olivia looking her way and she gave a little hopeful wave.

Olivia waved back, feeling more awkward than ever. Of course it was Caroline's birthday. She couldn't believe she'd forgotten.

'She sends her love,' Tom told Olivia. 'She was so pleased when I told her I'd seen you the other day, and now here we are again. Anyway, apologies, I've taken enough of your time. Enjoy your lunch.' With one more nod towards Olivia, he moved away.

Olivia felt Phil's eyes on her. She could also feel her face burning. 'Sorry about that.'

'You don't need to apologise. I'm more than happy to meet your friends. Who was he anyway?'

'That was Tom Boyd,' she said. 'My ex.'

'Ah,' he said and then his eyes shadowed slightly. 'The gem dealer who went to Spain. Hence the tan.'

She nodded, waiting for the inevitable next question. Phil was no fool. He was bound to pick up on Tom's comment about this not being the first time they'd met.

Instead, he said, 'Has he been back long?'

'About a month, I think. He turned up at my house on

Thursday night. He was waiting for me when I got back from seeing Eric. I was going to tell you, Phil, but I just haven't got round to it...' She broke off. She knew she was babbling, but it was hard to stop.

She looked at his face. Phil was always hard to read. But right now, it was impossible. He certainly didn't look cross, just maybe a little puzzled.

'So, what did he want?' he asked.

Oh my God – that was the last conversation she wanted to have. For one wild moment, she considered lying and saying that he'd just been passing and hadn't wanted anything at all. But she didn't want to lie to Phil. That was one of the things they'd both said early on in their relationship – no lies, they would always be straight with each other.

'He wanted me to go back to him,' she said haltingly. 'And I told him that I'd moved on and that I was happy with you.'

There was a pause. 'Didn't you break up with him because you wanted children and he didn't?'

It was the question she'd been dreading he'd ask. 'That's right.'

'So why would he think you'd want him back? Or did being over in Spain – the spiritual home of extended families – cause him to change his mind and make him broody for a family of his own?'

Phil's acute perceptiveness and his ability to home straight in on important truths was one of the things she loved about him – one of the things that made their relationship special and good.

'He had changed his mind. Yes,' she said finally.

For a few seconds, he didn't speak. He sipped his fizzy water – they were both driving. 'Were you tempted?'

'No,' she said and then again too quickly. 'No, of course I wasn't tempted.'

'Even though you've landed up dating an out-of-work actor who can't give you children.' His voice was so blank and quiet that she felt fleetingly chilled. All of the joy and excitement that had sizzled between them before Tom had arrived had disappeared. Sucked out of the air and leaving an atmosphere that was flat and brittle.

Olivia searched frantically for something to say that would put a smile back on his face, but she couldn't think of a single thing that wouldn't sound patronising.

They finished their meal in an uncomfortable atmosphere of small talk and awkwardness. They didn't order desserts.

When they left the pub, Tom and his mother had just been served champagne in an ice bucket and the waiter was making a big thing about popping the cork. Olivia was torn between going to say happy birthday to Caroline – none of this was her fault – and not wanting to make things any more difficult for Phil. Her loyalty to Phil won and she left the pub without looking in the direction of her ex and his mother.

Outside, she and Phil wandered towards their respective cars. They reached Olivia's first. There had been a space beside it when she had pulled in. This was now filled by a top-of-the-range, very shiny black Mercedes with a personalised number plate. Tom 100. He'd bought that number plate to celebrate his first hundred-thousand- pound commission.

'Nice car,' Phil said, glancing at it. 'So, he's rich, as well as family-orientated. Hard for a girl to refuse.'

There was a flicker of petulance in his voice that she had never heard before, but Olivia really couldn't blame him. He must feel terrible. And she had lied to him, even if only by omission.

'I don't want my ex back,' she told Phil, taking a step closer and touching his cheek. 'You're the only man I want in my life. Truly.'

Phil looked mollified. 'I'm sorry.' He rubbed his forehead with the flat of his palm. 'I'm acting like a jealous teenager. Ignore me.' He gave her a rueful smile.

'It's fine. I should have told you about his surprise visit.'

'You didn't really have the chance.' He gave her a get-out clause, his dark eyes going serious again. 'I know you have a lot of history with the man. I don't know what came over me.'

'And it is just history,' she said. 'Nothing to worry us.'

'Good. I'm looking forward to scuba diving next time we meet.'

'Me too. Very much. But that's not for two weeks. Aren't we meeting before then?'

'I'm not sure if I can. What with Clara being away.' He ran a hand through his hair. 'It's spectacularly bad timing. I'm sorry.'

'Yes.' She wouldn't bring up the subject of their future now – the timing for that felt spectacularly bad too, but she would do it on scuba diving Sunday. They had the whole day together and the whole night and they could talk properly then.

It was only when they'd said their goodbyes and had headed in their separate directions once more that Olivia thought about the significance of Tom parking his car next to hers. He must have known she was dining at The Rose and Crown before he'd even come in. It probably hadn't been a coincidence at all that he and Caroline had been sat at the table directly opposite them either.

He couldn't possibly have known she would be there though. That part must be coincidence. But the exaggerated surprise he'd shown when he'd seen her – that had definitely been fake. He'd known she was inside before he'd even entered the building.

23

Three events happened over the following fortnight – one of them lovely, and two that were distinctly unsettling. The lovely one was that Hannah phoned to tell Olivia she'd finally got a publishing contract.

'It's for three books and I'm thrilled to bits. It's almost unheard of to get a three-book deal in today's market.'

'That's brilliant. Congratulations.'

Olivia told her about the audition for *Nightingales*.

'You'll get that too,' Hannah said confidently. 'Our lives are running on parallel paths at the moment, I reckon.'

Olivia also told her about Tom's reappearance.

'Tell him to sling his hook,' was Hannah's response. She'd never had much time for Tom.

The first of the unsettling events was that Tom sent her a link to a house for sale on Rightmove with the message:

In case you wanted to refresh your memory… This is the house I'm renting with a view to buying. What do you think?

Olivia hesitated. It didn't matter what she thought about where he was living. It was nothing to do with her. She wasn't interested in getting back with him.

But she couldn't resist clicking on the link.

Her dream house swam into view. A big grey detached with eco-friendly solar panels on its roof sat prettily in a sea of lawns dotted with flowerbeds. In two smaller pictures to the right, the listing showed a gorgeous modern country-farmhouse kitchen, not unlike Ruby's but bigger, and a fabulous sea view.

Olivia skim-read through the details.

A substantial 4/5 bedroom detached family home built in the mid-1970s from handsome Portland stone under a tiled roof. The property is set in extensive grounds with its own private access to the beach a short distance from the Jurassic coastline. Superb sea views from three of the upstairs bedrooms. It is in the catchment area of two good schools.

Olivia stopped when she got to the bit about the schools and closed the link.

Estate agents didn't sell houses these days, they sold dreams. And this was certainly the kind of house she dreamed of in her wildest fantasies, but it wasn't the kind of house she would ever be able to afford from the profits of Amazing Cakes. It probably wasn't the kind of house she could have bought even if she did become a famous actress. There was a common misconception that once you got regular speaking parts on television you earned a fortune. But this wasn't true. Like many of the other creative professions, there was a world of difference between the people at the bottom and the people who were in the top five per cent of the success pyramid. It was like comparing a debut author to JK Rowling.

Olivia sighed. Once upon a time, and it hadn't been that long ago – maybe eighteen months earlier – Olivia would have jumped at the chance to live in a house like this with Tom. To be planning to bring up a family with him. To be dreaming about fixing up a rope swing to the old oak tree in the garden and building a Wendy house for their children to play in.

But that was before he'd trashed her dreams. And even if she hadn't been with Phil, she'd have thought long and hard before she took him back.

Tom didn't give her long to think about the house. An hour after he'd sent the link, he followed up with another text.

This is our dream house isn't it. A house to raise a family in. Mum loves it.

Olivia ignored both of the texts. She should probably phone him and put him straight. Tell him that it didn't matter if he magicked up a fairy castle with turrets in the sky on top of a cliff with a double rainbow arching over the top, she still wasn't going back to him.

But she was too busy to have that conversation. She was up to her eyes in work. More so because she'd had to rearrange some of it around the audition for *Nightingales* the following Thursday.

Phil was busy too. She was sure he was avoiding her now. Even though he'd backtracked on them not being able to meet until scuba diving Sunday. She'd arranged to call round to his after her audition for *Nightingales*. To let him know how it had gone. For the first time since their early days, she felt slightly awkward about seeing him.

The second unsettling event that happened was a phone call from Aunt Dawn that Olivia got on the Tuesday before her audition.

'Hello, darling, I know you're rushed off your feet, but I just wanted to let you know that I've had a fox incident.'

Olivia heard the distress in her aunt's voice. 'A fox incident,' she repeated cautiously.

'Yes. The worst of it is that it's my own fault. I left them unattended. It wasn't for long and it was in the middle of the day. I'd let them all out for lunch because it was such a nice day and then when I went back, I discovered... well, I discovered that Florence was gone and Greta, Emmeline, Madonna and Clementine were injured.'

'Oh my goodness. I'm so sorry. How badly were they hurt? Are they OK?'

'I didn't want to move them, so I phoned that nice Mike Turner. You remember the vet that we saw with Emmeline – and he came out to the house. Unfortunately, I had to have Madonna put to sleep, but I think we can save the others. He's pumped them full of antibiotics – Mike says that's the biggest problem with a fox bite – and now I've just got to pray and to hope for the best. Time will tell. They seem perky enough.' Beneath her optimistic words Olivia sensed her worry.

'Are the others OK?'

'Yes. I think I must have disturbed the fox. The others are fine.'

'I'm coming round,' Olivia said. 'Sit tight.'

'You really don't need to.'

'Don't be daft. I'm on my way.'

When she got to her aunt's, she found a subdued Lydia Brooks, her aunt's assistant, just locking up the shop. 'Hello, love. I'm so glad you're here. Your aunt's been that upset.'

'I just wish she'd called me earlier,' Olivia said. 'I'd have come round.'

'I don't think there'd have been much you could have done.

The vet came out very quickly and he was very kind. They've been dealing with the practicalities.'

'Even so...'

Lydia patted her shoulder. 'You know how proud and independent she is. I'm just locking up. Will you go up?'

'Thanks. I will.'

Olivia found her aunt on her knees in the back room of her flat – where she had set up an indoor crate of the type used for dogs, lined with newspaper and hay. She was adjusting a water container that was rigged up on a hook and when she heard Olivia's voice, she turned.

'Oh hello, darling.' Her face was tear-stained and a little pale and she looked incongruous, kneeling on the floor wearing a black vintage silk skirt which had bits of hay clinging to it.

'Lydia let me up. I hope you don't mind.'

'Of course I don't. It's lovely of you to come.'

She stood up and the two women hugged and Olivia breathed in the scent of hay mixed with apple hair shampoo.

'The worst of it is that I feel so terribly guilty,' Aunt Dawn said. 'Poor little things – they didn't stand a chance against that fox. If only I had put them away... I was distracted because someone came by earlier than I was expecting, to pick up some clothes.'

'It's not your fault,' Olivia said. 'Just bad luck. It could have happened to anyone.' She knew she was spouting clichés, but it was hard to find the right words.

'There are so many foxes around here. Apparently, there are more urban foxes than country ones these days. They come into the towns because food is in short supply in the countryside. I guess that's our fault too – humans, I mean. We're so busy developing the countryside. Putting up houses. We don't realise we're knocking out the habitats of the creatures that live there.' Dawn sighed.

'It's a good job you interrupted,' Olivia said. 'Don't foxes quite often kill the whole coop even if they're only going to take one hen?'

'Yes, they do, but that's not because they kill for fun – that's a misconception – it's because once they find a food supply, they kill all of it – but they can only carry one away. They come back for the others. I read that somewhere. I guess foxes need to eat too.'

She sounded resigned and sad, but not angry. Olivia guessed she'd gone through that stage. Only her aunt, who had always been such a staunch animal lover, could have defended the fox that had just tried to wipe out her precious flock.

'Why don't I make you a cuppa,' Olivia suggested. 'Unless there's anything I can help with in here?'

'No. It's just time. As Mike said, the main risk is infection from wounds. It's surprising how tough hens are.' She shut the door. 'I've brought them in so I can keep a close eye on them, but it'll be good for them to get some peace.'

As they sat in her aunt's little kitchen drinking coffee, she went on quietly. 'So how are you, my darling? How's the prep for the audition going?'

'I'm as ready as I'll ever be, which is just as well as there are only forty-eight hours to go. I'm trying not to get so uptight about it this time. And I've rescheduled my workload so I can't drop a cake the day before. At least I don't have to get up at the crack of dawn this time. It's in the afternoon.'

'That's a relief. How's Phil?'

'He's good. He's really busy too. I haven't seen much of him lately.'

There was a little pause in the conversation and Olivia let her gaze drift around the familiar kitchen. It was much more of a cottage kitchen than her utilitarian one at home. Over the stove was a novelty clock from Alderney, one of the Channel Islands. The time wasn't measured in numbers. Instead, it said, one-ish, two-ish, three-ish and so on. Apparently, time was measured at a much more laid-back pace on the Channel Islands. Aunt Dawn had bought it after being on holiday there one year.

On the windowsill, a pot of basil jostled against a pot of coriander. These were both susceptible to frost, which sometimes happened even in late May, and did better in full sun than outside on the more sheltered terrace.

The fridge was covered in magnets, many of them with inspirational quotes like 'Good things come to those who work for them' or 'Don't wait for opportunities – go out and create them.' Bang in the middle was one that Olivia had bought her aunt after a holiday with Tom. It said, 'Go confidently in the direction of your dreams. Live the life you've imagined.'

She cleared her throat. 'Tom came round to see me the other day. He's back from Spain.'

'Really?' Her aunt looked at her. 'How did that feel? Was it just a social call?'

Olivia hadn't been planning to get into an in-depth conversation about Tom, but now suddenly it all came tumbling out. How he'd come round to tell her he'd changed his mind about having children because of something that happened in Spain. How he'd asked her if she'd have him back. How he'd mentioned a fabulous family house he was renting with a view to buying.

'I told him that I'd moved on. That I was with someone else,' Olivia said. 'Not that he was in any mood to listen. You know what Tom's like. He knew about Phil anyway. He even knew he was an actor.'

'How did he know that?'

'I'm not sure. Apart from the fact that we have a few mutual friends still. He could easily have heard on the grapevine.'

'I see. That must have been difficult.'

'It was. Then I saw him again. Phil and I were in the Rose and Crown on Sunday and he came in with his mother. They sat at a table quite close to us. Then I dropped a fork on the floor and he used that as an excuse to come over and say hello. But I think he knew we were there all the time. He'd parked next door to my car outside, I realised later. He let slip to Phil that it wasn't the first time we'd seen each other. Which Phil didn't know – I hadn't told him.'

'Tricky.'

'Yes. I had a bit of explaining to do afterwards.' She paused. In for a penny, in for a pound. 'Then Tom sent me this text.' She pushed her phone across the table. 'Click on the link. This is the house he's renting.'

Her aunt did as she was bid and then she looked up at her niece. 'Are you tempted?' Her eyes were utterly non-judgmental.

'No. Well... I don't think so. I'm not actually sure what I think any more. Everything seems to be happening at the same time. Getting this audition, Tom coming back, Ruby's baby. I feel as though life's changing left, right and centre and it's hard to keep up.' She paused. 'It's funny, but Ruby asked me recently, if I had the choice of being a famous actress or a mother, which I would choose? And I didn't even know the answer to that.'

'One thing I have learned about life, my darling, is that if I don't know the answer, then I need to wait until I do. Sometimes the best course of action is to do nothing at all. Sooner or later, the answer will become clear.'

'How did you get to be so wise?'

'The best days give us great memories and the bad days teach us great lessons.'

'Brilliant.'

'It's not original. It's on one of my fridge magnets.' Her eyes crinkled with warmth. 'But it's true about lessons. Do you still have feelings for Tom?'

'Yes, I suppose on some level I do. We were together for just over ten years. It's hard to switch that off completely. I do still care about him, I know that.'

'And that muddies the waters, I'm sure,' Aunt Dawn said. 'The answer will come, darling.' She got up. 'I'm just going to pop in and check on those hens and then I'll make us another cuppa. Would you like to stop for your tea?'

* * *

Thankfully, the hens seemed to be fine and by the time they had eaten tea (scrambled eggs on toast and some of her aunt's home-made tea loaf spread thickly with butter for afters), most of the evening had disappeared.

'Thanks so much for coming over,' her aunt said as they hugged each other goodbye. 'I really appreciate it.'

'I really appreciate the chat,' Olivia said.

'Things will work out, darling. See what happens with the audition. Take things one step at a time. And never forget, I'm in your corner.'

'I know. Thanks.'

Olivia's step was much lighter as she crossed Town Bridge. Dozens of boats bobbed on their moorings at the quayside and the lights of the shops reflected on the dark water. A shimmering montage of red, green, blue and gold. The night air smelled of sea and diesel and takeaway food. One thing Olivia did know was that there wasn't a fancy house in the world that could make up for living a stone's throw from her aunt and being able to pop over the bridge to see her at a moment's notice. Nothing could change that.

24

The first thing Olivia did the following morning was to phone her aunt and ask after Emmeline and Greta.

'They seem fine this morning. Quite perky and both eating well.' Her aunt sounded much happier too. 'That lovely vet said he would be over this way later on today, so he's going to pop by and take a look too. He just phoned me.'

'That's brilliant,' Olivia said.

'And how are you feeling, darling?'

'I'm good, thank you. I slept much better last night. Which is a bonus. Only twenty-four hours to go until Bristol. Van fully fuelled, check; audition clothes, check; lucky necklace, check.'

'Belief in yourself – check?' her aunt questioned.

'That's the kind of thing Phil says.'

'Ah, well that's because he's one of the good guys.'

'He is, isn't he.'

* * *

Around lunchtime, Olivia got a phone call from Ruby wishing her luck and a text from her parents – well, it was from her mum, but it said:

Good luck from us both, darling. We'll be keeping everything crossed.

Olivia felt warmed for the rest of the day and it wasn't just the heat of her steamy, cake-scented kitchen. It was a warmth that came from her heart because she knew she was surrounded by love.

* * *

In the evening, Phil phoned.

'I'll be thinking of you,' he said. 'Give us a call when you've finished.

'I will. I'll call and give you the low-down on the sights of Bristol.'

'Can't wait. I will of course reciprocate, but I'll probably be at work. It won't be as exciting as the sights of Bristol.'

'I don't want to interrupt you at work. We can catch up when I see you afterwards.'

'Believe me, it will be a welcome interruption. I had another run-in with Mr B today. He's been a total pest since Clara's been away.'

'What was the run-in about?'

'There was a mix-up with an order for cocktail onions. They delivered twelve cases instead of twelve jars and we only use them occasionally. It was nothing to do with me. It was a genuine mistake, it turned out, and the supplier will take them back. But not until they're in the area next week, and they're cluttering up the storeroom. Mr B tripped over them and twisted his ankle. He wasn't happy.'

'Oh dear, so did the onions make him cry?'

'Ouch! Mean, but funny.' Phil chuckled. 'On a similar note, he's certainly made a few people's eyes smart this week.'

'I can imagine,' Olivia said sympathetically. 'I hope you're keeping out of his way.'

'I've made a point of it. But enough about Mr B. I'm looking forward to seeing you tomorrow.'

'Me too,' she replied softly.

Olivia's audition was at 2 p.m. at the Bristol studio and, as usual, she had allowed so much time, she was there early. It was strange, but she was much more relaxed than she'd been when she'd gone for the *Casualty* audition. She had driven there which helped. She always felt much more confident driving than taking the train because trains had an irritatingly unnerving habit of being delayed due to signal faults or leaves on the line or a dozen other problems out of her control.

It also helped that she hadn't spent the previous night panicking about cakes, she thought, as she arrived at the building, signed in and was directed to the studio where they were holding the auditions.

She felt much more relaxed through the audition too. It was as if there was some part of her that was no longer desperate to get this role. Maybe because there was a part of her that was worried that if she did get the part, she'd be away when Ruby's baby was born and she didn't really want to be.

Or maybe it was down to the pep talk Clarice had given her when she'd called yesterday.

'This is the perfect part for you. They're very keen. In fact, one of the casting crew actually saw you playing Gertrude, at Brownsea last year. He was impressed. So you're already off the start line. Good luck.'

Knowing that she'd been – if not headhunted – at least asked for, gave Olivia a quiet confidence. She gave the audition her all, but she didn't over play it. They'd thrown in a bit of a wild card and had asked her to act out a scene where the character she was portraying had to comfort someone who'd just had some really bad news about a relative who'd been in an accident.

Olivia's mind flicked back to the moment when she'd walked into her aunt's back bedroom. Aunt Dawn on her knees by her injured birds. Aunt Dawn's tear-stained face as she'd turned. Her guilt at leaving the hens alone at the wrong moment and the cracks in her voice when she'd said she felt responsible for what had happened. Olivia did not have to dig deep to portray the compassion she'd felt. As she spoke to the 'imaginary patient', her voice was gentle but fiercely supportive. 'This is not your fault. You are not to blame. I promise you that. It is one of those awful things that just happens. There was nothing you could have done to prevent it.'

All actors draw from their own lives. Just as all writers, artists and composers do – it's how it works. You draw the pain from your life and you channel it into your art and, in doing so, not only do you get others to identify with you because they have felt the same pain, but you also feel a cathartic relief yourself. It's a universal process – it has probably existed since the dawn of humanity when two cavemen first connected over a fire in an earthen pit.

What comes from the heart goes to the heart. If you believe it, if you really feel it, then your audience will believe it and feel it too. It was what she'd been taught at drama school.

And she had a feeling it had paid off today because when she came to the end of the audition, there was a stillness in the room. The kind of stillness that she knew meant they had been hanging on to her every word.

'Thank you, Olivia. We'll be in touch.' It was the same parting shot as always. But they were all smiling.

Olivia left the studio still feeling the same calmness that she'd felt throughout the audition. She bought a meal deal from a newsagent – she'd been too nervous to have lunch beforehand – and she took it back to her van, which was on the top floor of a municipal car park.

As she ate the cheese salad sandwich, she thought about what a strange life being a performer was. A roller coaster full of big ups and crashing downs. The ups were adrenaline-fuelled, exciting rushes, that exultant feeling when you got a part. The downs were gut-wrenching disappointments.

Running Amazing Cakes was much simpler. She felt much more on an even keel when she was baking, delivering, talking to clients and all of the essential accoutrements that surrounded it.

If she were to pack in acting and have a baby, she'd have a totally different life to the one she had now. She knew she would miss it badly. Maybe that was the reason she'd struggled when Ruby had asked her what she'd choose if the options were motherhood or fame.

Her phone, which was still on silent from the audition, suddenly buzzed in her lap. She glanced at the screen. It was Clarice.

This was it. Olivia's heart banged against her chest. They'd made that decision bloody fast. Or maybe her agent was phoning to tell her she'd left her jacket at the studio. That had happened once. Her hopes had soared to the sky and then been crushed underfoot again in a matter of seconds.

'Olivia.' Her agent's voice was triumphant. 'They loved you. You've got the part.'

'What?' There was a big bit of her that was so shocked she couldn't move.

Clarice repeated herself impatiently with more emphasis on the 'loved you' bit this time.

'Thank you,' Olivia said, feeling the whoosh in her ears as the roller coaster climbed steeply upwards, higher and higher. 'Oh my God. I've really got it.'

'You've really got it. Well done.' Clarice sounded as pleased as if she'd got the part herself. 'I'll email you the details, contracts, et cetera, but I thought you'd want to know as soon as possible. You're not driving, are you?'

'No, I'm sitting in my van.' She barely heard the rest of the conversation. But she knew that wouldn't matter. It would all be in an email. Clarice was highly efficient. All she could think about was that she would always remember this moment. The moment when she got her first huge break. And wasn't it a shame that she was sitting at the top of a multistorey car park looking at the most uninspiring of views – a concrete pillar which had been graffitied with the word 'fuck' in black paint. Although, actually, right now, that did seem quite apt.

After the call from Clarice, Olivia phoned Phil and told him her news.

'Congratulations. You are bloody amazing.' He couldn't have sounded more thrilled.

'Is this a bad time to talk?' she asked.

'No. of course it isn't. In fact, I'm on my way across to the lighthouse. I just took a call from a guest who left an hour ago. She thinks she left her engagement ring on the sink in the bathroom. I thought, as it was such a nice day, that I'd head over myself and check. So tell me more. What did they say?'

She filled him in and at the end of it, he said, 'Where are you anyway? What can you see?'

She laughed, high on adrenaline. 'It's not very inspiring. I can see a steering wheel and an empty sandwich wrapper on the passenger seat and through the window I can see a concrete building full of cars. Directly in front of me, there's a big concrete pillar which has the word "fuck" written on it in big black letters.'

'Sounds pretty apt to me. Is there an exclamation mark?'

'Yes, there is.'

'Well, that's a memory that's going to stick in your mind.' He chuckled.

'That's exactly what I was thinking.'

'So are you on your way back?'

'I am in a minute. Tell me what you can see?'

'Well... if you hang on just another minute...' He sounded out of breath. He must be climbing the spiral staircase of the lighthouse, which in Olivia's memory went up and up and up. 'Right, I'm there. I can see a circular room with huge, floor-to-ceiling windows. A room that once held the great light that warned sailors not to come too close to the rocks.'

'I can visualise it perfectly.'

'I have an almost panoramic view.' He hesitated and Olivia imagined him moving across to the window. There's the English Channel, which is dark blue and quite choppy today, although there are one or two boats out there.'

'What else? What colour's the sky?'

'The sky is mostly blue too, with patches of cloud, but the patches are moving fast and you can see the shadows of them on the surrounding hills.' He was into his stride now. 'I can see hikers on the coast path and dogs – and in the further distance I can see fields of yellow rapeseed.'

'Brilliant.'

But he wasn't finished. 'I'm looking back at the sea now. And in the distance, I can see the dark blue line of the horizon where the sky meets the water. I used to think that was the edge of forever when I was a kid.'

'I used to think it went to Africa,' Olivia said. 'Because I used to have this book all about Africa and when I asked our parents where Africa was, they said it was across the sea. For ages, I thought they meant just the other side of this sea. I was desperately disappointed when I found out it was just France over there. It's amazing isn't it – the fantastic images we conjure up in our imagination.'

'It is.'

Are you going to check for the ring?'

'I've already checked. It was on the sink. It's now safe in my pocket.'

'Great.'

Phil was silent for a second and fleetingly she thought she'd lost the signal.

Then she heard him breathing and realised he was still there.

'What?' she said. 'Tell me what you're thinking.'

'It'll sound mad.'

'Tell me anyway.'

'OK.' She heard him take a deep breath. 'I was wondering if a beautiful girl who's heading off to the big city with a rucksack of dreams on her shoulders would still want to know the maître d' she left behind when she came back all famous and successful.'

Olivia caught her breath. 'I think that the beautiful girl may well be a lot more enamoured with the maître d' than he seems to think,' she said softly.

'That's good to hear,' Phil replied. 'Because the maître d' is pretty smitten with the beautiful girl too.'

'We should talk about these things,' Olivia said then. 'But not on the phone.'

'I agree.' He'd gone back to matter of fact. 'I'd better go and let the owner of this ring know that it's safe and sound then. And you'd better get out of that car park before you run up a massive parking bill.'

'Good idea.'

'Drive safely, honey.'

They said their goodbyes and Olivia started the engine of the van. It was amazing what miracles could take place in a Bristol city-centre multistorey car park.

25

Olivia started the drive home on cloud ninety-nine, which was ten times higher than cloud nine but dipped dramatically when her van broke down halfway there. It didn't stop completely but lost most of its power and wouldn't go more than about eighteen mph. She managed to limp it to the next service station.

She called the RAC, who promised she'd be a priority because she was a woman on her own but who also warned that they were having a spectacularly busy day and would try to get to her within two hours.

Olivia wasn't too worried. She had a toilet and also a shop where she could purchase her tea, if necessary, although hopefully she wouldn't be waiting that long. She also had a phone, albeit one that only had forty-five per cent charge left, so it wasn't going to last indefinitely. This was the most annoying bit. She was itching to tell everyone she knew about her success. Aunt Dawn, Ruby and her parents were top of the list. But she didn't want to run her phone down too much, so she decided to wait. She also wanted to keep Phil informed because she'd planned to call by his house and celebrate.

The time stretched from two hours to three and then four with the RAC sending her text updates. In the end, the recovery truck didn't pull in until 8 p.m. and Olivia didn't think she'd ever been more pleased to see anyone.

It took him a further fifteen minutes of tests to tell her that she had an electrical fault which he couldn't fix on the spot so would take her and the van home. It was dusk by the time the van was safely on the low-loader and she was sitting up front with the driver, whose name was Benjamin Cox.

He was a similar age to her father, quite talkative, and every so often his chatter was interspersed by another apology and his dismay that she'd been kept waiting so long. He himself, he said, had done a record number of calls that day. Now he had finally got to her, he bent over backwards to help, and not only would he take her home but he agreed to drop her van off at her local garage en route.

'There's not a lot of point in you paying another tow truck to come out tomorrow,' he'd said kindly. 'And your van isn't going anywhere under its own steam until it's been fixed. It needs a crank sensor. It's probably a part they've got in stock, so it shouldn't be long. It's just unlucky that I don't have one on the truck. They don't let us carry much, these days.'

Olivia thanked him profusely and left a message on the garage's answerphone to tell them what her van was doing on their forecourt. Then she posted the key through the door with a note in an envelope, also helpfully produced by Benjamin Cox.

He drove her back to number five and they parted on good terms. She'd even told him about *Nightingales* – she hadn't been able to contain herself - and he'd said he didn't watch it, but he thought his wife did and that they'd look out for her.

It wasn't quite the same as telling her family, but it was better than nothing.

* * *

By the time she finally unlocked her front door, it was nearly 10 p.m. She considered phoning everyone now, but it was late. Ruby had been having early nights lately, blaming the baby for tiring her out, and Mum and Dad weren't nightbirds either. Aunt Dawn was the only one who was likely to be up late. And she'd be tired too – emotionally anyway, after the chicken tragedy with the fox.

Olivia decided reluctantly that it would be better to wait until the following morning and then tell everyone together.

She was sad that she hadn't had the chance to see Phil; she'd finally sent him a message to say she wasn't going to make it to his because of the van, but the memory of their conversation felt like a nugget of gold. They would have a proper chance to catch up on Sunday. They had planned a whole uninterrupted twenty-four hours together. They would have plenty of time for talking then. Olivia couldn't wait.

* * *

The next two days passed in a flurry of activity. The garage called and said her van would be ready late Saturday, which was a relief as she needed it for work. Olivia phoned the client who was expecting a cake delivery and explained the situation and he agreed to come over and collect it himself. This was handy as it saved her an hour and a half.

Her family were over the moon when they heard her news. She'd been quite worried about telling Ruby because of the dates of filming, but Ruby assuaged her fears. 'Don't be daft. Mum will be here anyway – just in case I change my mind at the last minute about having a birthing partner, which I can assure you I won't.' She paused. 'Besides, you won't be filming 24/7, will you? And

Bristol's only a couple of hours away. It's not like getting in and out of London.'

All of this was true.

Olivia decided to stop worrying and look forward to Sunday. Diving in the sea was very weather-dependent, but even though it was forecast to be fine, she and Phil had a backup plan just in case it changed.

On Sunday, when she woke up and looked out of her bedroom window, the sky was achingly blue and the sun felt warm through the glass. It felt like summer and the forecasters had promised a scorching bank holiday Monday.

The dive boat didn't leave the quay until nine thirty, but Phil was picking her up at eight thirty so they could allow for any hold-ups. Timewise, she was barely ten minutes from where they were meeting the boat, but dive kit was too heavy to carry that far.

They both had drysuits and stab jackets but had arranged to hire the heavy bottles and weight belts from the dive skipper. Dive bottles had to be tested every three years and hers had been well overdue.

Phil arrived on time.

'It's a fantastic day out there,' he said, bending to kiss her. 'I'm really looking forward to this. Are you?'

'I am, although I'm a little bit nervous. It's been ages since I dived.'

'Me too. But we're not going deep. Today is just about rediscovering the sport and deciding whether we like it enough to go again.'

'Absolutely,' she said.

'Do you remember all the hand signals?' he asked her.

'I think so. It's thumbs up if you want to go up. And finger and thumb together for OK?' she demonstrated.

'Exactly.' He held out his hand in front of him, palm facing the floor, and tilted it back and forth. 'This is the signal for, "I'm not sure." So if I ask you if you're OK and you do this, I'll know to wait until you are sure.'

'Yep. I remember that one.'

'And this one...' Phil did the cut-throat motion at his neck, followed by the thumbs up signal, 'means that I've got no air and I need to go up.'

'Absolutely. But that's not going to happen.'

'No. We won't be diving for that long. Forty-five minutes tops, Dan, the skipper, said. We're doing a drift dive across the Shambles, which is a sandbank off Portland. Nice easy conditions. It's going to be fun.'

The dive boat, which was called The Katherine – Phil thought she was named after the skipper's daughter – was moored up at the opposite side of the quay to Vintage Views, but it still wasn't more than a few hundred metres away.

There was a little heap of dive gear on the quay. Four air cylinders stood in a row. Next to them was a pile of dive bags, which Olivia knew would contain wetsuits, or maybe drysuits, like she and Phil would be wearing, which didn't allow any water in at all. Only the hardiest divers wore wetsuits in the English Channel at this time of year. Despite the air temperature, May was one of the coldest times of the year. The sea took a long time to cool down and an equally long time to warm back up again. Hence it was actually a lot warmer in December than it was in May.

Several people were already carrying gear from the quay to the boat and Olivia and Phil joined them. It was the kind of sport where everyone lent a hand and it gave them the chance to get acquainted with the other divers, most of whom seemed younger than them, Olivia observed, although there was one guy who looked a bit like Captain Birdseye, with white hair and bushy eyebrows, who Olivia decided must be the instructor Phil had mentioned. Until he put her right and pointed out a younger guy called Stephen, who couldn't have been more than thirty. Phil also introduced her to Dan, the skipper, who asked to see her dive qualification.

'Unbelievable health and safety these days,' he said, with an apologetic glance at Phil. 'And in our litigious society, I like to know who's jumping off my boat.'

'Absolutely,' Olivia said. She felt a little thrill of excitement in her stomach. It had been a few years since she'd last dived with Tom, but the familiar smells of sea water and neoprene, and the rocking of the boat as they went to and fro, carrying stuff on to it, with the cries of the gulls overhead – all of it whisked her back in an instant. Unlike many relatively new divers, she'd dived a lot more in England than she had abroad.

They'd almost finished packing the dive kit safely onto the boat – Phil was just helping a latecomer get the last of the heavy bits on – when Olivia saw a familiar figure striding along the quay. It was Tom.

She didn't know why she was so surprised. Her ex was a keen sailor and today was perfect for boating. And, of course, this would still be his closest harbour. Her first instinct was to hide so she didn't have to speak to him. This was difficult on a dive boat. There was a cabin, but it was quite small and it would look a bit odd if she suddenly ducked inside it.

With a bit of luck, Tom wouldn't spot her. He certainly wouldn't be expecting to see her here. Hopefully he wouldn't recognise Phil, who was in full view on the quay, chatting. Tom had only met him once, but then Phil was pretty recognisable. His darkly handsome brooding looks were head-turning and he had the kind of presence that men often looked at too.

But it did look as though Tom was on a mission. He was peering at the names of boats, stopping and starting as if he was searching for one. He had almost reached The Katherine – he glanced at a heap of weight belts and then at the boat, and Olivia found herself looking straight into his eyes.

Damn it.

He was about to head in her direction when she saw that Phil had seen him and was greeting him politely. Well done, Phil.

Both men turned slightly out of her view to speak to each other. She was too far away to hear what they were saying and could no longer see their faces, but she saw the body language suddenly change.

Tom was saying something and it wasn't friendly. He was gesticulating with his hands. Cross, impatient little gestures that Olivia knew so well. He was clearly pissed off about something. She saw Phil's shoulders stiffen and his back straighten. He and Tom were about the same height. Both of them were over six foot and there now seemed to be some kind of altercation going on. Phil was shaking his head.

Olivia was severely tempted to jump out of the boat and go and see what the hell it was about, but the skipper had just started the engines. The smell of marine diesel filled the air as they thrummed into life.

Phil was now the last person on the quay and Stephen was calling across, 'Come on, mate, or we'll be leaving you behind.'

Phil acknowledged this and shouted something in response, before he finally turned his back on Tom and headed for the boat. He was frowning, Olivia saw, and he looked pretty stressed out when he got to the boat.

'Sorry about that.' He hopped aboard as one of the divers cast off and they motored slowly through the calm waters of the harbour.

Including Stephen, the instructor, there were only four other divers, besides them, so three pairs of divers. Each of them sitting with their buddies. Olivia had saved Phil a seat on the bench and as he sat beside her, she said, 'What was that about? Did he have a go at you?'

'No. Not really.' Phil shrugged. 'I'll tell you later.' He gave her a slightly forced smile and she was aware of a tension in him that hadn't been there before Tom had rocked up. Whatever Tom had said had clearly jolted him.

* * *

They'd been going for about twenty-five minutes and were out on the open sea, along with dozens of other boats, clearly with the same idea, when Stephen, who was on the other side of Phil, leaned closer to say something to him.

Phil looked surprised, but then nodded.

'There's been a slight change of plan,' he said, leaning close to Olivia as the boat began to slow to a speed at which they could hear themselves more easily. 'They're not actually doing a drift dive today. Which is what I thought we'd be doing. It seems we're not very far off slack water, so they've decided to do a wreck dive instead. It's not very deep. Just over eighteen metres. It's a new shipwreck, but Dan has the co-ordinates so he's going to try and find it. Are you OK with that? Apparently, it's the perfect wreck dive for beginners.'

'I'm OK with that,' she said, feeling her stomach tighten. The other divers were clearly excited about the prospect and she didn't want to be a party pooper, although a wreck dive was a little more daunting than a drift dive – there were more opportunities to make mistakes when you were poking about amongst bits of old metal. 'Actually,' she continued, 'I did do a wreck dive once before. There are some old Valentine tanks that are sunk off Boscombe Pier. They were experimental flotation tanks but they sank.'

'Wow,' Phil said, looking at her with respect.

One of the other divers caught the word Valentine. 'I've dived those before,' he said, giving her a thumbs up sign. 'Brilliant, aren't they?'

The atmosphere had changed on the boat. There was a buzz of excitement at the prospect of exploring a wreck.

'I've never been on a wreck,' Phil said, 'But I'm up for giving it a go. And it makes sense if it's slack water anyway.'

Slack water was the point at which the tide turned and it was the best time to dive on stationary objects like shipwrecks because the current wasn't trying to sweep you off.

The skipper had now slowed and was circling around a patch of water – clearly, they had roughly the right co-ordinates – or marks, as divers called them – and was checking his echo sounder to find the wreck.

Stephen began to brief his divers.

'Right, guys, I know this isn't the first time most of you have been on a wreck.' He glanced at Phil. 'But I just want to run through the dive plan one more time. You don't separate. You always stay in sight of your buddy.' He checked over the side of the boat. 'It looks to be about four or five metres visibility down there so that shouldn't be too tricky. If you're not comfortable with anything, you let your buddy know and you both come up. You do not separate. We'll have about twenty minutes to mooch about on the wreck, which is mostly broken up, but there are one or two places where you can go right in. If you're not confident, steer clear. Got it?'

There were nods and grunts of affirmation.

Olivia wasn't the only woman on board. She caught the gaze of the other girl and they smiled at each other.

'Remember the incident pit,' Stephen continued. 'Who can tell me what the incident pit is?'

It was the girl who replied. Her clear voice carrying across the fresh sea air and the low rumbling of the engine. 'It's when one tiny incident leads to another, then that leads to another and so on and then, before you know it, you've got a major life-threatening incident.'

'Precisely,' said the instructor. 'It's not usually one big thing that catches divers out. It's a build-up of several small things. Not that we should have any problems today. We have almost perfect diving conditions.'

26

The skipper dropped anchor. 'We're pretty much on slack water now,' he called. 'And we're just south of the wreck. Have fun, you guys.'

Two by two, the divers entered the water. Each pair bobbing on the surface fleetingly before making their descent. Phil and Olivia were the last pair to go in. This boat was easier than some because it had a purpose-built platform on the stern which made the whole process much easier. Especially when it came to getting back on. There was none of the undignified scramble you had when you got back into a rib.

Traditionally, divers went into the sea backwards. It was easier to hit the water with your back because then you could protect your mask and regulator with your hands and make sure they stayed in place. Even so, it was always weird, stepping off a boat, into the water. One moment the sun was hot on Olivia's face, which was about the only exposed bit of skin there was in a dry suit, and the next there was the slight shock of cold water closing over her head. It was also odd making the transition from breathing air above land to breathing air from a regulator below the water.

Like the divers before them, she and Phil bobbed back up and stayed on the surface just long enough to gather themselves before agreeing they were ready to go down.

It was amazing how quickly it all came back to her, Olivia thought as they controlled their descent to the seabed, both of them taking it steady, keeping an eye on their dive computers, clearing their ears by gently blowing out through pinched nostrils, as they went.

It was ironic, she thought, that today had been the longest time she'd spent with Phil for ages. She was itching to talk to him, and now they still wouldn't get the chance because they'd be underwater for the next thirty-five minutes.

The instructor had been right about the visibility. She and Phil were face to face as they dropped down and she could see Phil's eyes clearly through this mask. He looked a little tense and she guessed he was still on edge because of whatever Tom had said to him. She wished they'd had a chance to speak about it before they'd left the boat. Being tense was not a good way to begin a dive. The episode had left her feeling uneasy and it had clearly unsettled Phil. Her mind flicked back to what the instructor had been saying earlier about the incident pit. It was so true. You needed to be totally on your game, not distracted, when you were about to slip down almost twenty metres in the sea.

Then, with a little thud, her dive boots touched the sandy seabed. She checked her computer – eighteen and a half metres.

Phil signalled to ask her if she was OK and she signalled back yes and returned the question to him. He patted the holster on his leg that was standard kit because it carried a dive knife which could come in useful if there was a problem and she saw that it was empty. He made gesturing motions to tell her it hadn't been in properly and must have come out when they'd hit the water.

She shielded her eyes with one hand and did peering motions around them and then opened her arms in a question – did he want to look for it? There was certainly no sign of it anywhere nearby, but they'd stirred up the sand quite a bit when they'd landed so that wasn't surprising.

He shook his head. His eyes were smiling. Olivia took this to be a no.

It was surprising, she mused, just how much conversation you could actually have underwater. Although, when she looked back on it later, she wondered whether the loss of his dive knife had been incident number two of the chain of mishaps that sent them hurtling into the incident pit.

* * *

There was no sign of the other divers. They must have already headed for the wreck. Technically, she and Phil weren't part of the group. So, the dive instructor wasn't responsible for them.

Olivia checked her compass and then headed south. Phil followed her. Both of them finning easily through the cool water. It was easier to see around once they got going and were out of the sandstorm they'd kicked up. The seabed was scattered with rocks and plant life, fat dark fronds of seaweed in clumps, and the occasional small fish swimming past. Very soon, they saw the dark shape of what must be the wreck looming up in front of them, and Olivia felt the tingle of excitement of imagining they were the first people to set foot on it since it had left the land of air. Apart from all the other dozens of divers that had been here lately, of course.

This particular shipwreck really deserved its title. It had

broken into several pieces, so it was hard to even see it had once been a cargo vessel. Chunks of rusting twisted metal were strewn about over quite a large area. In the distance, she could see one of the other diving pairs looking at something.

For a while, Olivia and Phil finned in and out of the various chunks of metal, taking care not to get caught on any of the sharp edges. Every so often, Olivia was aware of another diver's fin flicking in the distance, or they would drift over a piece of metal and she would see the trail of their air bubbles, so it didn't feel as though it were just the two of them, which was reassuring.

It looked as though one pair had ventured into the only closed-up section of the wreck that the instructor had mentioned, but she had no desire to follow them. And neither, it seemed, did Phil. It was nice to just mooch about and get her confidence back. Find her sea legs, if that was the right term when you were underwater.

About three quarters of the way through the dive, Phil gestured to her and she finned across to see what he was pointing at. As she reached him, she saw that he'd found a lobster. It was a big one, made even bigger by the magnifying effect water had on everything, tucked into a hole knocked out of the side of the vessel about a metre up from the seabed. One graceful blue claw was clearly visible, waving in the water.

Phil was now laying horizontally, his body tucked close to the wreck, to get a better view and Olivia manoeuvred herself into position beside him.

For a while, they stayed and just watched the graceful crustacean, anchoring themselves in the peace of the deep, which was silent but for the sounds of their breathing amplified in their ears. She was so glad they'd had the chance to see this. It was such a bonding moment.

Olivia glanced at her computer and it was almost time to go

up. She was about to tap Phil's shoulder and tell him, when suddenly he backed away from the lobster so fast, he bumped into her. At first, she wasn't sure what he'd seen or what had happened, but when she moved around him, she caught the edge of something grey and undulating on the edge of her vision. For a few moments, she wasn't sure what it was. A sea snake – were there such things?

A distant memory was stirring.

Not a snake. An eel. A conger eel possibly. She'd never seen one in real life, but Tom had once shown her a picture and followed it up with a dire warning. 'If you see one of these, keep well clear. They're vicious critters. Their teeth slant backwards. I once knew a guy who lost a finger. He got bitten and he couldn't get the damn thing off.'

No wonder Phil had been startled. The conger must have been in the same hole as the lobster. It was a big one too. Rather bizarrely Phil hadn't moved that far away though. He was still close to the side of the wreck and she realised in the next, gut-wrenching moment that he wasn't just gesturing to the conger but at his foot which now looked trapped. How was that even possible?

Olivia swam down for a closer look. His fin and foot had disappeared inside the wreck. She couldn't see what had happened. There was too much sand swirling about. He must have kicked out so hard when he'd glimpsed the conger that he'd dislodged something. He was aware of it too – his breathing was much faster than it had been a few moments earlier. Above her head, she could hear the frantic bubbles of his panic.

The first stirrings of fear trickled through her. She couldn't see a thing, but she did know that having a full-on panic attack underwater could be lethal. Making a split-second decision, she moved into his line of vision until they were face to face and held tight to his arm. How did you tell someone to calm down when you were underwater and the situation was actually quite bloody terrifying? Through his mask, she could see that he was fighting to control his fear. His pupils were huge.

Thanking God that she'd been trained in the chilly waters of this sea and not in some Caribbean tropical ocean like he had, Olivia took her regulator briefly out of her mouth and mouthed the words, 'It's OK. It will be OK. Stay calm.'

He seemed to understand. He gave her the OK signal with finger and thumb and his breathing slowed a fraction. That was a relief. He certainly wouldn't have air to waste. They were too close to the end of the dive. She moved away from him slightly so she could look around. It would be very handy if they could alert the other divers.

There was no one in sight. Shit.

Another glance at her computer told her that they were now bang on the time to make their ascent. And as they'd been last into the sea, the other divers were probably already on their way up.

They were alone. Whatever needed to be done, it was down to her.

She swam back down to where his fin was trapped inside the wreck. They had a quick-release clip. All fins had them for exactly this kind of eventuality. The only problem was the quick-release bit was inside. She unclipped her torch and had a closer look. The gap in the plates by the lobster hole had closed up. Something had definitely slipped. Phil was well and truly stuck.

After twenty or thirty seconds of trying to shift the heavy metal back a few inches, she knew it wasn't going to happen. God knows what they were made of, but they were too heavy to move. Phil had now regained sufficient control over his panic attack to try to help her, but even with two of them lifting, she knew it wasn't enough.

Olivia's computer began to beep – the audible alarm warning to tell her they were going into decompression time. They needed to go up. Fear hit her again, but this time it came in a wave, not a trickle. The most important thing was to keep calm. Once again, her training kicked in through the adrenaline.

Stay calm. Stay calm. Stay calm. She repeated the words in her head like a mantra. And suddenly there was an ice-cold part of her that knew what to do. If they couldn't get the fin off Phil's foot, she would just have to cut off the boot from his dry suit, then he could slip his foot out of both boot and fin. It was a risky strategy as he'd instantly fill up with water which would be freezing, not to mention weigh him down. The drysuit was part of their buoyancy. If she filled it up with water, they might have some trouble getting back up to the surface.

Olivia thought frantically. There must be another way. But she was going to have to work out what it was bloody quickly. They were running out of time fast.

27

Olivia's mind raced desperately as she looked down at Phil's trapped fin once more. It had gone in through the gap in the plates in the first place. Maybe there was a way she could manoeuvre it out again. She just needed to keep calm and let the sand that had been stirred up again by their efforts to move the plate settle so they could see.

She tapped his shoulder, indicated her torch and, with a series of gestures, got him to understand she was going to take a closer look.

He nodded, understanding immediately. Then he gestured to the gauge on his air supply. It was on red and the dial had just moved down to 10 bar left. Oh shit. Either he naturally used much more air than she did or he'd used it up while he'd panicked. It took no time at all to gulp through air underwater.

There was no time to mess about. Phil's computer was now beeping an alarm too, which did not help. She wondered if this was how the bomb-disposal guys felt when they were defusing a ticking bomb. The countdown to certain death if you made a mistake.

Don't overreact, she told herself, as she dived back down to Phil's trapped foot, taking care not to kick up the sand, and shone her torch back through the gap. This time, she could see the strap on the quick-release clip of the fin. It would be so much better if she could cut that. Quicker and easier than cutting through Phil's drysuit. But it meant reaching inside the wreck. How sensible was that when it was clearly so unstable?

Making a split-second decision and praying that the plates didn't shift again, she reached into the hole. At least the conger eel had made itself scarce. That was all she needed, a bloody sea snake lunging out with its snapping, sloping backwards teeth. She was terrified of snakes.

Oh crap. Focus. Focus. Thinking about malevolent sea monsters was definitely not going to help. It wasn't a snake anyway; it was a harmless eel.

That's not what Tom had said. Maybe he'd exaggerated.

Focus, Olivia, focus.

Gripping the knife firmly in fingers that were going increasingly numb with cold and fear, despite her neoprene gloves, she hesitated. She felt like a surgeon making the first cut. She could not get this wrong or she'd hurt him. And she'd need to be quick. The quicker she was, the less chance there was of them getting into any more trouble.

She steadied herself with one hand on the wreck and then gingerly stretched out with her other arm towards the fin. She could reach, but it was awkward. The rubber was thick and tough. It wasn't designed to be easily cut through and the job was three times as difficult when you were underwater and upside down and only had the use of one hand.

Olivia persevered, sawing at the rubber, and suddenly she felt it give. Still moving as slowly and as carefully as she could, she eased Phil's boot out of the fin and he must have felt the shift because he helped her until she could guide his foot out through the gap and then suddenly, they were both free. And they were vertical once more beside the wreck.

The adrenaline had sharpened her thoughts into icy clarity. She knew that Phil's impulse would be to shoot to the surface as quickly as possible, it was the survival instinct, but going up too quickly could kill a diver just as surely as being trapped with no air. Burst lungs, and the bends – caused by nitrogen trapped in the tissues – were just two ways you could die. Thanking God once again that she had done her training over several weeks and had the basics drummed into her so thoroughly, she looked at her air gauge. Still a quarter full.

Following her lead, Phil did the same thing. He shook his head slightly and pointed at the surface. Thankfully he seemed to realise he couldn't just go up.

If they'd ended this dive as they'd planned, they'd now be finning back to the anchor line that came down from the boat. That was the easiest and safest way to get back to the surface in a controlled fashion. But Olivia knew they didn't have enough time for that – or air.

They had never planned to do more than a one-minute safety stop on this dive. If they'd gone up at the right time, they wouldn't have needed to do more, but now it was critical that they stopped for a longer time to allow the nitrogen bubbles in their bodies that built up at depth to leave slowly and safely.

Free ascents were harder to control than having the steadying rope to hold on to. Olivia had only ever done one free ascent and that had been in training. But that's what they would have to do now.

They were about six metres off the seabed, very calm, very controlled, when Phil touched her shoulder again and then made the slashing motion across his neck. No air.

Sweet Jesus, that was all they needed.

Olivia grabbed his arm. Pointed to her own regulator, and then took it from her mouth and offered it to him. This was something else she had only ever done in the safety of either a swimming pool or very shallow waters. She had never dreamed she would have to do it for real.

Phil took it, breathed twice, handed it back. Textbook stuff. All divers were taught it. All divers hoped they'd never need to do it.

She did the same. It wasn't ideal, but it would work. The one saving grace was that she had plenty of air. And Phil was no longer panicking. Be grateful for small mercies.

Somehow in the elation of realising that they could actually do this though, Olivia had taken her eye off the ball. Something touched her feet and she realised with a sickening sense of shock that they were back on the seabed once more.

It was almost impossible to know, when you were neutrally buoyant in the water, how deep you actually were. Or even if you were going up or down. The only clue were the figures on the depth gauge of your computer. For a moment, they both stayed where they were, sharing her air, steadying themselves.

Then Phil signalled to her that they try again. Their positions were slowly reversing, Olivia realised. In the beginning, she'd been the one who was in control. The one who knew exactly what to do. Now Phil had conquered his fear and he was ice calm. She could feel it, even through the wall of water that was between them. She could see it in his beautiful eyes that were so very close to hers. There was a sense of calm purpose in them now, as if he were urging her on.

They ascended very slowly, back up to ten metres. Stopping every thirty or so seconds to share her air, holding on to each other tightly. Holding on as though their lives depended on never letting go. Which, of course, they did.

Nine metres, eight metres, seven metres, six. The surface was only just above them now. The last safety stop was at five metres and it was standard that this one should be for three minutes if you had gone into decompression time. Today, they'd unintentionally overstayed their diving time, so more would be better.

Phil held out his dive computer where she could see it and then held up five fingers. Five minutes then.

It was the longest five minutes Olivia could ever remember.

Breathe, breathe, swap. Breathe, breathe, swap.

And then, finally, the waiting was over and they moved, in unison, back towards the surface until it was shining brightly above them and they shot out once more into the world of air. For a second, they looked at each other over the slight swell. A mix of relief and elation.

Olivia had thought in her darker moments beneath the sea that the boat may have left them behind. Somehow forgotten them and headed back to shore. But, of course, it hadn't. She could see the dark bulk of it not far away. The welcome solidity of its hull in the water. The skipper would, of course, be waiting for them to come up on the anchor line as the others would have done. On board, the other divers were busy peeling off their wetsuits and chattering excitedly. Olivia realised that although it had felt like an eternity to her and Phil, they were probably only a few minutes overdue. Only Stephen was scanning the sea, looking for them.

'Divers up,' he shouted, and a few moments later, with the anchor safely heaved up from the depths, The Katherine began to move in their direction. 'Hey, you two,' Stephen called as the skipper manoeuvred the boat so the dive platform was in swimming range. 'You took your time. We were about to send out a search party.'

'No you weren't,' Olivia said, as they reached the safety of the ramp.

'No we weren't.' He grinned.

Both she and Phil knew enough about diving to know that it would have been dangerous for anyone to come back down and look for them. They had been totally on their own.

'You've lost a fin,' Stephen observed as he helped them up on deck. 'Did you have a problem?'

'Nothing we couldn't handle,' Olivia said.

Phil glanced at her with an expression in his eyes that she couldn't quite fathom. 'I managed to get my fin stuck inside a couple of plates. So, if you do happen to be down there again in the not-too-distant future, I'd appreciate it back.'

'I'll get you to fill out an incident form,' Stephen said, his voice sobering. 'For our records.'

'Sure,' Phil said, as he took off his empty air bottle and stab jacket.

Then they all gathered round, keen to hear more, and Phil told them the story of the conger and the lobster.

'Seriously though, guys,' he concluded, 'I was a total muppet. If I hadn't kicked out when I saw that conger, I'm pretty sure I wouldn't have dislodged those plates, and if I hadn't lost my knife in the first place, I'd have been better equipped to get myself out of trouble.'

And if Tom hadn't stirred up a viper's nest of emotion with whatever he said to you on the quay, Olivia thought, but didn't voice.

'Luckily Olivia was on the ball,' Phil was saying now. 'She saved my life.'

'Well done,' said the girl, her eyes on Olivia. 'It sounds like you did an amazing job sorting it. I'm not sure I'd have coped so well.'

'Hear, hear,' said Captain Birdseye. 'It's surprising how many divers don't have the wherewithal to get themselves out of trouble. They all learn to dive in the Caribbean and they think the English Channel's going to be as forgiving as a crystal-clear, warm, tropical ocean where you can see for ten metres, but it's not.'

This set off a big discussion about stories of divers who'd got into and out of trouble in the English Channel with varying degrees of success.

'I read this article in *Dive Magazine* about it once,' Stephen told them. 'The odds of getting out of trouble after a serious incident underwater are quite low. Ninety-four per cent of divers don't make it. Six per cent survive. Just *six* percent.' He whistled through his teeth. 'I've never forgotten that statistic.' He shuddered dramatically.

They moved on to stories of other divers they'd heard of who had and hadn't managed to crawl out of the incident pit.

Olivia was glad that the spotlight was off her and Phil. He'd seemed happy enough to share his story, but now he seemed quite subdued. She thought maybe for the same reason that she was, as they sped back over the glittering sea towards Weymouth Harbour. It was only when they'd got safely back on board The Katherine that the full shock of what had happened had really hit her. Things could have ended very differently today.

28

They were back at the quay by late lunchtime. They'd got changed out of their drysuits and back into jeans and trainers on the way back and now they unloaded the boat amongst the buzz of Sunday morning shoppers and tourists, and locals out getting the papers. Then Olivia and Phil said their goodbyes to the other divers who were going off to have a pizza.

'You're welcome to come along,' Stephen offered.

'I think we'll give it a miss thanks, mate,' Phil told him.

And then finally they were back at Phil's car and a few minutes later back in the car park at Olivia's house.

Neither of them had said a word. Phil turned off the ignition, but he made no move to come into the house. All of that peaceful closeness that Olivia had felt between them when they'd been trapped beneath the sea, sharing each other's air, had gone.

Was he embarrassed because of what had happened? She touched his arm. 'Phil, are you OK?'

'Yeah, I'm OK.' There was a deep sigh in his words. 'I made a right pig's ear of that, didn't I? I put both our lives at risk.' His dark eyes held hers. 'I'm sorry. I can't believe I was so stupid.'

'I don't think any of what happened was your fault.' She struggled for the words to reassure him. 'It was just unfortunate.'

'It wasn't unfortunate. It was careless. A series of careless incidents right from the beginning. I didn't make sure my knife was secured. Then when I did lose it, I didn't look for it. The batteries in my torch weren't working.' She hadn't known that bit. 'I shouldn't have freaked out when that conger put in an appearance. I should have been keeping a closer eye on my air – I always use a lot of air.'

'Stop it,' she said, hating hearing him beating himself up like this. 'We both made a decision not to look for your knife, I seem to remember. This isn't all on you.'

The heat of the sun felt hot on her face through the windscreen of the car. In the opposite corner of the car park, she could see a traffic warden putting tickets on windscreens.

'The fact is, Olivia, that if you hadn't been there, that would have been it. Game over.'

'But I was there. That's the whole point of the buddy system—'

He cut across her. 'I put your life at risk too.' There was something in his face that was hard, almost cold. She had never seen him like this.

A flashback of him standing on the quay talking to Tom flicked into her mind. She cleared her throat uncertainly.

'Phil, what did Tom say to you earlier?'

There was a little pause. 'Do you really want to know?'

'Yes, of course I do.'

'OK. He said that you still loved him. That the only reason you two weren't back together was because you felt obligated to me and couldn't bring yourself to end it between us. Oh, and he showed me a picture of the house he'd bought where you were both going to live and raise a family, as soon as you'd got round to dumping me.' A beat. 'He said that I was in your way. That I should let you go.'

Crap. No wonder Phil had been rattled when he'd got back onto the boat with all of that kicking about inside him. She looked at him in horror and for the first time since the diving incident, he met her eyes.

'Is any of that true?'

'Phil! No! Of course it's not true. He hasn't bought that house anyway. He's just renting it...'

The traffic warden was heading purposefully their way.

'So, he did show it to you then? The house.'

'Well, yes, he did.'

'And you were planning to tell me this when?'

'Phil, I have told you about him getting in touch. I—'

Before she could finish, the traffic warden, who had grey hair and a military straight back, reached the car and made a signal that Phil should lower the window, which he did.

'Are you planning to buy a ticket, sir?' He consulted his watch. 'Because this isn't a free car park.'

'I'm not stopping,' Phil said coldly and turned to her. 'Olivia, I need to go. I'll see you later.'

She stared at him in shock.

'You'll need to make that now please, sir.' The traffic warden was clearly one of those jobsworths who revelled in his work. 'I'm sure the young lady understands.'

Olivia got out of the car. 'Aren't you coming in? What about my dive kit?'

'We'll have to sort it later. I need to go.'

'Once I commit pen to paper, I won't be able to cancel the ticket.'

'ALL RIGHT.' This was aimed at the traffic warden.

Phil started the ignition. Olivia had no choice but to step away from the car and watch as he pulled away. He didn't even look back.

She stood for a few seconds, numb with shock. Then, not wanting to give the miserable little dictatorial traffic warden a second's more satisfaction, she headed for her front door.

Inside the privacy of her home, the shock of the last five minutes crashed in and Olivia felt like bursting into tears. What the hell had just happened? She and Phil had never even come close to a row before. So much for the amazing day they had planned together.

Scuba diving, followed by lunch at their favourite Italian, followed by delicious lovemaking and a chilled-out night at hers. She realised she was shaking. She couldn't quite believe he'd left so abruptly. Taking a few deep breaths, she told herself there was nothing she could do about it now. She needed to calm down first.

She got in the shower and washed off the smell of the sea and teased out the knots in her long hair. How had a day that had begun with such promise ended up like this? Should she phone him? No, he'd barely be home. And if he didn't answer the phone, it would be awful.

As soon as she was dry, she phoned Ruby instead and poured out the whole story to her, beginning with Tom turning up on the quay and dripping his poison into Phil's ear, then the change of plan from drift dive to wreck dive and ending with Phil's abrupt disappearance.

'Bloody hell, sis. That sounds pretty hairy.'

'It was. But we survived and I can't get my head around his reaction. He was so cold and dismissive.'

'Do you think he felt ashamed – about the getting stuck bit, I mean, and the fact that you basically had to rescue him. You know what men's egos are like. Maybe it was that?'

'That did cross my mind. Do you think I should phone him?'

'Maybe not straight away. Maybe let him cool down a bit.' She hesitated. 'It sounds like Tom is trying to do a hatchet job on your relationship. If you want to talk to someone, talk to Tom. That's a pretty nasty thing to do. The poor bloke's self-esteem is probably smashed to bits – Phil's, not Tom's. What was Tom even doing there anyway?'

'I don't know. Maybe going out on a boat. He likes boats. Although he did seem to be looking for something. He can't have been looking for us – he didn't know we were there.'

'Are you sure?' Ruby said slowly. 'Had you told anyone you were going diving today?'

'No.' Something was flickering in the back of Olivia's mind. 'Actually yes, I did. I put it on Facebook the other day when I was updating my business page. I was sharing a link to a cake that one of my colleagues had just won a prize for. It was in the shape of a diver swimming over a rock, it was gorgeous, and I mentioned when I shared the post that I was going diving on Sunday.'

'He might have seen that. Is he still on your Facebook page? Maybe you should unfriend him?'

'I have unfriended him. But my business page is public so anyone can look at it. Crap. He must have seen that. I even mentioned the name of the boat. The devious little so-and-so.'

'Yeah. And I bet it wasn't an accident that he and Caroline turned up at the Rose and Crown either. He's been stalking you.'

Olivia felt cold. Could that be true?

'I need to speak to him and put him straight,' she said. 'What he did this morning was completely out of order.'

'He's never been able to take no for an answer, though, has he?' Ruby's voice was indignant. 'Actually, Liv, and I know this is probably a totally un-PC thing to say, but it is quite something that you've got two guys fighting over you. I don't think anyone's ever cared about me enough to bother fighting over me.'

'They're not fighting,' Olivia pointed out. 'Tom isn't the fighting kind – he's just devious – and Phil is far too gallant. Although he did tell me that he's come close to having a punch-up with Mr B. He once chased him all round The Bluebell Cliff Hotel dining room with a steel frying pan.'

'I can imagine him doing that,' Ruby said with a thread of glee in her voice. 'Putting up with crap is probably in his job description, but I bet he's the type who you could only push so far and then one day he'd suddenly explode. An exploding doormat, Aunt Dawn used to call that. Do you remember?'

'Yes, I do.' Olivia sighed. 'Thanks for helping me get it in perspective. I'll speak to Phil in a bit. And I'll put an end to Tom's fantasies too. How are you and bump?' she asked.

'We're good.' Ruby's voice filled up with tenderness. 'I don't know how I could ever have thought of giving bump up.' She paused. 'Bump is a boy by the way. I found out on Friday.'

'Oh my God. Why didn't you tell me? I didn't even know you were going for your scan.'

'I didn't want a drama. Just in case anything was wrong. You're the first person I've told, as it happens.' Ruby sounded pleased with herself and slightly vulnerable. 'This is going to sound totally mad, but I feel as though this is mostly about me and bump – we're making this journey together – and everyone else is slightly outside of it in wider and wider concentric circles, like when you drop a pebble into a lake. Obviously, you're in a very close circle – the closest.' She paused. 'Does that make any sense?'

'Yes. Perfect sense. I think I'd be like that too. And you haven't had any more interaction with the...' Olivia chose her words carefully, '... sperm donor.'

'Nope. Although I did do some digging after what you told me about his wife. He's quite a wealthy guy. Or he was before his wife took him to the cleaners. According to my source – who's someone in the business – he's got a nice little nest egg stashed away in a secret art collection that she doesn't know about. He apparently has plans to sell it and buy himself another house. When his divorce has gone through, I'm going to instruct my solicitor to make a claim.'

'How on earth did you find out?' Olivia asked, catching her breath.

'Careless talk,' Ruby replied. 'It's still quite unusual for women to be dealers and some of the old-school guys treat me as if I'm invisible, so they let things slip that they wouldn't dream of saying in front of their male contemporaries.' She sighed. 'I've ended up with a few good deals because of that. I'm not a fan of sexism in the workplace obviously, but sometimes it works in our favour.'

'I'm really pleased. He should be contributing. Keep me posted and on you and Mr Bump.'

'I will.'

'I'd better go, Ruby. I need to make some phone calls.'

'Good luck, sis. Keep me posted too.'

Olivia then called Tom. Frustratingly, there was no answer. Now he'd got her attention, he'd clearly decided to ignore her. Fleetingly, she contemplated phoning Phil now too, but she wanted to speak to Tom first. So that she would have something to tell him. And she also agreed with Ruby – letting the dust settle was a good idea. She definitely had a point about men's egos. They both needed to be feeling calm.

Reluctant to waste the rest of the day, which was still gorgeously sunny and warm, she decided to visit Aunt Dawn.

She didn't phone in advance. Aunt Dawn would hopefully be

in and if she wasn't, she'd leave her a note. She walked over and went round to the back of the shop. On a sunny day like this, her aunt would most likely be outside pottering in her garden and keeping an eye on her chickens.

Olivia was about to open the back gate when she heard voices on the other side. Aunt Dawn's laughter and the deeper voice of a man. How curious. She hesitated, in two minds whether to go in. She didn't want to interrupt something private.

That was ridiculous though. It was probably just someone her aunt knew from the shop.

It would have felt odd knocking on a solid wooden back gate, so Olivia made a bit of a thing about rattling the latch as she opened it so that the people on the other side would be in no doubt they were about to be interrupted. Then she cleared her throat and went in.

She was greeted by the sight of Aunt Dawn and a man, who looked vaguely familiar, sitting at the wrought-iron table where she and her aunt so often had lunch or an evening snack. There was a half-drunk bottle of wine on the table and there was a hen having a dust bath in a nearby flower bed.

The couple both looked up and Aunt Dawn half rose. 'Hello, darling, I didn't know you were coming. Did I?' Two blotches of pink glowed on her cheeks. 'I haven't forgotten an arrangement, have I?'

'No, no, you haven't. I was just passing. Total impulse. I don't want to interrupt or anything.' She knew she was gabbling and she wondered whether she should suggest leaving again, but her aunt was smiling.

'Well, it's lovely to see you. I think you've met Mike Turner, haven't you?'

The man was standing up now too. 'We met in my practice when I treated Emmeline. It's good to see you again. Olivia?' His eyes warmed and she had the same impression she'd had the last time they'd met. He looked a bit like her old science teacher, grey-haired and rangy, with a slight air of eccentricity, but there was something very warm and laid-back about him too.

Mike pulled out another chair at the table for Olivia to sit on and there was a tiny silence as they all adjusted to it being three of them.

Then her aunt said, 'We were just enjoying the sunshine. Would you like a glass of wine, darling?'

Olivia was about to refuse – maybe it would, after all, be better to go, but Mike was nodding.

'Yes, please stay. Your aunt has told me so much about you.'

'Has she?' Olivia glanced at her.

She was nodding. 'Mike has been wonderful with my girls since the fox attack. He's gone well beyond the call of duty and all finally seems to be well, so we are tentatively celebrating.' She made a clicking sound with her mouth and addressed the hen that was having a dust bath. 'Isn't that right, Clementine?'

The chicken fluffed out her feathers, shifting slightly in a little flurry of dust before settling again with a contented clucking. She looked serene.

'I keep meaning to ask you who she was named after?' Mike said. 'I can't think of a famous Clementine.'

'Clementine Churchill. Winston's wife.' Aunt Dawn's eyes were bright with amusement. 'I mean, everyone knows it was Clementine who really ran the country, do they not?'

This started a discussion about famous men and their wives, and Olivia felt all of the tension and churning thoughts that had been in her head when she'd arrived, slowly dissipate beneath the sunshine and good humour. It was as though they had carved out a slice of peace and easiness, quite separate from the rest of the world. The secret garden had always affected her like that. But today it was more so than ever.

Neither Mike Turner nor her aunt were drinking very much – she guessed he was driving – but they seemed to be totally comfortable with each other. It was lovely. She couldn't remember the last time she'd seen her aunt so at ease. She found herself hoping that this was more than just a celebration drink.

29

In the end, Olivia didn't leave until just before 6 p.m. Mike was making going-home noises and she wanted to give him and her aunt some privacy, seeing as she'd basically gatecrashed their party. There had also been two missed calls on her phone from Tom and she wanted to call him and put him straight. She didn't want to be rude to him, but neither did she want to leave him in the slightest doubt that he was deluding himself about them getting back together. It was never going to happen. They were history. She needed to spell it out in a way that Tom would understand, which meant she needed to be blunt and firm, and probably repeat herself a few times.

Then she needed to speak to Phil and she had a feeling that this was going to be the trickier of the two conversations. She thought that Ruby had probably been right about his ego. Phil wasn't arrogant, but he was proud. And if he'd believed, even for a fleeting moment, that there was any truth in what Tom had said...? Blimey, no wonder he'd been so quiet on the boat. It put a very different perspective on everything that happened afterwards too. Anyone would have found it hard to concentrate after having that kind of poison dripped into their ear. Then when he'd asked her about it in the car – asked her if it was true that she'd seen the house and she said she had – Phil had probably assumed she'd meant physically 'seen' it. She hadn't told him it had just been a random text she hadn't even answered.

Even the most confident of guys – and Phil was pretty self-confident – would have been rattled by Tom's announcement that Olivia was planning to leave him. After everything that had gone on between them lately, at the very least, Tom would have planted the seeds of doubt. No wonder he was pissed off. She knew that if their positions had been reversed and Phil was being pursued by an ex-girlfriend hell-bent on getting him back, she'd have been pretty pissed off too.

She needed to speak to Phil sooner rather than later, and apologise. She was thinking about all of this when she put her key in the door of number five. It had barely closed behind her when the doorbell rang.

Her heart jumped and she opened it immediately, sure it would be Phil saying he'd regretted the way they'd parted too. It threw her completely to see Tom. He was wearing his hitman's coat and he smelled of expensive aftershave.

'Sorry I missed your call.' He was smiling. Confident. Sure of himself. One foot already over the threshold.

'Er yes. Tom. All I wanted was—'

He interrupted. 'Let's not talk out here. It's too public.' As he spoke, a couple brushed past on the walkway immediately behind him, both chatting animatedly on their phones.

Olivia let him in. It would be easier that way. She wasn't so insensitive that she would tell him on the doorstep to leave her alone. She could at least do this with integrity. But she would be firm. Before he had a chance to misconstrue anything else. Or cause any more trouble.

He followed her into the kitchen where she immediately took him to task.

'Phil told me what you said to him this morning. You were totally out of order.'

'I know. I'm sorry. I was just surprised to see you both there. It was a shock.' He went on smoothly. 'I reacted badly. Hands up. But I love you, Olivia. You know that and…' He pulled out a chair from the kitchen table and sat on it.

'Tom. I don't feel the same about you any more. I don't want to be with you.'

'Are you sure?'

'Yes, I'd like to know the answer to that question too. After all, you did let him in.' Olivia realised with a slow-growing shock that Phil was in the kitchen doorway; the front door clearly hadn't closed properly behind Tom. He must have been in the car park, maybe he'd been waiting for her. Maybe they both had. What spectacularly bad timing.

'Phil!'

Tom spun round in his chair. 'Ah, the rebound boyfriend. Always so tricky. But face facts, mate. It's me she wants. We'd still be together if—'

This time, it was Olivia who cut across him. 'Tom, that's not true. You're wrong. We would not be together. You're utterly deluded. And I want you to get out of my house.' She could feel her voice shaking with rage.

For the first time, her ex looked unsure of himself.

'Livvie…' Using her old pet name, he held out a hand. 'You know we're—'

'Get OUT, I said.' She didn't know where the rage was coming from, but it was there, boiling up in her. Pulsing in her head as though someone had unscrewed the tap on a lifetime of bottled-up anger and let it all out at the same time. It felt powerful. As though she could propel him out of her house by the sheer force of her anger.

Tom knew it too. He was on his feet now and he opened his mouth to speak, then shut it again and backed away from her, hands held out in front of him. 'All right. I'm going.'

He was out of the door and heading away before she could say anything else. And then she realised that Phil was gone too.

Olivia stood on the walkway, scanning the car park. She couldn't see his car. How had he gone so quickly? He'd been there one second and then gone the next. It was impossible.

She wiped her eyes, realising they were blurry with tears. Did rage make you cry? All of the emotions of today seemed to have got mixed up in some great cauldron, stirred with a stick of dynamite. She wouldn't have been surprised to hear herself hysterically screaming. And she was not the hysterical kind.

She strode across the walkway into the car park. Phil's car was there, after all. It was in the far corner, obscured by a black van, but she could see it now. She hurried across. She had to put this right. But as she got closer, she could see he wasn't in it.

Where else would he have gone? Wheeling round again, she saw him, coming back up the walkway, his hands in his pockets, in short, controlled steps.

Not caring any more about appearances, she raced across to him. 'Phil. Would you please give me a chance to tell you my side of the story.' The please came out as a command, not a plea.

He halted, standing in front of her, and she put her hands lightly on his forearms and looked into his eyes, which were black and unreadable.

She took a deep breath. 'I owe you an apology. I should have told you Tom had been in touch again and I didn't. But that was not because I was contemplating going back to him. He sent me a text about the house. I didn't even answer it, Phil. It was over between us a long time ago.' She paused and said the next words more slowly. 'It's been you, Phil. From the moment we met, it's only ever been you. I know we said in the beginning that we'd keep things light. Have some fun. But as I said when we were up on Ballard Down, my feelings have got deeper. I was too scared to tell you how I felt. Then today I was terrified I might lose you before I ever got the chance to tell you I love you. And today's made me realise that life's too short for messing about. So, I'm telling you now. I *love* you. Even if you don't love me. That is the score.'

She paused, searching his eyes for a reaction because he still hadn't spoken.

'Say something,' she demanded. 'Even if it's a no thanks, I'm off. See you around.'

'I will,' he said. 'If I can get a word in edgeways.'

She raised her eyebrows. Wow, it was amazing, all this anger. It was like having a superpower.

'I owe you an apology too,' he began. 'I've behaved like a sulky child today. You saved my life this morning and all I could do was stress about being a muppet. And messing things up. And yes, your ex didn't help turning up and having a pop, but I let my ego get in the way, Olivia, and for that I'm sorry.'

She opened her mouth to speak.

'Hang on,' he said. 'Let me get this out. You don't have the monopoly on being scared. I was pretty damn scared this morning getting my foot stuck in that pile of rusting metal.' She felt him shudder. 'But I'm more scared of losing you. When you said you wanted kids – which I knew, Olivia. I've always known that – I tried to back off a bit. Because I thought when you found out I'd have trouble on that front, it would be the end of us. That's why I've been so off lately. Your ex just added fuel to the fire. But the truth is I love you too. I've loved you since the first time I heard you say, "Good Hamlet, cast thy nighted colour off and let thine eye look like a friend on Denmark."'

She burst out laughing.

'What?' he said, his eyes widening in consternation. 'It's true. You were an amazing Gertrude.'

'It's not that – it's the irony. For our entire relationship, we've been too scared to talk about our feelings and now we've just had a full-on, no-holds-barred conversation about them in the middle of a public car park.' She gestured around them. 'At the top of our voices.'

There were loads of people about. Not that anyone appeared to be listening. Across the way, a couple had just got out of their car and were heading for the Indian takeaway and a girl with a dog strolled past. Closer by, an old man had just pressed the central locking on his car. Now he was humming tunelessly. No one was taking any notice of them.

'Maybe we do have a chance then,' Phil said with a spark of amusement in his eyes. He looked around them too. 'At least that bloody traffic warden isn't about.'

'Nope. I think even he has Sunday evenings off.' She was wearing flat shoes which made her about three inches shorter than him. She stood on her tiptoes. 'Shall we go the whole hog? Do you fancy a public snog as well?'

He kissed her and she felt her insides melt. It never changed – that honeymoon feeling. In fact, if anything, it grew newer, not older. How was that possible?

After a few more moments, she broke the kiss. 'Public car parks are all very well, but maybe we should go inside now. If you're planning to stop, are you?'

'I'm planning to stop for as long as you'll have me.'

Above their heads, the sky was beginning to streak with pink as the sun sank lower. It was almost eight thirty, Olivia realised, and she hadn't eaten properly all day. Her stomach rumbled. Tantalising smells wafted from the Indian takeaway. A guy had just emerged, swinging a white plastic carrier bag.

Phil glanced at him. 'Have you eaten, honey, because I'm flaming starving? Shall I get us some curry? Then we can continue this conversation over dinner.'

'That sounds like the best idea you've had all day.'

* * *

A little while later in Olivia's kitchen, now fragrant with prawn madras, pilau rice and peshwari nan, they talked some more. Now they'd started, it seemed that neither of them could stop.

At the moment, Phil was talking about his parents. 'Dad was a computer genius and Mum was a dinner lady. They'd probably never have met in the usual scheme of things – they were way outside of each other's social circles. But Mum was on holiday in Swanage and she and her friends were in a karaoke bar one night and Dad's mates had persuaded him to go along too. He used to joke that it was the first and only time he ever went clubbing – he hated clubs – but when he walked in, Mum was up on stage singing "Take A Chance On Me" and he was smitten. Mum's always had a good singing voice.'

'So, he plucked up the courage to ask her out?' Olivia asked, loving the romance of it all.

'Did he hell! No. Despite the fact that she was obviously interested in him – she was never slow in coming forward – he didn't do a single thing. In the end, she just marched across, grabbed his arm and said, "Mine's a gin and tonic if you're buying?" And that was that!'

'Wow, your mum wasn't shy then.'

'No, she was quite loud in those days apparently. Dad was the opposite. A total introvert and a bit antisocial, and Mum was a full-on, gregarious, social butterfly. I'm not sure who I take after. I guess I have elements of both. I'm massively shy and like spending time alone, like my father did. But I also have thespian tendencies – one of my aunts is in am-dram too. She's really good. Aunt Betty.'

'I'd like to meet your Aunt Betty. I'd like to meet your mum too.'

He touched her cheek. 'I'd love to introduce you to them. They'd love you. The only reason I've never suggested it is because I...' He paused. 'Well, it's because I thought that one day, we'd have the "do you want children?" conversation and then you might decide you don't want to be with me, after all.' He sighed. 'I do get it, Olivia. I totally get it if you want to break it off. You wouldn't be the first. I think that's why your ex got to me so much this morning. It was the kids thing. I thought maybe he had managed to tempt you back because he'd told you he'd changed his mind about kids. And I would never be able to compete with that.'

She looked at him and even though he was trying to disguise his pain, she could see it, glinting just below the surface. And she knew suddenly, with a total certainty, that this was how he coped. He gave off this moody, slightly brooding, untouchable persona, but when he was on stage, he threw all that emotion into his characters. Because that was the only way he could risk letting it out. No wonder he was such a good actor.

'I don't want to break it off. When I said I love you, I meant it. I meant it totally. I want us to be together – whether we can have kids or not.' She realised with a small shock that she really meant this. She put her hand to her heart. 'At the risk of sounding totally OTT and repeating myself, I'm going to say it again. You're stuck with me. I love you, Phil Grimshaw.' She paused. 'How come your dad had a northern name anyway? Grimshaw is a northern name, isn't it?'

'It's a Lancashire name yes. My ancestors originated from Blackburn. But my great-granddad moved south to get work. So, both my grandfather and father were born in Dorset. I think that was one of the things Dad liked about Mum and she about him – when they dug around a little, they found they had the same roots, amazingly. Mum's always been proud to have been born in Blackburn.'

'Family lines,' Olivia said softly. 'They're important.'

He blinked a couple of times.

'It doesn't have to be about blood,' she said quietly. 'We can adopt children – if you'd like to, I mean? I'd be happy to do that. If you would?'

He leaned across the empty tinfoil containers and took hold of both of her hands. 'It's not impossible for me to have children, Olivia. Just unlikely. I have looked into it. They put my chances of producing a baby at somewhere between six and ten per cent. That's not an absolute no-no. It does give us something to work with.'

Something was flickering in the back of her mind. A connection. And then it came back to her. 'Do you remember what Stephen said to us on the boat? About the percentage of divers who can get themselves out of trouble underwater. That was six per cent too.' She met his dark eyes, seeing understanding dawning as he nodded slowly. 'We've already beaten those exact same odds once, haven't we, Phil? I don't see why we shouldn't do it again.'

30

Phil stayed over at number five for the night. Even though they both knew they had to get up at the crack of dawn – Olivia to make cakes and he to head off to his house and then on to the Bluebell Cliff for work. They did it often enough that they both had the routine off pat. But there were still things that went backwards and forwards with them. Things that couldn't get left at each other's houses. Things like phone chargers and house keys, things they didn't want to forget. A gathering up and a separating until the next time they came together again.

It was odd, but since their chat tonight when they had smashed through so many barriers, everything had felt different. Even their lovemaking – or maybe especially their lovemaking, Olivia thought as they undressed in the warm shadowy darkness of her bedroom.

She felt closer to him than she had ever felt before. Closer than she had ever felt to any living being. His eyes, usually so dark and unreadable, were totally unguarded. Phil had always safeguarded his heart and now she knew why. She had done the same thing. Letting him in about ninety per cent, but fiercely guarding the last ten per cent of her self. For a very long time, they had both danced around each other, not quite daring to risk total vulnerability. But tonight, that changed.

Things had always been great between them in the bedroom department, but tonight it transcended 'pretty damn hot' and went into 'stratospheric' and she knew that this was because love had come into the mix. The kind of totally unconditional love that only happened when both parties are fully committed – no matter what happens – no matter what the future brings.

Even the afterglow felt different. As they lay face to face in her bed, each lying on their sides, propped on their elbows, Olivia felt as though they were seeing each other for the first time. Seeing into the very heart of each other – without being restrained, without being afraid. Without pretence. It was the weirdest sensation.

'What are you thinking?' she asked him.

'That I've never been so happy,' he replied with a smile.

'Even though we're only going to get about six hours sleep?' she teased.

'Sleep is overrated.' He stroked her cheek with the side of his index finger. 'I'd stay up all night just to watch you breathe. Isn't there a song with words like that?'

'I think there is. And I feel like that too. It's a pity we have to work tomorrow.'

'It's a pity we don't live in the same house,' he said. 'Maybe we should think about that. Maybe...' He hesitated. 'Maybe we should think about getting married.'

'Is that a proposal, Phil Grimshaw? Because if it is, it's not very romantic!' She sat up in bed, laughing.

'It's not, is it?' He sat up too. Then he flung off the duvet, swung his legs out of bed and jumped out. He was stark naked. He knelt on the bedroom carpet in front of her and he twisted off the gold sovereign ring he always wore on his middle finger. 'This was my dad's – I've worn it since the day he died. Mum insisted I have it and it's my most precious possession.'

She watched him, kneeling before her, holding out the ring in the palm of his hand and despite the craziness of it all, it still felt absolutely perfect.

'Will you wear it in lieu of a proper engagement ring, Olivia? Will you wear it until I get you the real thing? Will you do me the very great honour of becoming my wife?' His voice was steady, but there was the faintest of trembles in his hands and the ring wobbled on his palm.

'Oh yes,' she said, offering her finger for Phil to slide the ring on, feeling the emotion rise up in her throat and almost close it. 'Nothing would make me happier.' She gave him an elated kiss and drew back. 'And... Phil?'

'Yes.' He leaned forward, still kneeling, put his elbows on the side of the bed and rested his chin on his hands so they were face to face.

'One day, I will be telling our children about this moment.'

His eyes misted with tears. And she could feel them in her own eyes too. It was so mad – this moment, she and her man, talking about the future, talking about the children, which, however things panned out, were going to be at the end of a long and difficult road. One that they could only travel down because of love. Because right now that was all she could feel. Love was all around them in the room. Wrapping them together, giving them hope.

* * *

One of her first calls on Monday morning was from Aunt Dawn.

'Good morning, darling. Sorry to phone so early, but I wanted to talk to you about something. Have you got a moment?'

'I've always got a moment for you,' Olivia said. 'Did you by any chance want to talk about a certain vet that we both know who – er – goes by the name of Mike?'

Her aunt laughed. 'Not much gets past you.'

'I'm sorry I gatecrashed your evening.'

'You didn't. It was the perfect time for you two to meet and I'm really glad you did.' She cleared her throat. 'So, did you – er, like him?'

'He was OK. Did you have another chicken emergency – what with him being there on a Sunday afternoon and all?'

'Er, not exactly...'

'So, he was just checking in to make sure Emmeline, Clementine and Greta were fully recovered then. How lovely of him.'

'Um yes, but...'

Olivia couldn't carry on teasing. 'I thought he was absolutely lovely,' she said and she heard the sigh of relief in Aunt Dawn's voice.

'I'm so pleased. I think he's absolutely lovely too.'

'So how long has that been going on, you sly old thing? Does my mother know?'

'Oi. Less of the old – and no she doesn't. No one knows – except you. And nothing is really going on. We've just been talking and slowly getting to know each other. Mike's widowed too. We were both widowed at the same age. He's not been serious with anyone since his wife died either. Like me, he never wanted to meet anyone for a long time and then when he did feel ready, he didn't feel strongly enough to actively pursue it. I mean, he didn't go looking to join a dating agency or anything. Between you and me, I think he had a couple of offers through friends of friends, but he wasn't interested. He was happy alone.'

'Well, I for one, am thrilled to bits for you,' Olivia said. 'I really am. It's about time you had some fun.'

'I have lots of fun, darling.'

'You know what I mean.'

'Anyway, you sound happy. I thought you looked a bit stressed yesterday when you first came round – were you? Had you come to speak to me about something?'

'Nothing gets past you either. And yes, actually. I'd had a bit of a stressful morning.' Olivia gave her a very brief summary of what had happened on the dive and her aunt gasped.

'Oh, my darling, why didn't you say something? That sounds terribly traumatic. Are you OK? Is Phil OK?'

'We're both fine. We're both more than fine. Although there is a bit more I haven't told you.' She explained how Tom had turned up, both before the dive and after it, and how she and Ruby had worked out that he'd actually been stalking her. And how angry she'd felt to be manipulated. 'He was so cocky,' she said. 'He's always been like that, hasn't he? I just never saw it. I took it as confidence. I didn't see it for the arrogance and selfishness it actually was.'

'We live and learn. I think I've got that on a fridge magnet too, somewhere.'

Olivia laughed. She felt high on adrenaline. She and Phil had had even less than six hours sleep in the end, but she felt as though they had moved forward a massive step; as though their relationship had just graduated overnight from kindergarten to high school. 'At least it made me realise exactly what I wanted. And it wasn't Tom.' She took a deep breath. 'Phil asked me to marry him last night. And I said yes. And you're the first person I've told too.'

'Oh my darling, that's fantastic. I couldn't be any more delighted. That is the best news. It really is.'

'Don't tell anyone. We haven't even got a ring yet. We're going to go and choose one the next time we've both actually got a half-hour free.'

'Well, I think you should make it a priority. Neither of you have much time off, do you? You should have a proper holiday. Let me know if I can help out. I can make cakes.'

'You've got a shop to run,' Olivia reminded her. 'And talking of cakes, I've got one to make now. So I'd better get off the phone.'

Olivia disconnected, still smiling.

* * *

It was Wednesday before they got the chance to go and buy a ring. Olivia chose a sapphire and diamond one in a pretty wavy gold setting that reminded her of the sea and she handed back Phil's precious sovereign. After they'd bought the ring, he slipped the box into his pocket and said, 'You can't have it yet. We're doing this thing properly.'

'What does "properly" look like?'

'I'll book Harper's for a Saturday night.'

Harper's was Weymouth's answer to Gordon Ramsay's Union Street Café in London.

'You'll never get in,' Olivia said. 'Last time Ruby went there she had to book it three months in advance just to get a Thursday night and she's got a "privileged customer" card.'

'Yes, but I have friends in high places.' Phil tapped his nose. 'Watch this space!'

* * *

He clearly wasn't joking. Two days later, he sent her a booking confirmation text that said they had a table reservation for the last Saturday in June, which was just three weeks later.

Olivia phoned him immediately.

'How?' she gasped.

'Mr B trained with their chef. They're quite good friends, handily. Maybe the man does have his uses after all.' He snorted.

The booking threw Olivia into a spin of both excitement and panic and she phoned Ruby, who whooped with excitement when she told her about the engagement and sighed in exasperation when Olivia mentioned her concerns.

'I have absolutely nothing to wear to a place like Harper's,' she yelped.

'It's just a restaurant.' Ruby sounded completely unfazed. 'Wear what you'd normally wear to a restaurant.'

'I'd normally wear skinny jeans and a top that didn't matter too much if I spilled something down it. You know what I'm like when I get nervous. But then I'd normally be going to a pub or an Italian.'

'Well, if you haven't got time to go shopping, then you're welcome to raid my wardrobe.'

'Thanks. I might take you up on that. I'm seeing a client not a million miles from you this afternoon. Can I come after?'

'Of course you can. I'll be here.'

* * *

When Olivia arrived, Ruby answered the door to her wearing a daisy-print blue smock, which hid most of her bump, over leggings. Her fair hair was clipped up and her cheeks were rosy. She looked like an advertisement for a happy mum-to-be. To Olivia's surprise, she was also brandishing a paintbrush. But not the decorating kind.

'I've been dabbling with art again,' she told Olivia a little shyly. 'I'm up in the studio. Do you want to see?'

'I'd love to.' Olivia followed her sister up the second flight of stairs.

The loft which covered the entire top floor was a fabulous place to work. The three big Velux windows in the roof flooded the room with sunlight. There was an easel beneath one of them. On it was a piece of paper that was daubed with a wash of colour, lemon graduating into palest blue. On the long tables that lined the walls, several other paintings were spread out in various stages of drying. There were two palettes of paint, various-sized brushes on newspaper, and jars of murky liquid; the air smelled of turps and paint.

'I'm working on sunrises,' Ruby said. 'It's really hard to get the exact colour of the light at dawn. I'm trying different washes. But I'm having such fun, Liv. It's ages since I painted – just for the joy of it. Without having to think that anyone would ever see them. Apart from the people I love, I mean.'

Olivia hesitated over one of the paintings that looked more finished than the rest. It showed a couple – two stick figures walking with a little gap between them along a shingle beach by the sea.

'That's us,' Ruby said. 'Walking at Pebble Beach – talking about the future of this little one.' She smoothed the daisy-patterned smock over her bump. 'Do you remember?'

'Of course I remember.' Olivia glanced back at the image. The shingle was suggested with faint brushstrokes and there were white horses out in the bay, and when she looked carefully, she could see a couple of fishermen close to the water's edge.

'That's just a practise one. I'm going to paint a picture of you and me there at sunrise. I know we weren't actually there at sunrise, but that's poetic licence. I feel as though it was the start of a new dawn. A new beginning. Well, it was, of course. A massive new beginning. I shall call it "Sunrise Over Pebble Bay".' Her eyes sparkled and her voice was alight with passion. Olivia didn't think she had ever seen her so happy.

'I am so thrilled for you,' she said, moving across to her sister.

'I'm thrilled for you too. You and Phil – that's such great news. He's one of the good guys, isn't he?'

'Yes, he really is.'

'And I'm so glad you ditched the other one. What was his name again?'

Olivia almost said Tom before she stopped herself. Ruby was grinning widely. She moved in for a hug and Ruby held her arms out in front of her. She was still holding a paintbrush.

'Mind you don't get paint on yourself. I wear this smock because nothing shows on it.'

'Sounds like the same reason I pick clothes to wear out to dinner.'

'Which is, of course, why you're here. Let's get on the case then, shall we? Let's find you a "wow" outfit, worthy of being proposed to in.'

A few minutes later, they were standing next to Ruby's double wardrobe. She slid the door back and started riffling through hangers and pulling them out.

'It feels weird knowing that's what's going to happen before we even go out,' Olivia said.

'Weird, but also handy,' Ruby replied. 'I'm guessing you don't know the details of exactly what Phil's going to do, but at least you'll know not to swallow anything without chewing it carefully. I've heard stories where people have almost choked on their engagement rings because they'd been put in the chocolate mousse and served up for dessert.'

'Me too,' Olivia said.

'I bet he goes down on one knee, though,' Ruby continued. 'That's kind of obligatory, isn't it?'

'I hope so and at least I won't think he's dropped a contact lens – I heard a story where the lady in question thought that was what was happening and she leapt down onto the floor to help her boyfriend look for it and ended up putting her back out.'

'Ouch! Does Phil wear contact lenses then?'

'No, he doesn't.'

They smiled at each other. 'I take it you're going to wear a dress?'

'I guess I should.' Olivia's stomach clenched. 'But something that I'll feel comfortable in.'

'Not too tight then.'

'I didn't mean that really. But maybe nothing too low cut. You can get away with it with your cleavage, but I just look silly.'

'No, you don't, but OK. Nothing low cut.' She pulled out several dresses in quick succession and laid them out on the bed on their hangers. 'There we go. One of these might work. Try them on.'

Half an hour later, Olivia had narrowed it down to two. A slinky black and white number with flecks of maroon which was long and figure hugging and a shorter multicoloured one with a gorgeous scooped, but not too revealing, neckline.

'I could spill all sorts down that and it wouldn't show,' Olivia quipped about the latter.

'You'd better not, that's a Vivienne Westwood.'

Olivia gasped. 'I can't borrow that. I'd need to get it insured.'

'Don't be daft. You're not going to spill anything. Have some confidence in yourself. You're about to be the new star of *Nightingales* and you're going to Harper's to get proposed to by a gorgeous hunk of a man. You're on a roll, girl.'

31

Olivia didn't have time to worry too much about the dinner at Harper's. It was wedding-cake season. If she wasn't making cakes, she was icing them. Her schedule was rammed and so was Phil's. The author whose children's books he narrated had two more coming out in audio – the series was a huge hit – and he had become the voice the readers loved. 'I know it's only bread-and-butter work,' he said to Olivia, 'But actually it's quite cool knowing I'm the voice behind such a hit series.'

They were staying at each other's houses more than they'd ever done before. Otherwise, they'd hardly have seen each other. Or, to be more accurate, he was staying at her house because there was no real reason – other than having a longer journey to work at The Bluebell Cliff – that he couldn't be there.

'How are you going to manage Amazing Cakes when you're filming for *Nightingales*?' Phil asked her one lunchtime, when they were snatching a sandwich together.

'I've cleared my diary pretty much for October,' she told him. 'I've only had to turn down one or two bookings so far. But I know there'll be more.'

'I'm guessing that's not good for business. Is there any mileage in getting anyone in to help you?'

'Do you mean employing someone?'

'I suppose I do. Even if it was just part-time. It's very full on having your own business, isn't it? It's not like my job when I just swap shifts if I get a gig.'

'I don't really want to work with anyone else.' Olivia felt herself bristle at the thought of it. 'I like being self-sufficient.'

'How about your aunt?'

'She has the shop.' She stared at him in surprise. 'She won't want to work with me.'

'Are you sure? She's a really talented cake maker. I've seen that with my own eyes and it's quite hard work being on your feet in a shop all day. I don't want to be rude, but she must be coming up to retirement age.'

'She's sixty-two.'

'There you go. She might quite fancy the idea of making the odd cake and spending more time with her new man.'

'It's a little more complicated than making the odd cake,' Olivia said, her voice dripping with sarcasm, and he grinned in acknowledgement. But nevertheless, the seed was planted. And he was right about one thing – Aunt Dawn was a really talented cake maker.

* * *

The next time Olivia saw Aunt Dawn, having been summoned to the flat to collect two dozen eggs that her aunt said she needed to get off her hands, she asked her if she had any plans to take early retirement.

'Now you have a new man in your life, I mean,' she added idly as she packed the egg boxes into a carrier on the kitchen table.

'Not to mention a new great-niece or -nephew on the horizon.' Ruby still hadn't told anyone else the gender of her baby.

'What makes you think I'm going to get a look-in with your sister and your mother on the case,' Aunt Dawn said, laughing. 'Honestly, if your mother got any more excited, I think she'd explode.'

Olivia knew what she meant. Her parents, especially her mother, had been thrilled to bits when she'd told them on the phone about her engagement.

'I'll be back soon to help you with the planning,' Mum had said. 'Two new roles. Babysitter and wedding planner. How very exciting.'

Olivia had agreed, whilst crossing her fingers behind her back. With a bit of luck, Mum would be very busy on the babysitting front. She and Phil didn't want a lot of fuss. They'd already decided they wouldn't set a date until at least a year down the line. There were too many other things going on and they wanted to enjoy the build-up to their wedding, not fit it in around work and get stressed about it.

They weren't going to delay trying for a baby though. Olivia had already stopped taking the pill. 'Who knows?' Phil had said when he'd suggested it. 'Just because the medics say the chances aren't high, it doesn't mean it won't happen.'

Olivia had decided not to think about it. But it was a lovely feeling knowing that at some point in the future they would become parents, in whatever form that took, and that they both wanted it with all of their hearts.

'It's funny you should mention retirement, darling,' Aunt Dawn went on, bringing Olivia back to the conversation in hand. 'It's quite apposite timing, because Lydia and I were chatting about it the other day.'

'Really?' Olivia pricked up her ears.

'Yes. Lydia's interested in buying the business. She's asked me before if she could have a stake, but this time she's talking about buying me out altogether – she has a daughter who's in the rag trade too. Claire specialises in vintage clothes, but she does it online. She and Lydia could work very well alongside each other.'

'Wow. So do you mean you would sell up completely?' Olivia felt a start of shock at the thought, despite the fact she'd started this conversation. 'What about your lovely flat? And the secret garden? Would you have to give that up too?'

'It would make more sense to sell the flat and the shop together,' her aunt said. 'I know I've always been reticent to leave the place, lock, stock and barrel, but maybe the time is right. I can't keep it for ever.'

'But we have so many brilliant memories.' The words slipped out before she could stop them. Olivia knew she sounded selfish and petulant, but she couldn't seem to help it.

'We'll still have our brilliant memories.' Aunt Dawn's gentle brown eyes met hers across the kitchen. 'And places are only places at the end of the day. People are far more important.' She patted her niece's arm. 'I'm assuming you and Phil will want to find a new place to live when you're married. Or are you going to keep one of the houses you already have?'

'Phil rents his house,' Olivia said, blinking. She didn't want to confess that she'd barely thought about where they would live. 'We haven't talked about it yet, but I guess I'd made the assumption he'd just move in with me. Although it would be a long way for him to go to work.' She swallowed. 'I'm acting like a child aren't I. I want everything to be different, but I also want everything to be the same. I don't like change.'

'I don't think you're in the minority there, my darling. I don't know a single human being who's a fan of change. At least not the kind that involves giving up nice comfortable situations. Also known as ruts,' she added and raised her eyebrows. She tucked a strand of frizzy hair behind her ear. 'The only thing you can guarantee about life is that it will change,' she stated.

'Another fridge magnet?' Olivia asked.

'Definitely.' Her aunt glanced towards her fridge. 'I think I live my life via fridge magnets. Anyway, my darling, why were you asking me about my retirement plans? Was that just an idle enquiry?'

'No.' Olivia told her about Phil's suggestion and she knew immediately that her aunt's interest was piqued.

'It's not something I'd ever seriously thought I'd go into professionally,' she said slowly. 'But as I've said before I'm very happy to help out and if I didn't have the shop, well... there's no reason I couldn't help out more.' She paused. 'What if this role in *Nightingales* launches your acting career and you never have time to make another cake? What will you do then?'

'I guess we could cross that bridge when we come to it.' Olivia picked up the carrier bag of eggs again. 'Food for thought though.'

'Indeed.'

* * *

Eric and Brenda's wedding fell a fortnight before Olivia and Phil were going to Harper's and Phil had managed to wangle another Saturday night off to go to the evening do with her.

'I'm so glad you're coming,' she had told him as they got ready to go, at her's. 'Eric's one of my favourite clients and his fiancée, Brenda, is a right character too. She used to be in the business. As a make-up artist, not as an actress, but I bet she's got some fascinating stories. Not that she'll probably have time to talk about that on her wedding day.'

She had delivered the cake the previous morning. She had refused to let them pay for it at all in the end, which had caused an argument.

'It's my wedding present to you both,' she'd insisted as she had put the boxed cake carefully on Eric's worktop.

It wasn't a big cake, just the two tiers, and it had portrayed a couple sitting in a white Ferrari made from sugar paste. Brenda was wearing a cream hat and waving like the Queen.

'That's the closest we're ever going to get to owning a Ferrari,' Brenda had said, wiping her eyes as she'd leaned forward for a proper look.

'I could get in one, but I'd have a heck of a job getting out of it again,' Eric had said. He'd turned towards Olivia. 'Thanks a million, doll. You've done us proud. Are you sure you won't take anything?'

'One hundred per cent.'

'You are still coming to the evening do tomorrow, aren't you?' Brenda had asked. 'You and your plus-one. You're welcome to come to the wedding too, as you know, it's at midday, but we know Saturday must be a busy day for you.'

'Phil and I are both busy tomorrow lunchtime but we wouldn't miss your reception for the world. Thanks again for our invitation.'

'The DJ will kick off about seven. But don't worry if you're later, doll.' Eric had winked at her. 'We're planning on dancing till dawn.'

'It's easier when you've got a Zimmer frame to lean on,' Brenda had told Olivia in a stage whisper. 'No one notices if your knees give out.'

'My knees have still got plenty of dancing in them,' Eric had remonstrated. 'And don't you go mocking my Zimmer frame. They're hugely understated things, Zimmers – back in the day, we used to call 'em Zimmy shimmys – on account of them being helpful accessories for dancers who did the shimmy.' He'd tapped his nose, reminding Olivia of Phil, and added, 'I bet you don't know what a shimmy is, do you, doll?'

'A kind of dance?' Olivia had ventured, although her mind was already boggling when she tried to envisage any dance being accessorised by a Zimmer frame.

'Exactly that,' Eric had said. 'You'll see it in action tomorrow.'

* * *

'I can't imagine the party will go on that late,' Olivia said to Phil as they walked through the hotel foyer to the room where the reception was taking place. 'They are both in their eighties.'

The hotel manager had directed them. Not that they'd needed to be directed as they could hear the noise long before they got there.

Phil opened the door for her and they both did a double take. Olivia had expected to see a handful of octogenarians and a bunch of younger relatives sitting about serenely – Eric had told her they had a lot of friends coming and they both had large families – but the room was chock-a-block with people, most of whom were jiggling about on the dance floor.

A jazz band was set up in one corner and they were playing a lively jive. Couples were jiving, mums and dads were swinging each other round and teenagers bopped along, either alone or with their partners. There were even a couple of toddlers jiggling to the music. The room smelled of hot perfumed people, flowers, and food. Olivia thought she could see some familiar faces on the dance floor, but knew she must be imagining it. The chances of her knowing any of Eric and Brenda's friends had to be remote.

She glanced at Phil and he frowned at her and then leaned closer to speak in her ear. 'Did you say that Brenda used to be in the business?'

'That's right. She was known as make-up artist to the stars, back in the day. Why?'

'Because there's a few of the cast of *Coronation Street* here. That's William Roache over there and, if I'm not very much mistaken, that's Maureen Lipman. Either that or they're very good lookalikes.'

'Good grief, I think you're right.' Olivia tried not to stare as she looked around for the happy couple, finally spotting them, sitting at a table on the edge of the dance floor. 'Come on, I'll introduce you to the bride and groom.'

They went across the room, threading their way through dancers and tables.

Eric and Brenda looked delighted to see them. They were both red-faced and starry-eyed.

'We're pacing ourselves with the dancing,' Eric told them. 'But you hang around and you'll see some Zimmy shimmys, you mark my words.' He gestured to his Zimmer frame, which had been decorated with a yellow ribbon which went very well with the bride's yellow fascinator.

Brenda beckoned Olivia closer. 'Didn't you say you were in the next series of *Nightingales*, love?'

Olivia agreed shyly that she was.

'Good, because Simon Caine's here with his missus somewhere. I told him you were coming. I'll introduce you.'

Brenda was as good as her word. Twenty minutes later, Olivia and Phil found themselves in the middle of the acting faction of the wedding guests, all of whom were utterly charming.

* * *

It turned out that Eric hadn't been lying about the Zimmy shimmy dance either. One of the highlights of the evening was when the dance floor was cleared, and two young dancers, who turned out to be Eric's grandchildren, took to centre stage to perform a routine, the like of which Olivia had never seen.

It really did involve shimmying with a Zimmer frame, which they used as a prop with immense skill and flair. The applause that followed, especially when the bridal couple got up to join in, brought the house down.

'I think that tonight,' Phil told Olivia much later in the evening, 'has to be one of the most surreal and unexpected evenings of my life.'

'Me too,' she said, laughing. 'I had no idea it would be like this. I thought that Eric and Brenda would have sloped off by nine.'

Eric and Brenda did, in fact, finally leave the room around midnight.

'I'd like to stay longer, but my bride's getting impatient,' he announced from the stage to a cacophony of wolf whistles and rude remarks.

Olivia's last impression of Eric and Brenda was of joyous laughter. Not a yawn in sight.

She and Phil left soon after them.

'Maybe we should see if we can hire the Zimmy shimmy couple to do a turn at our wedding,' Olivia said to Phil.

'I'm not sure about that, but I do like this band. They're superb. And we definitely need to invite Eric and Brenda.'

'Top of the guest list,' Olivia replied, as they went out into the moonlit car park.

Phil's eyes were sparkling and he seemed hyped up. As he drove them back, he told her why. 'Did you see that dark-haired guy I was talking to in the white suit?'

'Yes, I think so. He laughed a lot.'

'That's the one. It turned out he's Simon Caine's agent and he's interested in taking me on. He's sure he can get me some work. In fact, he had a role in mind. He wants to sign me up.'

'Wow. That's brilliant.'

'I'm not going to get my hopes up. People say lots of things, don't they? But it can't hurt to go and see him in his office, can it?'

Olivia squeezed his hand.

The last thought she had, as she dropped off to sleep that night, was that she and Phil could both end up doing their dream job full time. It was such a precarious profession that they rarely talked about their hopes and dreams – they didn't want to tempt fate – and being a successful actor wasn't something that happened overnight. You were only as good as your last role. But they were definitely both going in the right direction.

That night, she dreamed that they were dining at Harper's. Phil had just dropped on to one knee to propose when Mr B suddenly leapt out from behind a pillar clutching an enormous bag of confetti, which he started to throw up in the air in handfuls. As it poured down on their heads, it turned out not to be confetti at all, but peanuts. A storm of endless peanuts like hailstones that bounced off the tables and chairs and everyone else in the vicinity, until soon it felt as though it was raining peanuts. And Olivia could hear Mr B's voice rising in glee as he continued to hurl handfuls of nuts in the air, 'Peanut-gate. It will never be beaten. Never, never, never...'

She woke up with her heart pounding and the taste of salt on her lips, which she thought she was imagining, until she remembered that one of the wedding buffet snacks last night had been the most delicious anchovy canapés, which she and Phil had both indulged in. She'd cleaned her teeth since then. Maybe it was just the memory of salt. But the dream reminded her that she was really quite nervous about going to Harper's in a posh dress, knowing that Phil was going to propose.

32

At least she had chosen the right posh dress for Harper's, Olivia thought, as she admired herself in the bedroom mirror and added the finishing touches to her make-up. She'd abandoned the idea of the Vivienne Westwood and had gone for Ruby's slinky black and white number instead.

'You can keep that dress if you like,' her sister had offered. 'I am never going to fit into it again. It was too tight in the first place.'

'Are you really sure?'

'Of course I am. You'll blow Phil's mind in that. You look amazing.'

Olivia hoped she was right, as she came out of the bedroom to meet Phil. She had splashed out on a new jacket, a soft maroon one that picked out the flecks in the dress, and some strappy gold heels that did wonders for her calves. Not that you could see her calves. The dress was floor length. Casual glamour personified. A spray of her favourite scent and her favourite bag and she was ready.

'Wow,' Phil said, giving a soft wolf whistle. 'You look stunning. I forget sometimes how beautiful you are.'

She felt herself blushing, warmed by the admiration in his eyes.

He looked pretty hot himself. He was wearing an expensive-looking pale blue shirt and dark trousers and he carried a jacket. Phil looked amazing in old jeans and a vest top, but he was one of those guys who scrubbed up well too. He had the kind of presence that drew the looks of both men and women alike. And the best thing about it was that he was totally unconscious of it.

He patted his pocket. 'What? Why are you staring at me?'

'I was just thinking how gorgeous you are.'

'Stop it.' He palmed his chin and frowned and changed the subject. 'I think I've cut myself. Is there blood?'

She leaned in. 'Can't see any.'

He took the opportunity to kiss her. 'You all set?'

Olivia nodded. She had no idea what he was planning. But knowing Phil there would be theatrics. And he had a suppressed excitement about him that he was having difficulty hiding.

They were getting a taxi to Harper's. 'Just in case we need champagne,' he quipped, slanting her a glance. 'I'm not taking anything for granted. You may have changed your mind now we've been living in sin for a month.'

They had fallen into the routine of living at her's because the studio where he was doing the audiobook recording was closer to Weymouth than Swanage, and because it had been harder than ever to tear themselves away from each other, lately.

There was a queue in the foyer of Harper's when they arrived. Men in suits, women in posh dresses. Expensive cologne mingled with the scent of the lilies in a vase on a table by the door.

'They're waiting for cancellations,' Phil told her as they

headed to the front of the queue. 'You can sometimes get lucky if you call in on spec.'

Olivia gulped. 'Good job Mr B came up trumps then,' she said, as a solemn-faced maître d', who looked like he had a curtain pole stuffed up the back of his jacket, showed them to a table.

Moments later, he was back with a wine list and two leather-bound menus, none of which had prices on.

'This is going to cost a fortune, isn't it?' Olivia said when he was out of earshot again.

'This is the version I'm going to be telling our children about,' Phil said, grabbing her hand and squeezing it tight. 'And for your information, I'm not totally broke!'

'Aren't you? That's good news.' She flashed him a grin.

'I've been investing in bitcoin for years,' Phil told her, eyeing her over the top of the leather menu. 'I've done quite well.' He rubbed his nose a bit self-consciously. 'I always thought I might need a backup plan – if my acting career didn't take off. Or...' He winked. 'If I ever needed to bail myself out of prison, having finally snapped and murdered Mr B.'

She looked at him in amazement. She was simultaneously both surprised and not surprised about the bitcoin investment. Phil had always played his cards close to his chest. He was a strange mix of very private and very up front.

'I thought I'd tell you that before I proposed,' Phil said. 'Just in case it makes a difference.'

'I'd marry you if you were a pauper.'

'I know that too.'

They ordered the soup of the day which was watercress. Both Mr B and the chef at Harper's had learned the recipe in training together. It had the most delicate and delicious of flavours and came with a selection of warm home-made olive breads on a board.

'This chef's even better than Mr B,' Phil said with satisfaction. 'And he's pretty damn good – even though he does say so himself.' He leaned forward. 'When I asked him if he could get us a table here, he made me promise not to try the watercress soup.'

'Really? Why?'

'Because he thinks he makes the best watercress soup in the UK. He said if we tried anyone else's we'd just be disappointed.'

'He didn't say that?' Olivia gasped. 'Is he really that arrogant?'

'Oh yes.' But there was a world of affection in Phil's voice.

For the main course, they had chateaubriand, carved at the table by the pompous maître d', who wasn't so pompous once they got chatting. The meat was accompanied by duchesse potatoes, tiny roasted mushrooms, stalks of braised broccoli and a divine pink peppercorn sauce.

'This is very possibly the best meal I've ever had,' Olivia told Phil.

'Good. Make sure you tell Mr B when you see him next. Don't forget the straws prank.'

She laughed. 'I'll tell him.'

After the maître d' had cleared away their finished main course, a surprise arrived. It wasn't dessert – they hadn't ordered that yet – and it came hidden under a small cloche, so Olivia couldn't see what it was.

The maître d' stood in front of Phil, and Phil pushed back his chair, stood up and took it from him. At the exact same moment that he dropped to his knees by Olivia's chair, all the lights in the restaurant dimmed.

Olivia half expected Mr B to jump out from behind a pillar, scattering handfuls of peanuts. To her relief, there was no sign of him. Her eyes adjusted to the light as Phil looked up at her. Then in a déjà vu encore of his first proposal – except this time he was dressed – Phil met Olivia's eyes.

'Olivia,' he said, 'would you do me the very great honour of becoming my wife?' He unveiled the cloche.

She'd expected to see the ring beneath it. But it wasn't just the ring. It was an edible scroll – about the size of a coffee mug, it had a cream background and blue writing which said, 'It's taken me half my life to find you. Please marry me. Please say we can spend the rest of it together?'

'Yes, and definitely YES,' Olivia said, leaning forward so enthusiastically that her chair tilted and she very nearly fell on top of him. How embarrassing.

He caught her amidst the sound of a rousing cheer. She hadn't realised there were so many other people in the restaurant, although several of the people cheering appeared to be staff. Then she realised that the group of people at the back of the restaurant weren't just staff. They were Ruby, Aunt Dawn and Mike Turner... and was that her friend, Hannah?

They began to move towards the table and then Ruby spotted two more familiar figures. Oh my God – her parents – what on earth were they doing here?

For the next few minutes, there was a lot of excited chatter and backslapping and congratulations. Two waiters came and moved an adjacent table close to Phil and Olivia's so everyone could sit together.

'It's a good job she said yes,' Hannah quipped to Phil. 'Or that could have been awkward.'

'I had a slight advantage,' Phil told her with an enigmatic smile and a wink at Olivia, who was relieved he didn't elaborate and tell everyone about the first proposal.

'You didn't need to come back especially,' Olivia said to her parents.

'Of course we did.' Her mother was all sparkly-eyed with excitement. 'Once we knew what was going on. We wouldn't have missed it for the world.'

'Quite right, Bean.' Her father was wearing one of his smartest lambswool jumpers. 'Hey, this place is grand, isn't it?'

Olivia smiled, feeling blown away that Phil had arranged all this – not least the number of seats they were now taking up – without her suspecting a thing. The entire party ordered dessert and coffees. Olivia noticed that Aunt Dawn and Mike were constantly touching each other – like a pair of teenagers who'd not long met. She didn't think she'd seen her aunt so happy for years.

'He'll be good for her,' Ruby said. 'He's nice.'

'Any more news on Scott's divorce proceedings?' Olivia asked her quietly.

'Not yet. But it's in progress. I've worked out all my finances though and I have actually made quite a few decisions.'

'What kind of decisions?'

'Some about money – that was essential. But I've also decided on what I'm going to do for the first year or two of Mr Bump's life.'

'Oh?' Olivia looked at her curiously. 'What's that?'

'I'm going to be a mum. And I'm going to carry on painting. I'm going back to my roots, Liv. And I'm really excited about it. It feels right.' She put her hand to her heart. 'In here, I mean. I've done a bit already, as you know. Some of it's really quite good – it has an energy I haven't managed to get before. I think it's all those pregnancy hormones swirling about.'

'I'm so pleased, honey, and are you OK? Emotionally, I mean, with…?'

'With being a single parent? Yes, sis, I really am.' Her eyes were clear and bright. 'I don't think I want to get involved in any kind of relationship, apart from the one I have with Bump. Not for ages.'

The two sisters hugged impulsively and Olivia felt Phil's eyes on her. He had a look of such tenderness on his face. He might not have thought he'd ever have a family, she realised, remembering his sadness when he told her about his father's premature demise. But, one way or another, he was always going to be part of one now.

The rest of the evening disappeared in a blur of laughter and champagne, which had duly arrived so they could have a toast. In fact, they had several.

At the end of the evening, Dawn and Mike dropped them both back to Olivia's, and Ruby took her parents and Hannah back to her's, where they were all staying over. Just before they left the restaurant, Hannah gave Olivia a huge hug.

'I'm so pleased for you,' she said. 'He's lovely. Did I tell you that I'm moving back into the area? I decided it was finally time to cut the apron strings from Mum. It's not as though she'll be a million miles away – it's only an hour.'

'That's fantastic news. So we'll get to see more of each other.'

'Indeed we will.'

By the time Olivia and Phil finally got to bed, it was almost midnight.

'I think that tonight has been one of the happiest of my life,' Olivia told Phil, glancing down at the ring on her finger. 'Thank you so much.'

'It was pretty cool, wasn't it? Thank you for saying yes, second time around.'

'I seem to remember I said yes, first time around,' she teased.

'So which version of our proposal are you planning to tell our children?' he asked her.

'I think it might have to be both,' Olivia said and kissed him.

33

'It's official,' Phil said, as he pulled up into a parking space on the road and switched off the headlights. 'I must be stark raving bonkers.'

'Is that because of what we're doing or what time it is?' Olivia asked.

'Both, I think.' He glanced at the clock on the dashboard of his car. 'I didn't even know three forty-five in the morning was an actual time.'

Olivia giggled. 'This was your idea, though, Phil.'

'I'd clearly drunk far too much when I suggested it.'

'Not that much,' she told him. 'Anyway, come on or we'll miss it.'

'We're not going to miss it. It's pitch dark. We could have had another hour in bed.'

'No, we could not. This is all part of the experience.'

Olivia opened the passenger door. It felt chillier right on the coast than it had when they'd left her house. Not that they were that far away. They were at Chesil Beach, more specifically at Chesil Cove. They'd just parked in Brandy Row, which was on the western side of Portland Bill, just as you crossed the cause-way. Chesil Cove was the place she had recommended would be good for a shore dive. 'That's if you still fancy going diving,' she'd challenged him a few nights earlier, 'after what happened last time.'

'If I'm going to go, I should probably make it soon,' he'd replied. 'So I don't lose my nerve. They say that about riding horses, don't they? If you have a fall, get back on straight away.'

'Mmmm,' Olivia had looked at him thoughtfully. 'The only problem is that Chesil Cove can get quite busy. It's really popular.'

'Maybe we should go at sunrise,' he'd said, flicking her a glance. 'That would be quite cool. Going scuba diving on Chesil beach at sunrise.'

'I'm up for it if you are?'

So now they were here, and sunrise, according to the website she had looked on, was due to happen in about an hour and a half. Not that there had been any sign of light as they'd driven over Portland causeway. The sky was pitch black and dotted with stars.

They began to get the heavy kit out of the back of Phil's car – bottles, regulators, weight belts, fins and drysuits. 'At least we can guarantee that I won't get stuck in any shipwrecks this morning,' Phil said.

'Oh, I don't know about that.' She smirked 'This road is named Brandy Row after a shipwreck.'

He slanted her a glance. 'Go on?'

'In 1872, a boat called the Royal Adelaide got smashed to pieces on the beach. Just up there.' She pointed into the darkness in the direction of the sea. 'It was carrying a cargo of brandy, and barrels and barrels of the stuff got washed up. Most of the crew survived the shipwreck, but then several locals who'd rocked up to help salvage the cargo started drinking the brandy and a few of them got so drunk that they fell asleep on the beach and died from exposure.'

'Unbelievable,' Phil said, giving a little shudder. 'Is the wreck still out there?'

'I think it pretty much broke up on the beach.' She grinned at him. 'Don't worry. I have it on good authority that the most dangerous piece of metal out there is a disused sewerage pipe – it's definitely disused. If we see anything that looks remotely like a shipwreck, we'll fin very fast in the other direction.'

'At least if there are any eels we won't see them,' he said thoughtfully. 'It'll be too dark.'

'You'd be surprised what you can see in the dark,' she replied. 'We have powerful torches and fish are more active at night. Except for eels. I've heard they're heavy sleepers.'

Phil laughed. 'Excellent. I'll take the bottles. You bring the lighter stuff.'

'That's what I like about you. You're such a gentleman.'

'I try.'

As they began the short but tricky walk across the shifting shingle, the sky began to lighten almost imperceptibly. They kitted up on the pebbles at the top of the beach. It was a steep walk down to the water's edge and the air was full of the sound of the sea, although it was a much gentler sea than when Olivia and Ruby had walked here after her scan.

'It's not shipwreck weather today,' Olivia said, glancing at the dark water. 'Flat, calm, and almost no wind according to the forecasts. It's been perfect diving weather for the last couple of days.'

'That's a relief.' Phil looked at the new fluorescent yellow fins he'd bought – it would be hard to miss them, even in the dark – and eyed the sea a little gingerly.

'Are you sure you're up for this?' she asked him. 'We could just scrap the dive and wait for the sunrise. I'm not sure we're going to see much of it underwater.'

'I am up for it. We're not going to be deep, are we?'

'Not at all – we'll have to swim out a bit to get ten metres depth. We'll have an hour if we want it, even at the way you gulp air.'

'Ouch!'

'There can be a strong swell though. And there's also a risk of fishing-net entanglement.' She tapped the holster on her calf. 'But I've got my knife.'

'I bought a new one too. While I was in the dive shop, I also bought a special cutting tool. Just to be safe.'

She nodded approvingly. 'Preparation is everything. OK, torches, check.' They switched them on and flashed them up and down the beach. There was no one else around yet. Not even a fisherman. 'I've brought an extra torch,' Olivia said, 'which will be fixed to our surface marker buoy. I shouldn't think there'll be any boats out there this early, but if there are, then they'll be able to see there are divers below.'

'Great stuff,' he said.

'OK. Computers, check; masks, check. What are you going to do with your car keys?' she asked him.

'Waterproof bumbag inside my drysuit. Full bottle, check. New fins, check! So, what's the plan? I'm letting you lead this one.'

'That sounds sensible.' She flashed him a look as she adjusted her computer, hoping he was as confident as he sounded. She'd been a little surprised he'd wanted to come. Most people would have been put off for life after the scare he'd had last time. Phil was definitely not a quitter. 'We won't go far and we won't go deep. I was thinking max depth ten metres, we'll fin parallel to the shore back towards Weymouth and if we get separated, we come straight up. Think of this as a getting-back-on-the-horse dive. Are you ready?'

'Ready as I ever will be.'

They arrived at the water's edge, carrying their fins, which they would put on at the last minute. Shore dives were harder work because you had to lug the heavy kit further, but you also had time to adjust to the water temperature. It wasn't such a shock as jumping straight in from a boat.

They clipped on their fins and then walked backwards through the lacy white frill of the tide and then on and over the fairly sharp drop-off, and into the cool embrace of the sea.

The sea at night was an eye-opener. Olivia had only ever done one night dive and she'd been amazed at how much there was to see. Chesil Cove was even better. It was a haven for marine life and today the visibility was amazing – the underwater world around them lighting up in the beams of their torches as they adjusted their buoyancy and began to fin through the water. Almost immediately, they saw fish flitting around across the clumps of dark red waving seaweed. Olivia's torch lit up the electric blue markings of a cuckoo wrasse and a crab scuttled away from them, its stalk eyes waving.

Twenty minutes into the dive, they came across a pair of squid undulating through the water with their strange fringed tentacles and round flat eyes. Olivia tapped Phil's arm and for a moment they followed them. The squid weren't at all fazed, they were clearly used to divers and they continued on their hunt for breakfast without hurry.

There was something almost miraculous about being underwater, Olivia thought. Such a strange and alien world, filled with the phosphorescent glow of cuttlefish, far from the traffic and hustle bustle of above, with only the sounds of their amplified breathing to accompany them and the trails of bubbles from their regulators, heading back to the world of air.

It was extraordinarily peaceful. Drift diving, she had thought, when she had first gone diving with Tom, was probably the closest you could get to flying. Drifting through the water, neutrally buoyant on the tide, gliding above a landscape of rocks, pebbles, weeds and tiny fish. There wasn't much current in these waters, but it was enough to make finning almost effortless.

The sea felt warmer today, even than it had a few weeks ago when they'd last been in it. She was probably imagining that. Her temperature gauge didn't show any difference. She was just so pleased they'd come and especially that Phil had been up for it. They had talked about their last disastrous dive quite a bit since the event. It had bonded them deeply. They had learned things about each other that took most couples a great deal longer. They had learned that when it really mattered, they could rely on each other utterly. They could work through problems – even when the situation was life-threatening. They had learned that they had each other's backs. That they could function as a unit.

She guessed that a near-death experience like they'd had would always be bonding, but, in a weird kind of way, much of the strong connection they now felt had come afterwards. It had come from talking. They had learned that it was OK to rescue each other. It was OK to feel strong emotions and to share them and it wasn't weak to apologise. They now knew that if they talked to each other, and were honest, they could probably get through anything that life threw at them.

Phil was finning alongside her and, as if by some telepathy, they looked at each other at exactly the same moment. He pointed at his computer and then gestured up and she realised that they'd had their planned dive time. It was time to return to the land of air.

Going up to the surface, the ascent towards the light had always put Olivia in mind of a kind of rebirth. That feeling was even stronger today because it had been dark when they'd gone in and when they surfaced, as planned, forty-five minutes later, on the nail, the sky had turned to a soft grey.

Then Phil took his regulator out of his mouth to speak.

'Oh wow,' he said as they floated in the calm sea. 'Just, wow. I think I'm hooked on night dives. That was fantastic.'

Olivia nodded enthusiastically. She loved the awe on his face. It was how she felt too. The sheer, elemental wonder of being alive, feeling as if every atom of your body was tingling. It almost, but not quite, beat making love.

'It was stunning,' Phil said and then got a mouthful of water as a sneaky wave went over his head.

He emerged coughing and spluttering a few seconds later.

Olivia glanced quickly around to make sure she didn't suffer the same fate and then whipped out her regulator to speak.

'Let's get you back to shore before you drown,' she admonished and saw his eyes dance with amusement.

There was definitely something to be said for bossing your loved ones about when they were in no position to retaliate.

They weren't very far from the beach, although they'd drifted quite some way from where they'd gone in and were now closer to Weymouth than Portland. They finned back into shore, which even with barely any swell was harder than it looked.

A few minutes later, they were back on solid ground once more. Well, semi solid, because the shingle on Chesil Beach was eternally mobile, reshaping with every footstep and every tide. Pebble Beach was a very apt name for it, Olivia thought happily.

Temporarily abandoning the heavy bottles and their fins at the bottom of the shingle bank, they climbed up to the top and then, breathless from the exertion and weak-kneed from the dive, they sank down side by side and looked towards the dawn.

Their timing couldn't have been more perfect. Above their heads, the darkness still lingered in purple swathes, but out on the horizon, in the direction of Portland Harbour, they could see the orange fire glow of the sunrise.

On one side of the sky, a huge moon the colour of custard still swung amongst the stars. But here, at the top of the shingle bank as they stared out to sea, they watched the sky slowly lighten from midnight blue, through smudgy grey, to softest lilac, while in the east, the horizon grew brighter – a montage of stunning pink and grey – and then, as the sun slid up over the edge of the world, a glorious flaming gold.

"Sunrise Over Pebble Bay". Olivia thought of Ruby's painting. And here she was experiencing it, first hand. Right now. Wow! Olivia wished she had her phone and could capture it for Ruby, but there was a part of her that knew it was impossible to capture the sunrise on film. It was better to just be in it, sitting in its glow, holding the hand of someone you love. She leant against Phil's shoulder, feeling the strength in him and the breath of a salt breeze against her face. It was so peaceful sitting in the sunrise with the soundtrack of the endless sea on shingle and the mewling gulls and the more distant muted sounds of a slowly waking town.

Neither of them spoke. They didn't need to. It was enough that they were there – together, side by side, watching a bright and beautiful dawn unfolding and lighting up a glorious, brand new day.

EPILOGUE

In October, Ruby had a little boy and called him Simon in memory of her and Olivia's much loved Uncle Simon. Simon junior's father showed no interest in being part of his child's upbringing but was made to pay Ruby a hefty one-off fee that Ruby has put in trust for their son's future.

Fortunately, as every female in the family agrees, Simon has a plethora of male role models, including his grandad James, his uncle Phil and Mike Turner.

James and Marie Lambert are proving to be doting grandparents. Their first gift to their grandson was a dinosaur onesie. Marie is much more hands-on, and has thrown herself into being the best granny ever. But even James can be tempted away from the past and into the present for quite long periods these days, while he gets to know his first grandson.

He has been heard to say that Simon has the hands of an archaeologist, and the sharp eyes of a historian, although how either of these things can be deduced when a child hasn't yet reached his first birthday no one knows. Not to be deterred Grandpa James has already bought young Simon his first toy trowel!

Dawn and Mike announced that time's too precious to waste and now live together on a Dorset smallholding a pebble's throw from Weymouth. They are working on creating a secret garden in one part of the grounds. They have much in common. Not least the fact that they're both pretty dotty about animals. It turned out that Mike had something of a menagerie of his own, including two cats – Sherlock and Watson – and an alpaca called Mrs Hudson. He also has six hens that Dawn is helping him name after famous women. So far, they have Madonna the Second, Twiggy and Cher. There is also a cockerel called Boris. They are never short of eggs.

Lydia Brooks and her daughter bought Aunt Dawn's shop, Vintage Views, and are very happy in their new family business.

Hannah has moved back to Dorset and doesn't live far from Weymouth quay. The first of her YA books came out to great reviews and not bad sales for a debut novelist. She was over the moon and is now working on book two.

* * *

Tom decided to go back to Spain after a holiday property company in Madrid he'd invested heavily in, turned out to be a scam. He is still trying to track down the perpetrators. When Hannah had bumped into him in Weymouth, just before he left, she said that his hair had gone quite white (and it definitely didn't suit him), which must have been the shock of losing so much money.

* * *

The new series of *Nightingales* was a smash hit and Olivia has just been signed up for another season. She now makes Amazing Cakes for a few handpicked clients, with Aunt Dawn's help.

* * *

Phil signed with the new agency and within a few months he finally got his big break as a heart-throb villain on a BBC drama. He is still maître d' at The Bluebell Cliff Hotel, but he can now pick and choose his shifts.

* * *

Phil and Olivia are planning their wedding at The Bluebell Cliff hotel. Ruby is going to be chief bridesmaid and there's a rumour that Phil is going to ask Mr B to be his best man. On condition that the eccentric chef promises there will be no funny business.

Mr B was so overwhelmed to be asked that he swore a solemn oath there and then that he would never play another trick on Phil for as long as they both lived.

No one, least of all Phil, was at all convinced by this. But as they all agree, a temporary truce is better than a broken promise.

* * *

Phil and Olivia are still trying for a baby. They have also begun the process of going along the adoption route. They both feel very strongly that the most important thing when it comes to babies is not how a life comes into being, or indeed who brought it into the world, the important thing is what happens afterwards. And the most important thing of all is, and always will be, love.

ACKNOWLEDGMENTS

It's impossible to write a book by yourself. There is such a big team behind you and every single one of them helps to make it the best it can be. Team Boldwood – you are amazing. As always, my special thanks go to Caroline Ridding, Judith Murdoch and Jade Craddock.

My huge thanks go to Tony Millward for his expert local knowledge of Weymouth and Portland and also for helping me out when I 'forgot' that the sun rises in the east! Thanks to Adam Millward for his London knowledge.

Thanks to Molly Carney, Angie Parkhurst and Sarah Doyle for their cake making expertise, and to Sarah for her expert knowledge of the business. Thank you so much to Shaun Scott for his insider knowledge of the acting business. Thank you to Jennifer McCormick for her knowledge and expertise of the art world. Thank you to Gordon Rawsthorne for his enduring support. He endures a lot!

Thank you to the huge support of my readers – without whom it would be pretty pointless writing novels. I love reading

your emails, tweets and Facebook comments. Please keep them
coming.

MORE FROM DELLA GALTON

We hope you enjoyed reading *Sunrise Over Pebble Bay*. If you did, please leave a review.

If you'd like to gift a copy, this book is also available as an ebook, digital audio download and audiobook CD.

Sign up to Della Galton's mailing list for news, competitions and updates on future books:

http://bit.ly/DellaGaltonNewsletter

Sunshine Over Bluebell Cliff, another glorious escapist read from Della Galton, is available to order now.

ABOUT THE AUTHOR

Della Galton is the author of 15 books, including *Ice and a Slice*. She writes short stories, teaches writing groups and is Agony Aunt for Writers Forum Magazine. She lives in Dorset.

Visit Della's website: www.dellagalton.co.uk

Follow Della on social media:

facebook.com/DailyDella

twitter.com/DellaGalton

instagram.com/Dellagalton

bookbub.com/authors/della-galton

ABOUT BOLDWOOD BOOKS

Boldwood Books is a fiction publishing company seeking out the best stories from around the world.

Find out more at www.boldwoodbooks.com

Sign up to the Book and Tonic newsletter for news, offers and competitions from Boldwood Books!

http://www.bit.ly/bookandtonic

We'd love to hear from you, follow us on social media:

facebook.com/BookandTonic

twitter.com/BoldwoodBooks

instagram.com/BookandTonic

.

Printed in Great Britain
by Amazon